FIGHT WITH THE DARK

CITY OF VIRTUE AND VICE
BOOK 5

SUSANNAH WELCH

CONTENTS

Cover Concept and Design by Art Muse (Patrisha E. Badalo)
Editing by Red Loop Editing (Victoria Basnuevo)

eISBN: 978-1-958568-02-6
Paperback ISBN: 978-1-958568-03-3
Hardback ISBN: 978-1-958568-04-0

www.susannahwelch.com

ALSO BY SUSANNAH WELCH

City of Virtue and Vice Series

Dance with the Wind

Dance with the Night

Dance with the Dawn

Fight with the Wind

Fight with the Dark

Fight with the Heart

For my crew

The Shining City

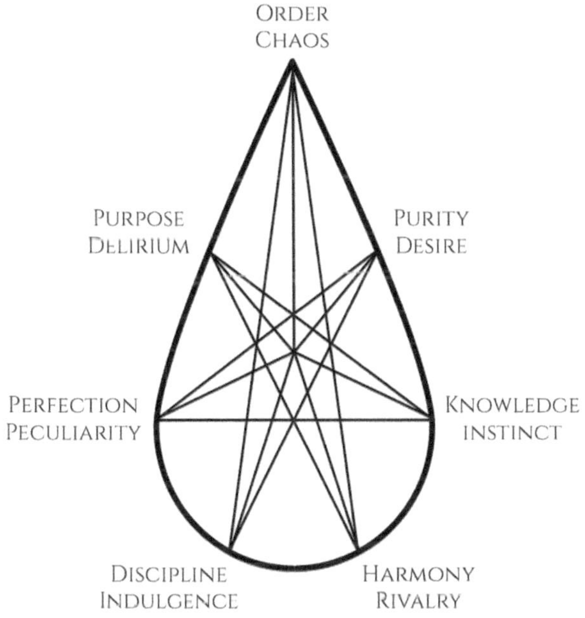

ORDER

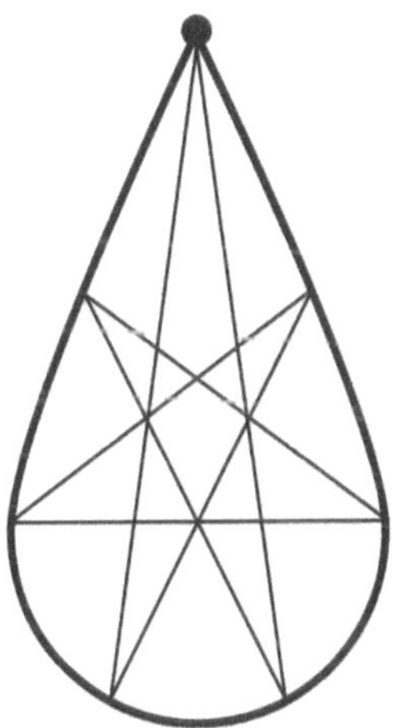

1

Rose wouldn't have made up the temple's steps if not for Wilder's strong arm around her. Her legs threatened to collapse, and her broken ribs throbbed so much she couldn't speak. Not that she wanted to. The Goddess had bestowed a Gift on Wilder without returning her own, and Rose had nothing to say.

Wilder broke his silence as they entered the inner courtyard. "I'm not sure how long we have until Vaylan sends Sentinels after us. We need to find the rest of the crew and make a plan."

She nodded weakly as he led her to the room she shared with Fitz. He shifted her body gently against his side as he opened the door. Her eyes widened in shock.

She had never seen so many people crammed in the small bedroom.

Tayeh stood by the door and relaxed her stance as they entered. Fitz sat on his own bed next to Rev, who nervously twisted her blond ponytail. Feather, the girl who had won the part of the Goddess in the auditions, perched lightly on Rose's bed next to Quinn. Kieran, the guy who won the part of the Companion, stood with his arms crossed, as far as he could from the others.

Wilder's face showed the same surprise as her own, but he recovered quickly. He pulled Rose inside the room while Tayeh eyed the courtyard before shutting the door.

As they squeezed inside the small room, Rose stumbled, and a gasp of pain escaped her lips. Rev and Fitz jumped up, and Wilder lowered her gently to the bed. She bit her lips to keep any more embarrassing signs of weakness from slipping out.

"What happened?" asked Rev. She lowered herself to the floor in front of Rose, but her one-eyed accusing glare was for Wilder.

"A lot," said Wilder. "I don't think we're safe here."

"No kidding," said Tayeh. Her voice was as calm as usual, but her fingers twitched as she fidgeted with her thick cloud of dark hair. "Something weird is going on."

Fitz pushed Kieran away from the closet and began digging through his bags. "I told you not to do anything strenuous, Rose!" He pulled out a thin cloth bundle and opened it to reveal a black twig. "Chew on this, but don't swallow it. It would be better if I ground it into a tea, but I don't think we have time for that."

Rose eyed the twig warily but gnawed on the end as instructed. It tasted even more bitter than the tea Fitz had given her before she left for the amphitheater and made her tongue feel tingly. She chewed on the twig with the end sticking out of her mouth as she spoke. "What are you all doing in here?"

Fitz absently rubbed his strawberry blond beard as he supervised her twig chewing. "Before you left, you asked if I would look after the acolytes who had won their spot in the audition. I told them what happened to Mayra and that we weren't sure would happen next. They all ran off. Except these two." He pointed to Kieran and Feather.

At seventeen, Feather was only two years younger than Rose, but her innocent expression made her seem much younger. Her skin was dark copper, and her black hair was pulled up in a sleek ponytail, highlighting her heart-shaped face. She ducked her head shyly. "I won the part of the Goddess. I'm not leaving that easily."

Rose turned to Kieran, who brushed his blond hair away from his eyes and crossed his arms over his chest as if he didn't care.

Quinn pushed his dark glasses up as he studied Rose. "Wilder warned us to be prepared before he left to find you. He said it was possible you would come running back with Sentinels on your heels."

Rose cocked her head to look at Wilder.

He shrugged. "I was right, wasn't I?"

She frowned as she imagined Vaylan mobilizing a troop of Sentinels to send their way.

Quinn continued, "Rev, Tayeh, and I gathered our things and came back here to wait for you."

"Why do I get the feeling that something else has happened?" asked Wilder.

The six of them looked at one another, silently fighting over who would be the one to explain. In the end, it was Rev who adjusted her hot pink eye patch and spoke.

"I was in the middle of a conversation with Quinn and Tayeh when I heard a clear ringing tone, like someone rubbing their finger against a crystal goblet. The sound pulled at me, summoning me to the inner courtyard and the glowing white crystal. I didn't know what happened to the Quinn and Tayeh, because all I could see, all I could hear, was the crystal vibrating through my bones. I felt compelled to lay my hand on the crystal, then it flared in a bright flash of light." Rev swallowed and took a breath. "When I opened my eyes, I saw the five of them blinking awake. We compared our stories. It was all the same."

Tentative nods agreed with her story.

"Okay ..." said Wilder with a slow drawl. "Yes, that is strange. And it was only the six of you?"

Quinn nodded. "We asked the Priests if they noticed anything odd, and they looked at us like we were crazy."

"Maybe we are," said Tayeh. Her normally proud shoulders were slightly hunched, her eyes unfocused as she stared at Rose.

Rose reluctantly took the soggy twig out of her mouth to talk. "I'm not sure what that means, but the person responsible for killing Brother Owyn, Mayra, and the other Priests knows we are in this temple. I'd rather not be here when he comes to find us. I'm packing my things and getting out of here."

She pushed herself off the bed and gasped as pain shot through her ribs. While seated, the bitter twig had brought some relief, but standing brought the pain back in a flash. Gasping made her ribs hurt worse, and she couldn't straighten fully. Wilder grabbed her hand to help her balance, and she closed her eyes to bring herself under control. After she caught her breath, she realized Wilder wasn't the only one holding her up.

Tayeh's warm brown eyes were still unfocused but shone brightly in the dim room. She clasped Rose's hand in a powerful grip but didn't seem aware she was doing it.

"Tayeh?" asked Rose. "Are you okay?"

Tayeh's attention snapped into focus. She blinked, and a single tear dropped to her cheek.

Rose gasped as the sensation of frigid air blasted against her chest. Her lungs tingled, and her ribs trembled before falling into place, a single painful moment before instantaneous relief.

Tayeh took a quick step backward, scrubbing her hand across her face to hide the fallen tears.

Rose slowly straightened to her full height and pressed her fingers tentatively against her ribs. They were still bruised, but not broken.

Even though the pain no longer affected her ribs, she couldn't raise her voice above a whisper. "You ... healed me."

Tayeh's eyes widened in fear and confusion, then she swallowed several times as if nauseous.

Wilder looked between the two of them, trying to understand what happened. Rose had let go of his hand and stood with eyes locked on Tayeh.

"The Goddess gave you a Gift." Rev covered her mouth with her hand and whispered, "Tayeh, you have the Gift of Perfection."

Tayeh looked at her hands like they had betrayed her. "How did this happen?"

"The strange sound from the crystal." Fitz's pale green eyes shone as he looked at the others. "It must have happened then."

Quinn adjusted his glasses with an excited grin. "That's extraordinary! All of us heard the sound. Does that mean we all have Gifts?"

Rose ground her teeth together. "Not all of us."

Wilder didn't meet her eyes but looked at Quinn. "It appears I do."

Feather cocked her head to the side as she looked at Rose. "But you didn't get a Gift? Aren't you a Priest?"

Rose snapped her head to stare at the girl, who scooted behind Quinn.

"Yes, I am a Priest." Rose clenched her hands into fists,

then consciously relaxed them. "But the Goddess does as she chooses."

Wilder looked at her with a pitying expression, and her hands curled into fists again. She would choke down her jealousy, but she couldn't tolerate his pity. Before she could decide where to strike him, the crystalline lamp went out.

Rose sucked in a sharp breath at the sudden darkness. She had never liked the dark, but now that she knew about Vaylan's Spark, the darkness held a different meaning.

"He's here." Wilder's timid whisper sounded so unlike his normally confident tone; it renewed her anger with Vaylan all over again.

Tayeh cracked open the door, letting the light from the crystal spire spill into the room. Her head snapped each direction looking for danger, then she swayed on her feet.

Wilder caught her under the arm before she could fall. "Tayeh! What's wrong?"

She swallowed loudly. "I am ... unwell."

Feather clung to Quinn's arm and whimpered, "What's going on?"

"It's Vaylan," whispered Wilder.

Rev shot up as if ready to attack. "Your father?"

Tayeh's head whipped around, and she grabbed a tighter hold on Wilder to keep from keeling over.

"He has a Spark that allows him to control crystalline." Rose pulled her blade out of her sheath at her side. "And I'm going to kill him."

Rev grabbed hold of her arm before she could leave the room. "Not alone, you aren't," she snapped. Rev spoke in her typical "girl talk" manner: cheerful but with a barely disguised threat. "You are part of this crew now. We are in this together."

2

After Rev reminded Rose that the crew worked together, Wilder seemed to regain some of his usual self-confidence. He hoisted Tayeh's arm further onto his shoulder and nodded for the others to follow him.

Before they made it to the outer courtyard, they heard crashing sounds from one of the common rooms. Wilder headed in the opposite direction, but Rose signaled for him to stop.

"We can't leave the Priests to deal with Sentinels!" hissed Rose. "They aren't fighters!"

Wilder's whisper was rough. "Neither are they." He inclined his head to the rest of the crew.

"Please," whispered Rose. The sight of Mayra and the other Priests in black surrounded by pools of blood rushed into her mind. "I couldn't save the others."

Wilder frowned but nodded for Rose to take the lead.

Rose slipped quietly down the dark hall and peeked around the corner into the common room. Priests had stacked tables and chairs against one archway into the outer courtyard, but Sentinels had burst through the other entrance. They silently examined the room as Priests hid behind the scattered furniture. When the Sentinels encountered no further resistance, they nodded at one another, then headed toward the door where the crew hid.

Rose pulled back and signaled to Tayeh and Wilder that two Sentinels were approaching. Wilder gestured at the rest of the crew to fall back, and Tayeh let go of his shoulder and assumed a somewhat shaky fighting stance.

As soon as the first Sentinel crossed the doorframe, Wilder fell upon him and wrestled him to the ground. While they grappled, the second Sentinel stepped toward Rose. She slashed with her knife, but it slid off his matte black armor. Tayeh lunged at him, twisting his arm behind his back, and he squirmed in pain. The High Priests' Sentinels were always silent, and it appeared Vaylan had trained his Sentinels to be the same. The man raised his free hand in a gesture of surrender.

Tayeh narrowed her eyes suspiciously, but then her eyes glazed over, and she staggered back a step. The Sentinel reached his hand inside his armor, into the pocket that held their poisonous dust.

Rose's eyes widened. There was an antidote, but she didn't have it. She felt time slow, as it had right before the mob had closed in on her. No one could save her this time.

Tayeh caught herself from her fall and lunged forward, stabbing the Sentinel through the gap in the side of his armor. He stiffened as she slid the blade in further. Tayeh's eyes opened wide, unblinking, and the man sank to his knees. As she removed her blade, he slumped all the way to the floor.

When he dropped, his hand fell out of his pocket. He didn't hold poisonous dust.

He held a letter.

Rose bent down slowly and pulled the letter out of his limp hand.

It was addressed to her.

She blinked several times, trying to understand why a Sentinel was delivering her a letter.

Feather let out a quiet sob, and her pouty lips trembled. Rev wrapped her arms around the shaking girl, who stood with wide, terrified eyes.

"We need to leave," said Wilder. "Now."

He herded them toward the open door, but Tayeh didn't move. She stared at the blood on her hands and the dead men on the floor.

Wilder took her gently by the arm. "Tayeh? Are you okay? You did what you had to do." He dropped his voice, but Rose was still close enough to hear. "We've had to do worse before."

"I felt it ..." Tayeh choked on her trembling whisper. "I felt it when his heart stopped."

Wilder blew out a soft sigh. "I'm sorry, Tayeh." He gripped her forearms until she looked him in the eyes. "We will sort this out, but I need you to help me get them out of here. Can you do that?"

She didn't respond.

Wilder turned to Rose with serious eyes, and he didn't have to say aloud what he was thinking: the crew was in no position to fight. Rose chewed her lip, trying to find some way the crew could win a fight against Vaylan. Tayeh stood only because of her arm around Wilder's neck. Her other arm wrapped across her stomach as if she might vomit any moment.

Feather trembled in Rev's arms, and even though Rev and the three other guys were from Rivalry, none of them were armed, and Rose had no idea about their fighting abilities. If someone was going to stop Vaylan, it had to be her.

She shoved the note into her pocket, adjusted the grip on her blade, and headed toward the courtyard.

Wilder hissed, "Rose! Don't you dare go out there alone!"

Even if she hadn't heard the tentative sound of Wilder's voice earlier, there was no way she wanted him to fight his own father. She planned to do whatever it took to kill Vaylan but decided to give Wilder the more optimistic version.

"Fighting him alone isn't my plan," she said. "I'm going to reason with him."

Wilder raised a disbelieving eyebrow.

Rose huffed. "Fine. Stand in the doorway and listen. I'll call you if I need help."

Tayeh snorted, then clapped a hand over her mouth, squeezing her eyes shut.

Calling for help wasn't an option. She stepped into the outer courtyard and found Vaylan standing at the foot of the temple stairs.

"Hello, Rose. It's good to see you again." He held one clenched fist near his shoulder, as if he held all the temple's crystalline in his hand.

"Turn the lights back on, Vaylan," she growled.

His lips curled into his usual grin, revealing his dimple. "Are you afraid of the dark? Surely you weren't alone in there, were you?"

Judging from the hissing whispers behind her in the dark hallway, she knew there was a heated debate about who should step outside to join her. She didn't know who would win that debate, but if Wilder stepped out here, she swore she would kill him herself.

"What do you want, Vaylan?"

"Not what," he said. "Who."

He wanted Wilder. And judging by his reaction in the amphitheater, his intentions weren't paternal.

She dropped her voice to a deadly whisper. "I won't let you have him."

His grin remained, but his eyes locked on her face. He cocked his head, as if learning something new, then said, "I don't want just one. I want them all."

The whispering behind her suddenly stopped, and her heart lurched in her chest. How did he know about them? They hadn't revealed their Gifts to anyone.

"All of them?" she whispered.

His grin widened. "Yes. I want all the Sentinels you command."

She shook her head. "My ... Sentinels?"

"Yes. All of them. Not just the ones that murdered Brother Owyn. I demand that you release all your Sentinels to me."

"I don't command any Sentinels!" she snapped.

"The Sentinels belonged to the Goddess, and the Priests have used them for years. But I've come to give them the freedom Brother Owyn promised."

It wasn't until he spoke these words that she realized a crowd had gathered. Vaylan's words weren't for her. He spoke to them.

She clenched her blade harder. "We don't have any Sentinels. You are the one who had Brother Owyn killed."

He shook his head sadly. "You don't need to protect them, Rose. You are no longer a Priest. Just let them go."

Her eyes flared with fury, and she opened her mouth to attack him with a string of curses, when a dozen Sentinels flowed out of the archways to either side. The crowd gasped and stepped backward in fear.

The Sentinels walked calmly down the stairs and stood at attention in front of Vaylan. He didn't relax his clenched fist, but he raised his other hand in a sign of benediction.

"You are no longer held captive by the Goddess and are

not to blame for the orders you followed under her command. You are free to do as you wish. Serve who you will from now on, without compulsion."

As one, they lowered onto a bent knee and bowed their heads.

Rose stared at the scene with unblinking eyes. She wasn't surprised the Sentinels followed Vaylan's direction. She already knew they did. Their reaction was expected.

But she didn't expect the crowd to believe it.

They murmured in excited whispers, pointing at the Sentinels, covering their shocked expressions with their hands. The symbol of fear and intimidation the High Priests had used for centuries now bowed at Vaylan's feet.

He had adopted a serene expression, but Rose could sense his grin of self-satisfaction lingering below the surface.

"I appreciate you handing them over to me, Rose. I truly chose well when I marked you as my own."

Her hand floated up to the wound on her collarbone against her will.

"It's time for you to join me, Marked One." He held out his hand in summons.

"I'm not going anywhere with you!" she spat.

His dark eyes glittered with the light from the crystal spire. "Hiding from me inside a temple is unwise, Rose. Priests have already taken much from me. I won't allow them to take one of my own."

Her eyes blazed at his assumption that she belonged to him. She raised her blade, and the Sentinels stood, shuffling into an attack formation.

Her hand stilled as she imagined the Sentinels swarming the temple with Vaylan raining burning crystalline on everyone inside.

The corner of Vaylan's lip twitched. "You might not be

ready to join me today, but I know you will. If you leave here tonight, I will assume the Priests have released their hold on you, and I won't be forced to fight them to retrieve you."

She heard the threat clearly in his words, and she lowered her blade almost imperceptibly.

He cleared his throat, and the Sentinels relaxed into an at ease position. "Because you handed the Sentinels over so obediently, I will return the light to this temple. As long as they let you leave, I will not harm these Priests." He paused dramatically, knowing the crowd was hanging on his every word. "For now."

He released his fist, and the crystalline flowed back to life, temporarily blinding her. But not before she saw him grin as he turned away, his midnight-blue cape flaring behind him as the Sentinels followed.

3

Once they made it back to Rose's room, she tried to convince the others to stay at the temple, but her arguments were short-lived.

"I know you aren't suggesting that you should run off on your own, Rose," growled Wilder. "Because you are not leaving here without me."

She was happy to see some fire behind his eyes, even if it meant he was messing up her plans.

"She's not leaving without *us*. We already had an escape planned before Vaylan suggested it." Rev nodded at the rest of the crew, who each hefted a getaway bag onto their shoulder while Fitz handed Wilder a bag of his own. Rev crossed her arms over her chest, eyeing Rose. "So, pack a bag, hon, and let's get going."

Rose sighed as she admitted defeat, then stared into her closet, trying to decide what to take with her. Everything she owned was black. And wearing the color of Priests felt like a lie.

She took count of every weapon she wore. She had strapped them into place when she went hunting Vaylan, and they turned out to be wholly ineffective against him. Yet they were the only possessions of any value to her now.

"Let's go," she said.

Wilder frowned as he examined her empty arms. Then he looked in her closet and sighed. He handed her the gray cloak she had draped over the chair.

He knew.

He understood her.

She turned away from his look of sadness and opened the door. The inner courtyard shone with the bright white of the crystal. Rose felt exposed, both to the hunting eyes of the Sentinels and the weighing eyes of the Goddess.

She had seen the Goddess in the flesh. Or at least, what appeared to be flesh. Rose had seen her and knew she was real. Knew she planned to return the Gifts. Knew she welcomed Rose as her chosen.

And yet, the Goddess had failed Rose once again.

Tears from the pain of her broken ribs had dried on Rose's face, but there was nothing within. The wind blowing through the inner courtyard didn't answer her call. Even indoors, it pushed against her, trying to trip her up, flowing along currents outside her control. The hateful breeze blew right past her.

To curl lovingly around Wilder.

The thick spirals of his hair bounced in the gentle breeze, floating on currents only for him. No one else's clothing stirred, yet his shirt clung to him with a faint sigh of wind.

He frowned as he studied her expression. Of course he didn't even notice how the wind blew only for him. Answered only him. Loved only him.

Rose never considered the wind's gender before, but now, she realized it was a woman.

Her jaw clenched as she considered the thought, but Wilder's hand on her arm brought her out of her musings.

"Rose? What is it?" He looked around the empty hallway for a threat.

She couldn't confess who her enemy was, so she cleared her throat and didn't meet his eyes. "We need to disappear immediately. We should take the stairway to the Underneath at the bottom of the temple."

Wilder nodded, and the crew followed her down the stairs to the secret doorway, which was previously the only way to enter the Underneath.

The door was locked.

Of course it was. Even though people could freely travel from the Underneath up the giant looping bridges, the Priests didn't want people traipsing through the temples all day.

Rose combed her stray red locks away from her face with a sigh. "Sorry. I didn't consider a locked door."

Rev chuckled quietly. "You're becoming good at apologizing, but this time, there is no need." She patted Quinn on the back.

Quinn grinned and pulled lock picks out of his bag. He had the door unlocked in a matter of seconds.

Rose stared into the dark cave beyond and couldn't move.

Wilder gestured for Rose to lead. "Let's go."

She could see a thin line of crystalline running down the length of the stairway, but she couldn't see where it led.

Wilder sighed gently as he realized the truth. "You've never been to the Underneath."

She knew she probably looked like an idiot, standing there staring into the darkness, but she couldn't take the first step.

Quinn gave her a friendly pat on the shoulder. "The

tunnel looks dark, but the Grottos themselves are actually bright. The crystal shines there, too." He tilted his head in thought. "Although when the crystals went out, the darkness in the Underneath was absolute. But it's highly unlikely the crystals will go out again."

Rev rubbed her forehead. "Quinn, you aren't being very helpful."

Kieran had been silent the whole night, so it surprised Rose when he spoke. "Are you afraid of the dark, Rose?" He flipped his blond hair away from his eyes and turned up his nose like he smelled something foul. "How very ... common of you."

His words sent a flash of pride down her spine. She turned to him with a haughty glare. "I'm not afraid, Kieran. But since I've never been here, I'm considering the best option for who should lead."

Wilder stepped forward, and she sighed inwardly in relief. "I'll lead," he said. "Rose, will you take the rear with Tayeh?" His eyes roved over Tayeh, who alternated between sharp awareness and nausea. "I need you to watch our back."

"Of course," she said with a haughty look in Kieran's direction.

He rolled his eyes and followed Wilder and the rest of the crew through the door.

Tayeh was staring mindlessly at the floor again, so Rose took her by the arm. "Come on, Tayeh. I need you to help keep us safe."

She nodded distractedly, and Rose led her through the door.

Rose couldn't bring herself to close the door behind them, even though the light from the hall barely fell inside. She knew she should hide their escape, but she rationalized it by thinking the picked lock would give them away anyway. She might as well savor the last bit of light while she had it.

Tayeh stumbled, and Rose caught her under the arms. "Tayeh? Are you okay?"

Tayeh's voice fell flat in the dark tunnel. "I hear your heartbeat ... It seems fast. Is it fast? I'm not sure ..."

Rose pulled Tayeh ahead so they didn't fall behind the rest of the group. "Yeah, it's probably a little fast." Rose didn't like the darkness, but she distracted herself by keeping Tayeh walking forward.

"I feel so strange ... I can barely concentrate because all I hear is your speeding heartbeat. I feel the muscles along your ribs that I'm not skilled enough to heal yet. I sense that deep burn on your collarbone ... Is it a fingerprint?"

Rose drew in a sharp breath. "It's hard to explain without telling the whole story."

"I can't heal it." Tayeh shook her head. "I feel the wound, but it's not something I can heal. I'm not sure why ..."

Rose tried to keep her voice steady. "Some things can't be healed."

"I've heard that." Tayeh took a deep breath through her nose and swallowed loudly. "Do you think it will be like this for the others the first time they use their Gifts?"

"I'm not sure."

"It's good to have you with us." Tayeh gripped tighter to Rose's hand on her arm. "You can help us figure out how our Gifts work."

Rose mumbled a weak confirmation.

Tayeh let out a sigh. "We made it."

Rose blinked and realized there was a white glow up ahead. "That didn't take as long as I expected."

Tayeh straightened and pulled gently away from Rose. "I feel a bit more like myself." She twitched her neck from side to side, and Rose heard it crack. "I need to be careful not to cry. Unexpected tears could be dangerous."

Rose turned her head and surreptitiously wiped her face on her sleeve. "Yes, exactly."

They stepped out of the tunnel to find the rest of the crew waiting.

Wilder tried to catch her eyes, but she ignored him and stared wide-eyed at the sight before her. The crystal from the temple above continued below ground and lit up the whole Grotto in a soft white light. The cave arched high overhead, and in the distance, she could see the giant stone bridge that curved through the air to the City above. If she looked closely, she could see the night sky at the top of the bridge.

"Wow," she said. "I expected it to feel more ... cave-like."

Quinn patted her shoulder again. "See? I told you it wasn't so bad."

Wilder drew all their attention to him. "This is Grotto Chaos. None of the Grottos are safe, but this one least of all. We need to get somewhere safe for the night, then sort out all the details in the morning. Rev, you know the way."

Tayeh stepped to Rev's side. "I'm feeling more like myself. I'll take the lead with you."

Rev smiled, and they headed off, followed by the rest of the crew.

Wilder held back, forcing Rose to finally look at him.

"I'm okay," she said. She didn't like how her shaky voice betrayed her.

"I know you will be," he said gently. He looked at her with expectation. "So ... what does it say?"

Rose blinked before realizing what he meant. She quickly dug the letter out of her pocket and smoothed the crinkled parchment, turning so that the light of the crystal shone on the page.

Dear Rose,

There is no need to fear me. I have no desire to hurt you. I have marked you as my own and have a lot of plans for you.

I know things don't make sense right now, but trust me. Everything will work out as it should.

You will come to understand me and believe as I do.

Blessings,

Vaylan

CHAOS

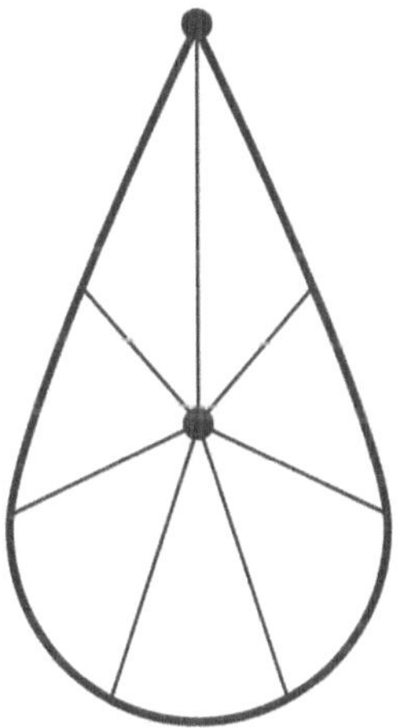

4

———

When Rose woke the next morning, she thought she was back at Mims's house with all her brothers and sisters. While she floated in the space between dreams and consciousness, she heard someone cooking breakfast. Two voices argued about who had the next turn in the bathroom. Another pair of voices bickered in whispered hisses.

Her name.

Her eyes shot open to find Wilder and Rev seated on a pile of ragged blankets nearby. They saw her wake and ceased their whispering.

Wilder cleared his throat awkwardly. "Good morning, Rose. There's a line for the bathroom, but Quinn and Feather are working on breakfast."

She raised an eyebrow. He was going to pretend he hadn't been in a conversation about her. She decided to play along for the moment.

"Good to know." She rolled onto her stomach as she looked around the shabby living room. When they'd arrived last night, a man and woman ushered them inside with a quiet nod at Rev. The crew had pushed the tattered couch and two stiff-backed chairs to the edges of the room, and the woman brought them a stack of old quilts and a few flat pillows. Rose had fallen asleep the moment she lay down on the floor.

Rose pushed herself up to a crossed legged position on her rumpled blankets and rubbed her tender ribs. Tayeh had healed the worst of the injury but would need more practice before she could heal completely. Rose was grateful for the partial relief. Her mind felt clearer without the crippling pain.

"Where are we?" she asked.

Rev answered. "This house belongs to Clayr's son and his wife. He's the one who hired us to find his mother when she went missing."

Wilder frowned. Rose knew he was disappointed that they had never found Clayr. The last they heard about her was that she recognized someone from the Underneath. She was from this Grotto, Chaos. The same Grotto where Vaylan had lived, though he denied knowing her.

Rose's chest tightened. "She lived in this Grotto when Vaylan lived here, and she recognized him when she moved Upstairs. So, did she go into hiding? Or did he ... find her?"

Wilder didn't answer.

"Are others at risk?" she asked.

Rev frowned. "Several people from Vaylan's time in this Grotto are missing. That doesn't mean much, though. Many people in this Grotto go missing."

Rose eyed Rev and Wilder sitting close together on the same quilt. "So, you already filled Rev in on everything that happened last night?"

Wilder's gaze lingered on her mouth, his eyes dark as night and deep as the Abyss. Her thoughts locked on their passionate kiss inside the amphitheater. Her lips blazed with the memory.

"I didn't tell her everything," he said with a secret smile.

Rose's cheeks threatened to burn, so she cleared her throat and straightened her messy quilt as a distraction.

Rev chuckled. "My imagination is good enough to fill in the details just by looking at you." She nodded toward the kitchen. "But you'll need to fill in the rest of the crew on what we are up against."

"The crew?" asked Rose. "You act like we are all together in this, but I'm not sure we are. We don't even know what's going on."

"We know something strange happened to us last night. And based on Tayeh's sudden Gift, I think we were all affected."

Rose scowled. "Not all of us."

Wilder looked at her but thankfully without the pity he showed last night. "Rose, you are tied into this more than the rest." He brought his hand to his collarbone. "He marked you."

Rose's hand reached tentatively for the burning fingerprint at her throat. If she didn't touch it, she could almost ignore the wound, but the slightest touch caused the pain to flare.

"The Goddess has tied us together," said Rev. "She didn't say why, so it's up to us to figure it out." Rev reached across the blankets and squeezed her hand. "You aren't getting rid of us."

Rose nodded but kept her blasphemous thought to herself.

They were chosen by the Goddess.

But Rose was chosen by Vaylan.

Quinn and Feather put together an impressive breakfast for the crew. Clayr's son, Trev, and his wife, Laryn, hadn't known eight extra people would invade their house, so they hadn't stocked extra food. However, Quinn and Feather somehow whipped up pancakes with an odd assortment of toppings and enough coffee for everyone.

After they ate breakfast and took turns in the bathroom, Rev called everyone to the living room. Her voice was sweet, but she let them know they needed to hustle. She reminded Rose of Mims rounding up all of Rose's brothers and sisters for a family meeting. Rose smiled at the memory as she plopped down on the couch. Wilder sat beside her and scooted close, making room for Fitz on his other side.

Wilder's warm body against her side reminded her it was not quite like a family meeting after all.

Rev plopped down on the floor. "Tell us what happened at the amphitheater last night."

Rose's thoughts immediately went to her kiss with Wilder, but when she noticed the hesitant look in his eyes, she realized Rev meant their confrontation with Vaylan. Rose told most of the story to save Wilder from having to do it himself.

But when it came to their interaction with the Goddess, Wilder took over. Even though Rose had been awestruck during their conversation, her feelings about the Goddess were complicated once again.

Wilder spoke about the Goddess without the doubt that had resurfaced in her own heart. His eyes brightened as he spoke about how they had met her and the Companion, the blessing she had spoken over them, and the Goddess's promise to return some of the Gifts.

Feather bounced excitedly from her seat on the floor. "That's us, right? That's why we felt called to the crystal and then passed out!"

Kieran leaned back on his hands and spoke in a bored voice. "Just because Tayeh has a Gift doesn't mean the rest of us do. Why would she choose me? I'm not one of her followers."

Rose bit her lips to keep from asking the same question.

"Tayeh's not one of her followers either," said Quinn calmly. "But she obviously can heal now, so something out of the ordinary occurred last night."

"I want to find out." Feather stood and took a vase with a single cut flower off the shelf. "I saw this flower last night when we came in. No ... it's more like I *heard* it. Maybe because I had tears drying on my face?"

Kieran muttered, "Or maybe because you have an active imagination?"

Feather ignored him. "I think my Gift is Order."

Tayeh shifted from her spot by the door. "I don't know if you should. Using the Gift was very ... disorienting. If Rose hadn't carried me down the staircase, I might have passed out. I don't know if my Gift is working like it's supposed to."

Rev studied Tayeh's face. "That's concerning. I've seen Tayeh take on a gang of street thugs on her own. If something is strong enough to knock her out, it's a big deal."

Feather stared at the flower, her eyes a shade of darker copper than her skin. She blinked, then collected the tear from her eye. She stretched forward a shaking hand and brushed her fingertip across the petal.

Thick roots shot from the bottom of the cut flower, and the glass vase shattered with a crack. Feather leaned back, her pouty lips opened in surprise. The roots spread in front of her across the wood floor, curling around the scattered quilts, and small green sprouts popped up. The growing plant slowed to a halt before any flowers bloomed.

Everyone stared silently at the little plants growing amid the glass shards.

Feather swallowed loudly. "I ... think I need ... sunlight to make it grow more." Her lips twisted into a grimace. "I don't feel so good ..." She jumped up and ran to the bathroom.

Tayeh raised her eyebrows but didn't offer an "I told you so."

"Well, that's two Gifts," said Fitz. "Three, if you count Wilder calling the wind. I'd love to find out if I have a Gift as well, but I'm not sure I want to vomit up pancakes to test it out."

"Is that normal, Rose?" Quinn asked. "Do all Priests react that way when they use their Gift the first time?"

Rose choked down her bitterness and tried to answer his honest question as calmly as possible. "I don't remember the first time. Priests manifest their Gifts when they are babies. They cry, as babies do, and their tears trigger their Gift."

She felt all their eyes on her. They wondered why the Goddess left her out. Why the Priest was the only one who didn't get a Gift. Why the Goddess chose them and not Rose.

She wondered the same things, but she couldn't handle the confusion and pity in their eyes. She took a deep breath and prepared to let them know what they could do with their pity.

Wilder stood suddenly, and the loss of his warmth at her side shocked her into silence.

"The return of the Goddess's Gifts isn't our only concern. Vaylan is planning to take over the City. We need to find out more about him. He lived in this Giotto fourteen years ago. We need to find someone who knew him to tell us what really happened. If there is anyone like that still alive." He said the last sentence quietly. Trev and Laryn must know that Clayr was probably dead, but Wilder was sensitive to their presence in the next room.

"I propose we split up and see what information we can gather," said Tayeh. "This group is too large to sneak around easily." She gave an annoyed glance at Kieran. "And I'm not sure how beneficial it is for us all to stick together."

Kieran narrowed his eyes at her and seemed to wonder the same thing.

Rev nodded. "I agree. Tayeh, take Quinn with you. Wilder, you can take Fitz and Kieran." Rose saw Wilder's lips turn down in the hint of a scowl. He'd told her Kieran was mean. Apparently, the others agreed; no one wanted Kieran on their team.

Rev finished assigning their roles. "We will leave Feather here with Trev and Laryn. Let's hope she recovers quickly."

Rose looked around as the others began moving toward their different tasks. "And what are we doing?"

Rev looked her up and down. "We are taking you shopping for clothes that won't get you killed."

5

———————

Before they could leave, Rose had to borrow clothes from Laryn. Her black shirt and pants were caked in blood and sweat, so she felt no remorse in throwing them away. The sweat was all hers, but she realized with a start that some of the blood on her pants belonged to Mayra.

Yesterday seemed like a lifetime ago.

Rev ogled her approvingly when Rose entered the kitchen. Laryn had given her a tank top with skulls printed on the front and a short red plaid skirt. She said it was her "work clothes," then laughed with Rev. Rose had no idea what kind of work Laryn did, but at least the clothes were cute.

The shops in Grotto Chaos were a lot different from any she had seen in the City. People shopped quickly and didn't linger inside the dimly lit stores. There didn't seem to be as many crystalline lamps as Upstairs, but that suited Rose's current attitude toward crystalline just fine.

Rose had never considered clothing for herself that wasn't black, so she appreciated Rev's help. She found a cute pair of turquoise boots, a few brightly colored crop tops, and pants so perfectly form fitting that Rev couldn't stop waggling her eyebrows.

Rose found the variety of colors disorienting but wearing something besides black gave her a feeling of anonymity that she had never felt before. She couldn't decide if she loved the feeling or hated it.

As they stepped up to the counter, Rose was grateful that Rev paid for the clothing, since she still couldn't understand how people earned money. She didn't know what she would do if she didn't have wealthy friends.

She really needed to find a marketable skill.

After clothes shopping, they stopped by a market to replenish Trev and Laryn's pantry. Rose tried to help Rev carry all the bags of food and coffee and clothes, but Rev shook her off.

"It's best if I carry everything," said Rev. "You are the better fighter, so you should keep your weapons ready."

Rose widened her eyes but obeyed. "It's really that dangerous here?"

"Yes. All the Grottos have their own dangers, but Grotto Chaos takes its Vice seriously. You never know who will jump out and get you."

Rose eyed the dark shadows around corners warily. "I've noticed a lot of ... unusual people here."

Rev sighed. "Yes. There are many people with illnesses of the mind here. They are often celebrated, but the literal chaos of this Grotto tends to make their situations worse. It's a bad cycle."

"Why doesn't anyone help them? There are healing centers in the City to care for people with illnesses that Priests can't cure."

Rev snorted. "I don't know if you've noticed this, Rose, but the Underneath is much different from Upstairs."

Rose straightened her shoulders in response. "Obviously. I just think there are ways to help the people here. It doesn't have to be like this."

Rev's voice softened. "I agree. And there are those of us who attempt to do what we can. But it's never enough." She sighed. "I always think how different Wilder's life would have been if there had been healing centers down here."

"What do you mean?"

Rev hesitated, as if unsure if she said too much. "How much has Wilder told you about his parents?"

Rose thought back to the conversation she had with Wilder and Fitz about their families. "He said his father did a good deed for a Warden and won his way Upstairs." She wondered how that tied into Vaylan's story about spending over a decade in a High Priest's prison. "His father left him alone with his mother ... Wilder said she should not have been allowed to have children."

Rev's expression turned sad. "Most of the sick people in Chaos aren't violent. But Wilder's mother was. He doesn't speak much about his childhood with her, but what he has said is awful. If there had been a place for her to get help, maybe his childhood would have turned out differently. As it is, I'm not sure how he survived."

Rose considered the story in silence.

Rev's face brightened. "But he didn't just survive. He grew into one of the best people I know. It's one of the surest signs of the Goddess I've ever seen."

Rose studied her out of the corner of her eye as they continued to walk. She envied Rev's faith that the Goddess caused good things to happen. There was a time when Rose believed that. Now nothing was clear.

When they arrived back at the house, Feather was sitting on the couch with hunched shoulders. Wilder came out of the kitchen with a steaming mug in his hands. He smiled at Rose and Rev before sitting down next to Feather.

"Drink this," he said. "It will help settle your stomach."

Rev carried their food into the kitchen while Rose looked at the plant growing in the middle of the room. Small red flowers had sprouted among the vines while they were gone.

"Thanks, Wilder." Feather took a tentative sip. "You're so nice."

"I guess you definitively proved your point. You actually *heard* that plant last night."

She tilted her heart-shaped face at him and gave him a beatific smile.

Rose narrowed her eyes at the girl but was distracted by Rev coming back into the room.

"Did you discover anything while you were out?" Rev plopped down on the arm of the couch, practically in Wilder's lap.

"I heard rumors about weird stuff happening at the former Warden's Den. Not that weird stuff hasn't always happened there, but we should probably check it out." He bit his lip, not meeting her eyes. "No one in my old neighborhood remembers Vaylan. They are all new or didn't know him back then."

Rose considered him. "You went to your old neighborhood? To the house you grew up in?"

He shrugged and studied the plant on the floor. "It wasn't pleasant, but it needed to be done."

Feather looked confused but continued to drink her medicine as she was told.

Rev frowned. "I think we are too late to find anything here. Vaylan knew who to look for and had the element of surprise on his side. I'm sure they never saw him coming."

"But why would he need to kill people that knew him back then?" asked Rose. "What's his motivation?"

Wilder met her eyes. "His life in Grotto Chaos was just

like everyone else's. He was one of the many people struggling to survive. But that story is too common, and he believes he is something extraordinary. That means he needs to eliminate anyone who knew him before. Including me."

Rose slumped against the wall like he'd punched her in the gut. Her mind played out a dozen different ways that Vaylan could kill Wilder. Poisonous dust, knife in the back, burning him with crystalline ... Vaylan murdered him over and over, and she saw the bright spark in Wilder's eyes go out. A terror seized her like she had never known.

The flame of her anger roared to life.

"I. Will. Kill. Him." Each word was a promise. A vow. She had already planned to kill him for the way he'd used her as a pawn while murdering Brother Owyn, Mayra, and the other six Priests. But the thought of him killing Wilder filled her with such fury that she felt her blood heating in her veins.

"Rose." Wilder's soft voice shattered her rage.

She blinked and found him looking at her with the same ferocious desire in his eyes as the day she threatened to burn the heretics who sold Knowledge.

The two of them would storm libraries and challenge mobs together. And together, they would defeat Vaylan.

Her lips curled in a small smile, and she nodded in agreement at this unspoken communication.

They didn't break eye contact until Rev laughed. "I knew this would be fun. Didn't I say it would be fun, Wilder?" She patted him on the shoulder, but he still looked at Rose. "But the two of you shouldn't have such long silent conversations with us in the room. Just look at poor Feather here!" Feather's mouth was open wide, and the empty mug dangled in her hands. "Goddess bless her, she doesn't know what to make of the two of you."

Rose wasn't sure she liked how easily Rev could read the moments that passed between her and Wilder. Rose liked to believe she was good at hiding her emotions, because the alternative seemed weak. She smoothed out her plaid skirt and stood tall.

Rev pulled a still shocked Feather to her feet. "Besides, we need to get ready if we are going to arrive on time." She gave Rose a mysterious smile.

Rose asked the question Rev was begging her to ask. "Where are we going?"

She grinned. "We are going to watch Trev and Laryn work."

6

—————

Rose had never heard music so loud in her life. Even before they entered the nightclub, the rumble of the bass pulsed through her boots. When they opened the doors, a wall of sound slammed into her and rattled her down to the bone.

She shivered in delight.

The guys had left early for the club, but the girls had stayed behind to finish preparing for their night out. Once suitably dressed, the four of them headed out together. As Rose walked between Rev, Tayeh, and Feather into the nightclub, their steps fell in time to the bass drum. The music filled her with a joy she hadn't felt for days.

The people inside the club danced with a wild abandon Rose found intoxicating. She wanted to fling herself into the churning mix of people around the stage and lose herself among them. But she held back, sticking close to her well-dressed girlfriends.

Rev glittered in the dark room. Her tiny dress was shocking pink with strategic rips revealing hints of pale skin. She flipped her blond ponytail over her shoulder as she bent to needlessly adjust her gold thigh-high boots.

Tayeh wore a fitted leather vest and tight pants, as usual. Her burnished brown skin glowed in contrast with the light gray leather and polished silver buckles. She always appeared to be above trivial fashion concerns, but Rose knew Tayeh's beautiful dark cloud of hair didn't just style itself. Tayeh surveyed the crowd with confidence. She knew she looked good, and Rose appreciated that about her.

Feather wore a strapless white romper that flowed gently as she walked. Her sleek black ponytail slid across her copper shoulders whenever she turned her head. Despite only being seventeen, her outfit was that of a strong, confident woman. And she could have pulled it off, if not for the wide-eyed look of innocence frozen on her face.

Rose still wore the borrowed red plaid skirt, but she had added ripped fishnets along with her new turquoise boots. She'd traded out the tank top for a deep purple corset with shimmering swirls. She was already questioning the decision of wearing a tight corset with still bruised ribs, though it wouldn't be the first time she suffered for the sake of a cute outfit.

The Underneath lacked many things, but luckily, fashion was not one of them.

Rose bent closer to hear Rev speak. "I thought we would make a grand entrance by showing up late and walking in formation through the front door. But no, they pull off an even more dramatic entrance." She frowned and gestured across the bar.

Rose stood taller to keep the corset boning from stabbing her, and as she turned, her mouth fell open. Wilder led the other guys down a giant stone staircase looping through the club. Quinn smoothed a hand down the front of his cream jacket. The bright teal shirt underneath made his blue eyes shine, even from behind his dark-rimmed glasses. Kieran adjusted the collar of his well-tailored floral jacket, examining the crowd with a haughty look. And Fitz's strange, mismatched, grungy outfit suddenly made sense with the other fashion inside the club.

But Wilder ... He strutted down the stairs like a Goddess-damn work of art.

In many ways, he looked exactly as he always did. Dark leather pants tighter than necessary. A deep burgundy shirt unbuttoned further than necessary. It was a look most men could not pull off without looking ridiculous. But everything about him fit together perfectly. He walked in time with the slow thump of the bass line, as if his footfalls vibrated the floor beneath her feet.

As he drew closer, she spotted it: the extra bounce of his raven black curls. The way his shirt pressed gently against his chest. But it was the cool breeze that slid along her shoulders in an otherwise still room that brought her up short.

He stepped in front of her with a wide smile and had just opened his mouth when she hissed at him. "What in the Abyss do you think you are doing?"

He leaned back and blinked. "What are you talking about?"

She moved closer to him and slitted her eyes as she studied his face. He genuinely seemed confused, but she knew what he'd done.

"Did you call the wind to yourself to make a grand entrance?" At this accusation, the others drifted off to find somewhere else to be.

"Did I call ...?" He shook his head in confusion. "I called the wind at the amphitheater, but I barely knew what I was doing. Do you seriously think I would experiment with that here?"

He was practically shouting over the loud music, and she was angry enough to shout back.

"You are vain enough to try it! Don't deny it!"

His eyes blazed in response. "I'm vain? I bet you're accusing me because you've done it yourself!"

She bit her lips, refusing to answer, because the accusation was dead-on.

He leaned closer, and though he had to yell to be heard, his voice was a soft breeze against her ear. "I look this good with no help from the wind. Don't take your anger at the Goddess out on me."

She stepped back with a growl. She threw him one last angry look over her shoulder, then plunged into the surging crowd of dancers.

Rose let the crowd sweep her closer to the stage. As she drew near, she recognized Trev playing guitar and Laryn on drums. Discipline Priests could control the intensity of music by controlling the air around the instruments, but these instruments were locked on to stone bases covered in crystalline. She shook her head in wonder. They had used the crystalline to amplify the sound without a need for a Priest. She followed the shining liquid along its path into a stone case that pointed out to the crowd. She didn't enjoy thinking about another task that rendered Priests unnecessary, but she appreciated the religious significance. The Companion was, above all, a musician. It was quite poetic that his blood could project music to the masses.

Her thoughts didn't remain on the instruments for long. The music itself could not be ignored. Each strum of the metallic guitar buzzed along her skin, and the pounding drumbeat overtook the rhythm of her own heart. She focused on the girl standing center stage. Her hair was wrapped into two messy buns in shocking blue, and her lips were painted black. She sang-screamed into her own crystalline contraption that blasted her voice over the crowd.

Rose found it difficult to make out all the lyrics, but the sentiment was clear enough. Overthrow. Rebel. Burn it all down.

Rose recognized the fact that, as a Priest, she was part of the system the girl sang to overthrow. But there was something so raw and primal in the girl's song. And there was a deep part of Rose that desperately agreed.

Burn it all down.

She raised her fist in the air and jumped in time with the rest of the crowd. She screamed lyrics she didn't know, but the music was so loud that it didn't matter what she sang wrong. Her physical pain disappeared as she moved in time to the beat. All her doubts and fears sank below the surface of the anger burning inside her chest.

There were no Gifts.

There was no Goddess.

There was only this one perfect moment of rage.

She stopped her dance and screamed out a bellow of fury as she had never done before.

And no one even noticed.

She stood panting, wanting to lean over and catch her breath but unable to bend thanks to her corset. Her furious scream sank into the crowd unnoticed by anyone except her.

She felt unreasonably light. A weight had lifted from her chest that she didn't know was there. She threw back her head and laughed, letting it turn into another scream, swallowed up in the crowd.

As she lowered her head, she found a guy standing in front of her. There were a lot of men dancing around her, but the unusual thing was that this one stood completely still.

The other unusual thing was that he was gorgeous.

His hair fell to his shoulders in tousled waves of caramel, and his skin glistened bronze beneath his white cotton shirt. He stood perfectly still, staring right at her. She sensed his intention a moment before he moved.

There was time for her to react. But she didn't.

He pulled her into a kiss that was tender yet furious. Her laughing rage from a moment before blossomed into a reckless surrender, and though she didn't kiss him back, she allowed herself to melt into his strong arms, offering no resistance to his daring kiss.

He released her, and her body sagged. He bit his bottom lip playfully as he pulled a slip of paper out of his shirt pocket. Without breaking eye contact, he slipped it gently into the top of her corset.

With one last glance, he stepped backward and melted into the crowd.

She couldn't move, frozen in place. What just happened? The entire experience was completely foreign to her. And yet, with passion and adrenaline and the lingering rage coursing through her veins, she couldn't say that she regretted it. She turned around to find Wilder and Rev watching her.

The regret quickly kicked in.

Rev's cold blue eye fixed on Rose with an accusatory glare. Wilder had also seen the kiss, but his face was unreadable. There was no jealousy. There was no anger.

There was nothing.

Rev pulled her by the arm through the crowd into an alcove where the music wasn't so loud. "Who in the Goddess's name was that?"

"I don't know." Rose looked at Wilder for a hint of anger, but she still couldn't sense anything.

Rev crossed her arms over her chest. "So, you just kissed some random stranger on the dance floor?"

Her judgmental blue eye stirred Rose's anger back to life. "He's the one who kissed me! What was I supposed to do? Punch him in the throat?"

Rev regarded Rose with a calmly raised eyebrow. "Yes, actually. That's what I would expect from you."

Rose wanted to protest, but honestly, that sounded like her typical behavior.

Rev turned her eye on Wilder, looking at him as if checking for injuries. His face hadn't shifted from its neutral expression, and Rev turned back to Rose with a glare.

Rose had the feeling she would soon receive another "girl talk."

Rev blew out a frustrated breath. "So, that gorgeous guy kissed you, then just wandered away? In exchange for creating such drama, he could have at least left a way for me to find him later for a kiss of my own." Her pink lips curved into a pout.

Rose blinked, suddenly remembering the note he had tucked down her corset. She pulled out the slip of paper.

Rev's eye lit up. "I'm still upset with you, but you can redeem yourself if that has his address on it. Maybe he has a brother." She bit her bottom lip. "Or a sister." And then an evil grin. "Or maybe both ..."

Rose rolled her eyes and opened the folded slip of paper. Her skin still felt overheated, but when she recognized the familiar handwriting, her blood ran cold.

Rose,

I'm glad you made it to the Underneath. I am visiting the Grottos myself, and I'd love to chat with you. Please come find me in what was formerly the Warden's Den at your earliest convenience. My mark will grant you entrance.

Blessings,

Vaylan

7

Rose stormed through the streets of Chaos. She wasn't exactly sure where the Warden's Den was located, but knew it was close to the crystal, which was an obvious landmark. Even though she was alone, no one harassed her as she made her way down the strangely winding streets. She wondered if her expression scared them off or if they were all too tired to fight because of the early hour.

After Rev had snatched Vaylan's letter from Rose's hands the previous night, they'd had a lengthy discussion about what should be done, even though a loud nightclub was not the best place to discuss serious matters. Rose wanted to discover what game Vaylan was playing, but Rev and Wilder disagreed.

Wilder believed the letter was Vaylan's way of luring Rose in with an innocent request so he could use her to accomplish his nefarious plans. But Rose knew Wilder suspected her deeper purpose.

She planned to kill Vaylan, no matter the cost.

After Vaylan invited her inside, she planned to stab him as soon as he turned his back. Vaylan had so many deaths on his hands, and Wilder was in his sights. Rose planned to use this invitation to stop him now.

She didn't speak her plan aloud to Rev, but Wilder saw it written on her face. He hadn't confronted her with the accusation, though she wished he had. She longed to see something other than the casual indifference on his face since he'd seen her kiss the messenger on the dance floor.

They agreed to leave the club and discuss it in the morning when they didn't have to scream over loud music. Rose appeared to comply.

But instead, she woke early and left before anyone noticed.

She didn't want to get into a conversation with the whole crew about whether she should meet with Vaylan. Especially not if Rev told the others how Vaylan issued his invitation. Rose's gut clenched when she imagined Vaylan giving his letter to that gorgeous man and sending him to find Rose. How dare he think that was a reasonable method to summon her!

She attempted to overlook the method's effectiveness.

As she drew closer to the crystal, she found the former Warden's Den, a roughhewn building carved into the side of the cave wall. It seemed like a very strategic location in the Grotto, so she couldn't imagine it standing vacant these last few weeks. When had Vaylan found the time to take it over?

"At least you are taking a moment to consider this monumentally bad decision." She spun around at the sound of Wilder's voice. He stood with his arms crossed, Tayeh at his side. "I expected you to run the entire way here with a blade in your hand. The fact that you stopped, even briefly, is a definite improvement."

She put her hands on her hips. "I'm going in there."

His jaw flexed as he ground his teeth together. "Not alone."

"If you go in there, he won't let you back out."

"Not me." His voice was halting, as if he hated saying the words. "Tayeh's going with you."

Rose looked at Tayeh, who raised a calm eyebrow in response.

"Oh," said Rose simply. "That's not a bad idea."

Wilder's mouth twisted. "It's an idea we could have decided together. If you hadn't run off on your own. Again."

Rose cleared her throat. "Well, yes ... I can see that now." She took a deep breath and spoke calmly. "I will attempt to be more reasonable next time, okay?"

His eyes said that he didn't believe her. He thought she would run off on her own again. He thought she would continue to act without thinking.

He thought she would break his heart.

She bit her lip. "About last night ..."

Tayeh grunted once, then wandered away a few steps. She fell into a watchful stance, observing everything but the two of them.

He shook his head. "You don't owe me—"

"I'm sorry, Wilder." She tugged on the front of her fuchsia jacket, searching for the right words. "While I didn't kiss that messenger on purpose, I didn't stop him. I got caught up in the music because I was angry." She huffed out a breath, and her shoulders sagged. "I'm always angry lately, so that's not a good excuse. I wish I could go back in time and punch him in the throat like I should have."

His dark eyes searched her face, and she saw the question that still lurked below the surface. The question that haunted him because he had been hurt before.

Even though they stood in the middle of a busy street and her cheeks blazed with heat, she whispered the answer he needed to hear. "I only want to kiss you, Wilder."

The tightened muscles around his mouth relaxed, and

suddenly all she could think about was his lips on hers. She licked her lips unconsciously, and his mouth curled in a gentle grin. She leaned toward him but was knocked backward by a scruffy child running past.

Suddenly, Tayeh was at her side. "A group is gathering."

Rose straightened her jacket, trying to regain a semblance of her previous focus. She nodded at Tayeh and turned to the Den.

"Wait!"

Rose turned back at Wilder's sharp call. His face was solemn, but the question in his eyes had fled. "Be careful," he whispered.

She gave him a small smile, then walked toward the Den.

Tayeh fell into step beside her, and they melted into the crowd of people surrounding the Den. Each person they passed had slumped shoulders and a vacant stare. They passed a messy-haired woman staring at the Den with hungry eyes. It took a moment for Rose to realize there was a small child huddled in the woman's ragged skirt. The woman's eyes focused on the two of them for a moment, then she clutched the child tighter and continued her close watch of the Den.

"What has Vaylan done to these people?" Rose's eyes caught on an old man leaning on a cane. He pulled his jacket tighter around him, as if that would protect him from her, before he shuffled away. "All of them look half-starved and terrified."

Tayeh frowned. "Vaylan isn't solely to blame. Food is harder to find now." She looked at the massive closed doors of the Den. "But I don't know what everyone is doing here."

"We're here for food," said a quiet voice at their side. A young woman tugged at her low-cut blouse with an anxious look over her shoulder. The rouge on her cheeks didn't hide her sickly complexion, and she bit her chapped lips nervously.

"Someone here gives you food?" asked Rose.

The young woman looked Rose and Tayeh up and down. "You're both strong. They might have someone you can rough up in exchange for food. If not, they are usually willing to accept other ... favors."

Rose watched the young woman shuffle forward in line, and a sick fury bloomed in her chest. Vaylan talked about freedom and equality—is this what he was really after all along? Taking advantage of starving, desperate people?

Rose pushed forward through the crowd, but Tayeh caught her arm in a rock-solid grasp. She opened her mouth to hiss but followed Tayeh's gaze to the back of the crowd.

A hush fell as Vaylan strode through the hungry people, his midnight-blue cape streaming behind him, along with a formation of six Sentinels at his back. The crowd parted as he strode up to the entrance of the Den. He didn't say a word but raised his hands over his head, his fingers shaping into claws. With the tendons on the back of his hands straining, he pushed his hands firmly out to his sides.

Every drop of crystalline around him slid away, casting the entire area in shadow.

The crowd murmured in anxious whispers, terrified yet too hungry to leave. Tayeh's hand slipped from Rose's arm, but Rose was too shocked to stage an attack.

Eight burly men stormed out of the Den, looking for the cause of the sudden darkness. Vaylan wasted no time. He kept his arms outstretched, but he tipped his head, and the Sentinels took that as their cue.

The burly men fell quickly. Some fell to poisonous dust. Some fell to swords. Some fell to truly spectacular kicks aimed right at their heads. Despite her terror at seeing Sentinels, she admired their skill. Vaylan's Sentinels appeared to be better trained than the High Priests' Sentinels ever needed to be.

The murmuring crowd slipped into silence as Vaylan turned around to face them, outstretched arms still holding back the crystalline. The Sentinels slid into formation around him, and an older woman bit back a choked sob.

Vaylan turned his warm smile on the woman. "There is no need to fear the Sentinels. I have taken them from the Goddess, and now they follow me. They will no longer hurt the innocent but will hunt down those that have harmed you."

"Who are you?" whispered the young woman in the low-cut blouse.

Vaylan heard her quiet whisper, and his eyes blazed with religious fervor. "I am the one Brother Owyn foretold. He said, 'Seek the light.'" He grinned, revealing his dimple. "That's me."

He clapped his hands over his head, and the crystalline blazed a bright silver. Tiny crystalline rivers flowed over the rough-hewn stone of the cave wall, bathing the Den's entrance in a glittering web of light. Tendrils of crystalline snaked up the walls of the underground cavern, creating a beacon of light pointing straight at the Den.

Tayeh whistled quietly. "I see where Wilder gets his showmanship."

Wilder's name snapped Rose out of her open-mouthed stare. "I have to stop him. Go tell the others Vaylan took control of the Den."

Tayeh looked up at the crystalline beacon and raised an eyebrow. "I think they will figure it out on their own." She shook her head and took Rose's arm again. "We need to leave."

Rose started to protest, but Vaylan's voice stopped her.

"I am the leader Brother Owyn foretold—the one who

will bring about his vision for the future. A City of equality and freedom, with no more Goddess controlling your life."

A few people whispered nervously, but most of them stared at Vaylan as if he was their savior. Rose shook off Tayeh's grip and pressed through the crowd.

A Sentinel stepped smoothly in front of Vaylan to block her path.

She stared into the unnerving, faceless black mask and tried to calm her breathing. The Sentinel's head tilted to the side, then they stepped back, granting her access to Vaylan.

She touched the wound at her throat self-consciously. Vaylan's note said her mark would grant her entrance. Tayeh watched with hard eyes on the other side of a wall of Sentinels, perched on her toes and ready to attack. Tayeh was good, but Rose knew the outcome if they were forced to fight. She ground her teeth together and promised herself to remain calm.

Vaylan's eyes twinkled, as if he knew it was a struggle for her not to attack him. "I'm so pleased you came, Rose. I wasn't sure you would."

"You sent an interesting messenger," she said coldly.

"Ah, yes. What a nice young man! I told him to hand you the letter in whatever way he thought would get your attention. I'm glad to see he was successful."

Rose crossed her arms over her chest and glared at him.

Vaylan looked up at the sparkling beacon he had created. "It's only right that you would be here at the beginning. I'm heading to Delirium next. I hope you join me there as well."

"So, this is just the first stop on your path to dominate the entire City?"

His lips curled in a paternal smile that made her stomach churn. "I still believe in everything I told you before. I believe in equality and no separation between the Upstairs and Underneath."

She studied him, looking below his peaceful exterior. "Under your firm hand."

He grinned, and his dimple reappeared. "I haven't met anyone with a better plan than mine. Have you?"

Her voice was a rough growl. "The only people I knew with a plan were those setting themselves up as High Priests, and you killed them."

He shook his head, looking at her as if she was a forgetful child. "Those Priests were killed by a mob, not me."

"A mob you led to their door!" She clenched her fists. "You invoke Brother Owyn's name, but your Sentinels are the ones who killed him."

His easy smile faltered, and sadness passed behind his eyes. "Brother Owyn died to bring about the future he dreamed of." He sighed and clasped his hands together as his patient smile returned. "Everything happened as it should, even though it grieves me. But I can't avoid my destiny. I must do what it takes to unite this City."

"Don't act like you will be some benevolent ruler. You aren't interested in anyone besides yourself!" she hissed.

He leaned forward. "I'll make you an offer, Rose. Follow me as I go about my work. Watch me. Judge my worthiness for yourself. If you find someone with a better plan to lead this City, I promise you, I will listen. But if not, all I ask is that you consider what I offer and judge it fairly."

She studied him with narrowed eyes, wondering if it was wise to make a deal with a power-hungry murderer. But if he trusted her, she could get him away from his Sentinels and kill him.

He didn't wait for a response but turned back to the crowd and raised his voice. "Even though their Goddess is false, I have permitted the Priests to live. Since they surrendered their Sentinels willingly, they are free to remain inside their temples." His normally smooth voice took on a sharp note. "However, if any of their Priests—or *former* Priests—strike at me, the truce will end."

Vaylan turned his head, and she was the only one who saw him wink.

He turned back to the crowd with arms spread wide. "This Den is now a Haven for my followers. All are welcome."

And with those last dramatic words, he walked inside the bright Haven, followed by Sentinels and a crowd of hungry followers.

8

———

Rose and Tayeh had barely made it a few steps away from the crowd when Wilder stepped out of a side street. "Are you okay?"

Rose pointed at the glowing crystalline beacon. "Vaylan says he's taking over all the Dens like that. And he's holding the Priests' lives as collateral to make sure I don't attack him."

Wilder shook his head. "You can't meet with him again. It's too dangerous."

"I'm fine— "

He raised an eyebrow. "Too dangerous for the other Priests."

Rose let out of a huff of irritation, even though she knew he had a point. She rubbed her bruised ribs absently as she considered her next argument.

Tayeh's normally confident voice was hesitant. "I can try to heal you again ... if you want."

Rose's hand on her ribs stilled. "It's not that bad. Not bad enough that I want you to have a negative reaction from it. Maybe we should wait until it's something serious."

Tayeh shrugged. "I should practice. And it's best to practice when we aren't in the middle of a fight."

Rose sighed. "You're probably right."

Tayeh closed her eyes for a moment, then blinked, forming a tear. She took hold of Rose's hand.

Nothing happened.

Tayeh frowned. "Am I missing something? This is exactly what I did last time. In fact, it was so easy it was almost unintentional."

Rose pasted on a comforting smile. She was once again in the position of training someone to use a Gift despite not having her own returned. "The ability to use your Gift in skilled ways takes time. However, you should feel *something*, even if the results aren't what you wanted."

Tayeh closed her eyes and scrunched her face in concentration. She dropped Rose's hand with a huff. "Nothing."

Wilder turned to her with sharp eyes. "Did you drink any tea at the Den?"

Tayeh rolled her eyes. "I'm not an idiot, Wilder."

He had the good sense to look apologetic. "Sorry. Of course you aren't."

Rose forced her lips into an encouraging smile. "You can try again later."

They walked the rest of the way in silence, which made it easier to hear the yelling coming from inside the house when they arrived.

"I'm not doing it wrong!" shouted Feather. Rose was surprised to hear the usually soft-spoken girl yelling as they entered the house.

Kieran casually flipped his blond hair. "Well, you obviously aren't doing it *right*."

"I'm doing it exactly the same!" she huffed. "And what do you know? You haven't even figured out what Gift you have." She murmured under her breath, "If you even have one."

Rev groaned. "Seriously, you two. Cut it out."

Wilder closed the door behind him. "You're having difficulties with your Gift, too, Feather?"

She looked up at him hopefully. "Too? You're having the same problem?"

He ducked his head. "Oh ... I didn't try. It was Tayeh."

Feather sighed. "I'm glad it's not just me. That means it's something we can figure out together." She looked up at Rose with teary eyes. "Do you know why it's happening?"

Rose pushed down her irritation and took a seat on the couch next to Quinn and Fitz. "No. I'm not sure." At Feather's downcast face, she added, "But try again, and I'll see if I notice anything."

Rose knew that was ridiculous. Other than seeing someone produce a tear, there were no other visible signs of a Priest using a Gift.

Feather nodded her head solemnly, then touched a tear to an offshoot of the plant she had caused to grow the day before.

Roots and vines shot outward, and small red blossoms popped up among the green.

Feather's eyes glowed with pride. "It's working! And I even grew flowers this time! Why couldn't I—" She swallowed sharply and ran toward the bathroom.

Kieran rolled his eyes, but the rest of the crew studied the flowers in bloom.

"What was different this time?" asked Fitz. "Did you do something, Rose?"

"Me?" she blurted loudly. "What could I do?"

"I just thought ..." His voice trailed off.

"I couldn't help Tayeh earlier, so it wasn't me." She crossed her arms and sank back into the couch.

Tayeh reached out her hand. "Can I try again?"

Rose shrugged. She knew she was being petulant, but she had reached the limit of her ability to pretend.

As soon as Rose touched Tayeh's hand, an icy blast of air wrapped around her ribs. Vaylan's fingerprint still burned at her throat, but Rose finally took her first full breath without discomfort.

She sighed and gave Tayeh a sincere smile. "Thank you, Tayeh. That's much better."

Tayeh staggered but kept her feet. She nodded a response, breathing slowly through her nose.

"So, what's different?" asked Rev. "Feather has been trying since you left this morning. What changed?"

"That's what changed!" said Quinn excitedly. "They came back."

Fitz leaned forward in his spot beside Rose. "It makes sense. The Gifts have traditionally been about balance. The numbers of Priests with each Gift have always been very stable. It's one way the High Priests knew the Wardens were up to something. The numbers were out of balance."

Kieran made an irritated sound. "So, if we want to use these Gifts at all, we are stuck with each other?"

"Is there somewhere else you need to be, Kieran?" Rev crossed her arms across her chest.

"I auditioned for the Pageant. Not this." He gestured at their scattered blankets across the floor from where they slept.

"We are still having a Pageant," said Rose firmly.

Everyone but Wilder turned to her with open mouths.

Kieran started laughing. "Still having a Pageant? How are we supposed to do that?" He ticked the obstacles off on his fingers. "There are roaming factions who want to murder anyone involved in the Goddess's religion. They already murdered the Priest in charge of the audition, along with six others. And the eight of us are currently on the run from Wilder's dad, who loosed Sentinels on us."

Rose answered with as much dignity as she could. "It's unclear if those Sentinels were trying to kill us."

Kieran laughed louder. "It's ridiculous, Rose. Give up. There's no Pageant. And by sticking together, all we can do is use a Gift that makes us sick."

Rose's voice dropped to a low growl. "We are having a Pageant. And you will play the Companion as planned. I don't know when it's happening or how, but I will not let you out of my sight until you sing every note perfectly and the Goddess returns all her Gifts."

Kieran prickled like she stroked his fur the wrong way. He grabbed his bag and looked down his nose at them. "Unlike the rest of you, I have better things I could do right now."

He stomped to the door, but Rev smoothly intercepted him. She looked him up and down with her sharp blue eye, and though he was over a foot taller than her, he stepped back.

"This is the break you've been waiting for, Kieran." Her voice was a warm yet dangerous purr. "Your chance to be special. It's true you have to share it with the rest of us, but it finally happened. Someone picked *you.*" She poked him in the chest, and he took another step back. "That doesn't happen every day. And in the Underneath, it rarely happens at all." She smiled pleasantly and whispered her last sentence as a sweet threat. "You will take your place as a member of this crew .... or else."

Kieran was stunned speechless by her pronouncement. He blinked several times, and his mouth moved as if he would speak. Eventually, he walked back to his blanket, lowered his bag, and sat back down.

Rev turned to Wilder as if nothing had happened. "So,

what's the plan? We can't stay here with Trev and Laryn forever."

Wilder was still staring at Kieran, who now sat calmly on the floor, and shook his head before answering her. "You're right. We need to find another place to stay, but we don't have many contacts in Chaos."

"I think we should go to Delirium," said Rose.

"Why?" asked Quinn. "What's so special there?"

"I don't know," she answered honestly. "I've never been. But that's where Vaylan is going next. I don't trust him, and I want to stay close enough to watch him."

The crew turned to look at Wilder, and he nodded as he considered the idea. "It's a good plan. We have a lot more contacts in Delirium, so we can probably discover what is happening both Upstairs and down here."

Rev nodded. "We'll leave tomorrow. I'll check on Feather. Everyone else, no tears until we make it to our next home."

DELIRIUM

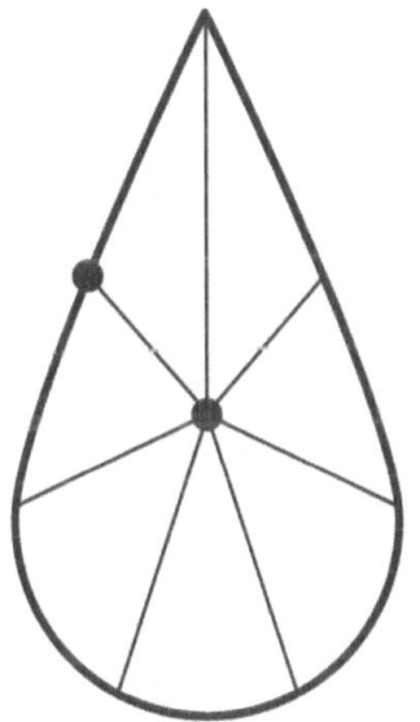

9

———

When they arrived in Delirium the next afternoon, a crystalline web already glowed at the far end of the Grotto. Rose grumbled, "Looks like Vaylan didn't waste any time moving in."

Rev crossed her arms over her chest. "Before you go running off, we need to divide up to buy supplies for the new safe house. You can go with Tayeh and Kieran to pick up some more weapons."

Wilder stepped in before Rose could object. "I usually agree with the wisdom of your assignments, Rev, but I have my own plans for Rose."

Rev gave Rose a smoldering look. "Mmm ... Lucky girl."

Wilder's lips twitched but he didn't correct her assumption. The group was watching, so Rose attempted to look calm, even though her cheeks threatened to flush.

Rev's expression shifted and reminded her of Mims. "Be back before it gets too late. We can't practice any of our Gifts until we are all together, so please be considerate."

Wilder gave her a small bow, then took Rose's hand and led her away from the group.

"Where are we going?" she asked.

He looked back at the rest of the group still conversing before they split up. "Does it matter? I got you out of a group with Kieran."

His eyes twinkled with mischief, and she laughed. She looked down at their clasped hands. She was walking through the streets of the Underneath hand in hand with Wilder. Her mind couldn't comprehend how much her life had changed in the last few weeks.

She grinned. "No, it doesn't matter where we go."

He smiled, and their footsteps slowed to a leisurely stroll.

Wilder pointed out a few interesting shops as they walked. Grotto Delirium had a completely different vibe from Chaos, and Wilder's personality seemed more relaxed. He stopped in front of a window with little bottles and jars lined up in neat rows.

"This is what I was looking for." He opened the door and led her inside.

Dark wooden shelves filled with glass bottles lined the walls. Wilder nodded at the woman shopkeeper, and she gave him a warm smile. A few customers roamed among the shelves, picking up jars and sniffing the contents.

"It's an apothecary," he answered her unasked question. "The Underneath doesn't have the benefit of healers, so we've had to find other remedies." He picked up a pale blue glass jar. "This elixir is good for upset stomachs. I thought I'd pick it up to see if it helps with the side effects the others are dealing with."

She raised a haughty eyebrow. "Only the others? I guess you're so strong your Gift hasn't affected you?"

He ducked his head. "Well, I haven't tried it again since the amphitheater and..."

She tilted her head to catch his eyes. "I'm teasing you."

He gave a rueful smile. "The next time I test out my Gift, I'll try to vomit on your shoes to prove it."

She laughed, then looked around. "So, what else do they have here?"

"Remedies for headaches or the inability to sleep. Although believers in the Vice of Delirium use those for their own sort of worship." He shrugged. "Like everything else down here, there's always a hint of darkness mixed in with the light."

"Sounds the same as Upstairs." She picked up a pink glass jar. "And what's this one?"

He cleared his throat. "Um ... for someone seeking to prevent pregnancy."

She stared at the bottle a moment before realizing what he meant. She cleared her throat and set the bottle down a little too quickly. "Oh. Well, Priests don't need ..."

No one knew why Priests couldn't conceive children, though they assumed it was connected to their Gifts. The strange girl, Ylena, was the exception to the rule, the only child born to Priests. But the bigger question in Rose's mind was, if she didn't have a Gift anymore, did that mean she could get pregnant some day? The thought was so foreign to her she couldn't imagine the implications.

Wilder was studying her face, and she realized her thoughts were probably written plainly. She smoothed her expression and looked around at the other jars hopefully. "Anything else interesting?"

He didn't drag her into a conversation about all the thoughts racing through her mind, instead picking up a small green glass jar and holding it out for her to smell its contents.

"Lavender?" she asked.

His expression was pleased. "Yes. Blended with aloe and

a few other remedies known only to this shopkeeper. It works on burns."

Her mouth dropped opened. Other than healing, she hadn't considered a remedy for the crystalline burn on her collarbone. But Wilder had. Even though she hadn't mentioned the pain, he'd guessed how badly the burn still hurt and brought her here to help.

She looked into his eyes, and her heart beat so loudly she was sure he could hear it. "Did you bring me on a date to buy me medicine?" She wanted her voice to sound coy, but it came out breathless.

His eyes twinkled as he raised the jar. "May I?"

She unbuttoned her collar with shaking fingers. She was self-conscious of the mark and kept it hidden, but that meant her clothes rubbed against the wound, making it sting worse.

He frowned at the sight of the bright red mark lined with a black fingerprint. He scooped out the clear gel and brushed a careful finger along the wound.

She closed her eyes with a quiet indrawn hiss. Despite Tayeh's attempt at healing, the mark had not healed at all. The wound itself never stopped burning, but the balm soothed the irritated skin along the edges. It was the only relief she had felt for days.

Wilder's touch was so tender she wanted to weep. She leaned back with a moan, and as she gripped the table for balance, the little jars clicked together like bells. Wilder's finger circled the inflamed skin with slow, deliberate strokes, and despite her closed eyelids, her eyes rolled back in her head.

When Wilder pulled his hand away, she sighed. She opened her eyes to find him watching her with the hint of a smug smile curving his lips.

"What?" she asked.

"We've spent too much time cooped up with the crew. I'm savoring the fact that I finally got you alone."

She looked around the shop and noticed several people staring at them with wide eyes. "I wouldn't say we are alone."

He chuckled. "We should probably pay and leave these people to finish their shopping in peace."

He paid the shopkeeper for the burn remedy and stomach elixir, and the woman gave Wilder an appraising smile that Rose found quite familiar. Then the woman tilted her head to study the wound on Rose's neck.

Rose quickly buttoned her collar.

"That doesn't look like a normal burn." The woman tapped a finger against her lips, then grabbed a black jar from behind the counter. "If the other remedy doesn't work, try this. It won't help it heal any faster, but it will numb the pain."

Rose accepted the jar with careful hands. "Thank you."

Wilder moved to pull more coins out of his pocket, but the shopkeeper waved him off. "No need. It's on the house." Her eyes sparkled as she studied them both. "And you are welcome to come back anytime to sample my products. I'm going to sell a lot of that burn remedy today thanks to your little ... demonstration."

Rose turned to find the other customers plucking green glass jars off the table she had sprawled against.

Wilder bit his lips to hide his smile and pulled Rose out of the shop before she could express any indignation.

10

After their visit to the apothecary, Rose and Wilder joined the rest of the crew back at their new safe house. Since many people from the Underneath moved Upstairs, Wilder said it was easier for him to find better lodgings than usual. Plus, she didn't think it hurt that he had a lot of money.

They opened the door into a large living room where Kieran lounged on one couch and Tayeh sat on another, sharpening knives spread out on a low table. In the kitchen, Quinn and Fitz sat a long table with a stack of books between them, while Feather chatted happily with Rev as they put food into the cabinets.

Wilder took a seat at the table. "It looks like you were successful at your tasks."

Rev put her hands on her waist and raised an eyebrow. "And it looks like the two of you took the long way to get here."

Wilder grinned. "Possibly. But we picked up some stomach elixir for the next person who uses their Gift." He handed her the pale blue jar.

"I guess I can forgive your tardiness," she said. "I'm

excited to attempt using my Gift, but I admit I'm worried about the effects. Earlier, when I took a bath, I got this strange sense that I could manipulate the water if I tried."

Rose snorted. "Of course that's your Gift."

Rev gave her a curious look, and Wilder laughed. "If anyone should have the Gift of Purity, it's you, Rev."

She leaned against the counter and nodded her head sagely. "The Goddess is full of wisdom."

Feather sat down at the table across from Wilder. "How are the other Gifts divided?" She looked at Fitz and Quinn. "Do either of you know what you are?"

"I think I'm Purpose," said Fitz. "Every stone building we pass and street we walk on resonates strangely to me now. It's very distracting being in the Underneath, where the entire Grotto is stone."

"That's fascinating," said Quinn. "I've sensed nothing unusual. Maybe I—" He paused and cocked his head as if he heard something.

Rose heard nothing, and the others appeared just as confused by his reaction.

Quinn stood quickly and walked into the living room, the rest of them close behind. They discovered Tayeh in front of the closed door with a blade in her hand.

"Someone's out there," she whispered. "Are you expecting anyone?"

Quinn's face lit up, and he flung the door open.

Two white wolves leaped into the room. They ran in circles around Wilder's legs before coming to rest at his side. They sat on their haunches and faced Rose with bowed heads.

"Where have you been?" Rose shook a stern finger at them. "Do you realize how much danger he has been in?"

The wolves whined softly and dipped their heads further.

Quinn's eyes widened. "They're speaking, and I can almost understand them. With a tear, I bet I could fully communicate with them."

Rose continued to glare at the wolves. "Good. Tell them I'm going to find Wilder a new pair of wolves if they don't shape up."

They whined and lowered onto their front paws.

"I think they understand you pretty well." Despite his laugh of delight, a tear formed on his lashes. He bent down to study the wolves.

The wolves' blue eyes didn't move from Rose's face. Quinn turned to look up at her. "They call you 'Lady Fire Wolf.'"

Feather cooed. "Oh, that's so sweet! They think your hair looks like fire, Rose!"

Rose crossed her arms. "And what are their names? I want to know what to shout the next time they wander off."

Quinn cocked his head. He pointed to the wolf at Wilder's right. "Her name is Storm Fang." He looked at the wolf on the left. Then he shook his head and whispered, "Really?"

He stood and shrugged. "And her name is Pickles."

Feather clapped a hand to her mouth to stifle a giggle.

Rose put her hands on her hips. "Storm Fang and Pickles?" Both wolves gave a short yip in response. She slapped her hands down to her sides. "Fine. That's what I'll yell the next time I find him in a dangerous situation without you."

Wilder was staring at the wolves with a confused expression on his face. He flinched when he noticed she was watching him. He bent down to scratch the wolves behind the neck and avoid her eyes.

"There's no need to be self-conscious, Wilder," she said. "They are the ones who believe you belong to them. I plan to hold them accountable to that."

He chuckled but still didn't meet her eyes as he patted their backs. "It's just weird that Quinn can talk to them now. It's going to be very useful."

Rose tried to smile, but it felt more like a grimace. "The Goddess's Gifts are always useful."

"Quinn?" Rev grabbed him under the arm. "Are you okay?"

His eyes unfocused, and he swayed on his feet. "I don't feel so good."

Tayeh grabbed him under the other arm, and they carried him to lie down.

Rose tried to catch Wilder's eye, but he remained firmly focused on the wolves. She shook her head and went to the kitchen to grab the stomach elixir for Quinn.

Once Quinn had slightly recovered, the crew met together in the living room. Quinn took a seat on the couch next to Wilder and the wolves, forcing Rose to sit in a chair across from them.

"I guess this cleared up one of the last unknowns about the Gifts," said Rev.

Feather looked to Kieran. "Does this mean you have the Gift of Knowledge?" She held out her hand. "Do you want to try it on me?"

Kieran's lip curled. "I'd rather not."

She frowned and put both hands in her lap.

"The stomach elixir helped with the nausea," said Quinn. "But I still feel pretty weak."

"We should alternate practicing with our Gifts so we aren't all weak at the same time," said Tayeh.

"I agree," said Rev. "And since we can only practice when we are all together, our time is limited. So, who else would like to practice tonight?" She looked around the room. "Wilder? What about you?"

His head snapped up from blindly staring at the wolves at his feet. "Me? No, that's okay. The others can go first."

"I'd like to try," said Fitz. "Since there is no stone in here, I'll have to go outside. It will be interesting to see if it works with the rest of you inside."

"Good point!" said Quinn. "We should measure the proximity needed to make it work." He grabbed a notebook. "I'll take notes."

Tayeh studied Fitz and shrugged. "I'll carry you inside when you puke."

Fitz smiled. "Thanks!"

The three of them went out the door, leaving the rest to discuss their plans for the next day.

"I'm going to check in on Vaylan," said Rose. "I want to know what he's planning."

Wilder looked up at her with a frown. "I don't trust him."

"I didn't say I trusted him. I just want to get close enough to figure out what he's trying to accomplish."

"I don't know if it's smart, Rose," said Rev. "Vaylan has something to gain in this, even if we don't know what. It might be safer for us to avoid him."

Rose crossed her arms. "I thought your crew was all about discovering valuable information? He invited me into the heart of his operations. Why shouldn't we seize the opportunity to understand his motives better?"

"Because he's making it too easy," said Wilder. He sat up taller on the couch, and the wolves looked at him to see if he had any directions for them. "Why does he want you there? What does he gain from showing you around? And why did he mark you in the first place?"

She consciously kept her hand from moving to touch her mark. "I don't know. But he spoke to me just like he did at every audition Upstairs. He seems to enjoy talking to me. He's always trying to convert me to whatever it is he believes."

Wilder narrowed his eyes. "And is it working?"

She jumped to her feet and glared at him. "What? Why would you ask me that?"

He studied her with shrewd eyes. "I was a child when Vaylan left, but I was smart enough to realize how smooth he could be. He's a liar, Rose. I don't want to see you manipulated by him."

She crossed her arms over her chest. "You don't think I'm smart enough to see through his manipulation?"

"It's not about you being smart enough. It's about him being a predator."

The two of them glared at each other in silence until Rev jumped in. "I think we need more information. And since Rose has an invitation, we should take advantage of it."

Wilder slumped back on the couch, and the wolves settled back down at his feet.

Rev looked at him with a sympathetic eye. "But I agree we need to take precautions. Rose shouldn't go alone. Tayeh can go with her."

Rose sat back down, trying not to gloat. "She might as well stay here. I don't think Vaylan will talk to me unless Tayeh is out of earshot."

Wilder perked back up and hissed, "And that doesn't seem suspicious to you?"

"Of course it's suspicious!" said Rose. "He's definitely plotting something, and we need to figure it out. But I think bringing Tayeh will make him less likely to speak openly about his plans."

"You could take the wolves," said Feather.

Rev, Wilder, and Rose turned their heads to stare at the

girl sitting timidly with her hands in her lap. Rose had forgotten she was still in the room.

Feather's voice was quiet but persuasive. "Quinn can give them instructions on what to look out for. They can warn you if they sense any danger. And I assume they would be handy in a fight?"

Rev nodded her approval. "I think it's a great idea, Feather." She looked between Wilder and Rose. "Don't the two of you agree?"

Rose nodded sharply. Wilder looked down at the wolves and nodded begrudgingly.

"Terrific," said Rev. "Tomorrow, you and the wolves can see what Vaylan is up to, and the seven of us will stay here and take turns using our Gifts."

A sound at the door caused them to all look up. Tayeh dragged Fitz inside, carrying him stumbling into the bathroom.

"We all saw that coming," said Kieran. Rose forgot he was lounging on his own couch and ignoring them. "The Goddess really *blessed* us with these *Gifts*. Maybe she should have picked someone with a stronger stomach."

"Shut up, Kieran." Wilder stood and glared at him. "If you don't want to help, fine. But you don't have to be a jerk."

Rose wanted to catch his eye to give him an encouraging smile for standing up to a brat, but he left the room without a backward glance at her.

11

———

Rose approached Vaylan's new Haven with two wolves stepping quietly at her side. She was determined to prove to the crew that she could gather information about Vaylan without letting him manipulate her, no matter what Wilder said.

The thought of Wilder was enough to make her stomp, and the wolves growled softly in response. She couldn't figure out his problem. She was familiar with dealing with moody people like Caed, but it seemed out of character for Wilder. Not that she hadn't made him furious occasionally, but he seemed on edge. They'd had such a lovely time at the apothecary, but after that, it fell apart.

She didn't understand why he couldn't trust her to use her head regarding Vaylan. She didn't trust him, but she needed to get close enough to figure out his plans. What did Wilder think was going to happen? How much did Wilder truly know about Vaylan?

She thought back to her own childhood growing up in Temple Discipline, raised by Mims alongside Caed and Kai and her older brothers and sisters. She imagined herself as a five-year-old, Wilder's age the last time he saw Vaylan. All her memories were fuzzy, filled with laughter and childish arguments and the calm protection of Mims. What were Wilder's childhood memories like?

She tried to picture her five-year-old self in the middle of Grotto Chaos, in a run-down house with a violent, unstable mother. She imagined Vaylan in the scene and couldn't reconcile his patronizing smile and grandiose beliefs with the idea of him as a father. What must it be like for Wilder to think about Rose casually chatting with Vaylan?

At the stirring of guilt in her chest, she vowed to be more sensitive the next time she spoke to Wilder about him.

People in white aprons moved in and out of the Den. A man dressed in all white stopped her at the door. "Good morning, sister. Do you need help?"

Rose pasted on a smile as pleasant as she could manage. "I'm here to see Vaylan."

The man gave her a patronizing yet sweet smile. "He's very busy."

Rose pulled down the high collar of her pale blue jacket to reveal the scorched skin of Vaylan's crystalline fingerprint at her throat. "I was invited," she growled. His eyes widened, and he gave her a quick bow before ushering her inside.

She had never been inside the Den when Wardens controlled it, but Rose assumed it used to be much darker. Crystalline webbed across the ceiling in intricate patterns and cast a bright glow. More people in white aprons scrubbed the floors of the long hallway. Vaylan must require a cleaner headquarters than the Wardens did. Especially since the bright lights would reveal any dirty footprints.

The man led her down the hallway and waved her through a door to her left. Crystalline lattice continued along the ceiling, lighting up the large room. People in white stood at counters, chopping vegetables and dumping them into pots of boiling broth. A woman scooped bowls of soup for children dressed in ragged clothes. A man in white bounced a baby on his lap while next to him, a woman with tired eyes ate a bowl of soup with a grateful smile.

Rose stood with her mouth open, trying to comprehend what was going on. Of all the things she had pictured Vaylan using a Den for, this was not it. The wolves scanned the room for danger and, finding none, sat quietly at her side.

She heard a familiar voice and turned to find Vaylan seated before a crowd of children, who listened to him with rapt attention. He was telling them a silly story, complete with funny voices and dramatic facial expressions. The children giggled and clapped when he finished.

"Rose!" He patted a child on the head as he made his way over to her. "I'm so glad you stopped by. What do you think?"

"It's ... surprising," she said honestly. She looked at his navy shirt, rolled up at the sleeves, and navy slacks. "I guess the dress code is different for you?"

He grinned, and his dimple shone. "I don't demand any sort of dress code. But my Adopted choose to wear white to set them apart."

"Your Adopted?" She looked around at all the men and women in white and wondered what they had gotten themselves into.

He chuckled. "It's their interpretation of one of Brother Owyn's prophecies. 'The Adopted glow in the reflected light of power.'" He gestured to the crystalline lattice he had shaped along the ceiling. "They translated the prophecy literally."

She blinked. "You believe ... and they believe ... that Brother Owyn was a prophet?"

"I have seen so many of his prophecies fulfilled that it's easy for me to believe." He smiled at the people working on the soup. "They've not only seen it happen, but are working alongside me as we fulfill it together. Brother Owyn said, 'Devote yourself to the powerless.' I have. We have. And we are making a difference."

"But you had Brother Owyn killed! Those Sentinels were under your control, not the Priests. Do Brother Owyn's followers know that?"

He shook his head in his head as if explaining something remedial. "No one believes I murdered Brother Owyn. He believed his own prophecies so much that he allowed it to happen."

Rose's mouth dropped open. "You're blaming him for his own death?"

"He knew the Sentinels would come, and he chose to act on that knowledge. You saw him that day ... Did he seem surprised the Sentinels came for him?"

Rose remembered holding the dying old man in her arms. He said he knew they would kill him. She had screamed at him, asking why he hadn't brought an antidote. He'd said he knew she would weep.

He'd known.

Vaylan nodded as if reading the memory on her face. "During our long captivity in the High Priests' prison, he spoke of his death often. He believed it would usher in a new age for the City. I believe he's right."

Rose shook her head. "I don't understand what your angle is here. What do you hope to gain by feeding these people?"

"Isn't feeding people its own reward?" His voice was pious, but his eyes twinkled.

She raised an eyebrow. "For you, I think it's probably more than that."

He smiled as if proud that she saw through him. "I've made my intentions plain, Rose. I intend to rule. The people in the Underneath and Upstairs have had poor examples of rulers. I will show them that there is a different way. I offer exactly what I've told you from the beginning: freedom. Something your former colleagues could never give them."

"Why do you say former? I'm avoiding the temples because of your threats against them, but I'm still a Priest."

He looked at her with a sad smile. "But are you, Rose?"

She growled. "I have always been and will continue to be a Priest. The Goddess chose me, and that hasn't changed."

"Hasn't it?" he asked coolly. "Brother Owyn made another prophecy that you might find interesting. 'After the end, the Seven will return.' I know she has returned her Gifts. And I know you were not one of her Chosen."

Rose flinched like he'd punched her in the gut. She couldn't breathe, and the glowing room felt too bright. The wolves whined softly, but there was no visible enemy for them to attack.

Vaylan put a steadying hand on her arm. "We were both forsaken by the Goddess, Rose. She might look out for others, but you and I have had to make our own way. When I climbed out of the High Priests' prison, I was born into a new life. A life free of her restrictions and rules. And you are free in the same way. This is your chance to discover who you really are. Without the Goddess."

She shook off his arm and stumbled back a step. "No ... I don't have a Gift, but she still chose me."

He shook his head sadly. "No, Rose. There are other prophecies about the Chosen. And they aren't about you."

She swallowed but couldn't find words to say.

His voice was a soft whisper in her raging mind. "You aren't one of the Chosen, Rose. But you are Marked. You still belong. With me."

She took another step backward, almost tripping over the wolves. They perked up and flowed menacingly around her ankles, looking for danger. Rose couldn't communicate to them that the danger wasn't out there.

It was within her own heart.

She turned and ran out of the Haven, the wolves streaming behind.

12

____

Rose wandered around the streets of Delirium for a long time before heading back to their house. She knew what she would find when she returned: the seven of them together, practicing their Gifts. She couldn't bear to see that after her conversation with Vaylan.

How did he know the words to say to pierce her to the core? He said they were the same. Is that how he knew? Had he wrestled with the same doubt and fear and anger? Their lives were nothing alike. After living in Chaos with a wife and child, the High Priests had thrown him in prison for fourteen years. How was that like her lifetime spent as a Priest? He might have his own doubts, but they couldn't be the same as hers.

How did she wind up in the middle of this? If the Goddess wanted to leave Rose out of her plans, why couldn't she have made that choice at the beginning? Why did Rose have to be part of the audition, meet Vaylan, meet Wilder ...

She wanted to add Wilder to the mess she was in, but he was the one bright spot in the middle of it all. Despite his moodiness and their arguments, the thought of him was enough to warm her to the core. She wanted to be here with him. But it would have been a lot easier if he wasn't one of the Chosen.

She frowned at the ungracious thought. It should thrill her he'd received a Gift. If she was a good Priest, she would be happy for him.

But she wasn't a good Priest.

Maybe she wasn't a Priest at all.

The Goddess could have chosen her, but she hadn't. Rose had no Gift to offer in service of the Goddess. Without her Gift, she could have children and live a normal life. A boring life.

A common life.

She thought back on the words Rev had said to Kieran. He wouldn't leave, because this was his one chance to be special. To be chosen. He wouldn't let that go.

Rose knew what that feeling was like. And losing it felt like losing a part of her soul.

Her mark scraped against her shirt, and she hissed. She unbuttoned her collar to stop her shirt from irritating it further. Even though the burn was several days old, it had not healed at all. That wasn't normal for crystalline burns. They normally healed at the same rate as a burn from a hot stove. But Vaylan's fingerprint shone just as clearly as it had the night he gave her the mark.

At least she was special in that way.

She couldn't avoid the crew forever, so she finally arrived back at the house. She had barely made it inside when Wilder grabbed her hand and led her back out.

"I'm so glad you're back," he said. "The rest of them are sick and cranky, and I need to get out. Want to escape with me?"

At his words, butterflies stirred in her stomach. His effect on her was embarrassing, but she had already admitted it to him. That feeling was worth more than her pride.

"I'd love that," she said with a soft smile.

He led her to a tea shop that smelled like eucalyptus and chamomile, and the wolves followed them inside. A woman played a stringed instrument with a hypnotic sound and sang with a deep, melodic voice. Wilder pulled Rose into a booth for two and discussed what kinds of tea were safe to drink in Delirium.

After her strawberry peppermint tea arrived, she stared at him over the edge of her cup. His iced tea had the faint scent of cinnamon. His dark eyes sparkled as she studied him. Her eyes followed the line of his neck, and she imagined tracing it with a gentle finger.

His eyes followed a similar path down her neck but snagged when they saw the uncovered mark on her collarbone. She moved to cover it, but he took hold of her hand.

"Don't," he said. "Covering it hurts you."

She frowned. "Displaying it hurts in a different way."

He nodded in understanding. "How did it go today?" His voice was hesitant, as if he didn't want to stumble into an argument. "Did you discover his plans?"

"He turned the Den into a soup kitchen and calls it a Haven."

Wilder blinked in confusion.

She smiled wryly. "Exactly what I thought. The people in white call themselves the Adopted." She shrugged. "It's some prophecy from Brother Owyn."

Wilder tapped the top of his glass of tea absently. "Interesting. I'm sure he has some evil plans, but I'm not sure how that fits." His eyes refocused on her face. "You were right. You did learn useful information. I feel out of sorts right now ... I'm sorry for doubting you."

Her voice warmed into a playful purr. "You know how much I love it when you apologize."

He grinned. "Then I'll do it again. I'm sorry that I was worried about Vaylan manipulating you. You're too stubborn to be affected by anything he says."

Her smile froze on her face as she considered the rest of the conversation. She didn't want to admit how shaken she felt by everything Vaylan said.

Before Wilder could notice her hesitation, she took a sip of tea, then cleared her throat. "I'm glad to hear it. Why don't you tell me about your day?"

His face fell. "It was rough. Kieran refuses to use his Gift, but luckily, he stays so we have a complete seven. Rev lifted water from a pitcher and swirled it in patterns near the ceiling. Until she soaked us all when she lost control as she ran for the bathroom." He sighed. "The whole process was exhausting."

She spun her tea around her cup. "So ... did you do anything fun with the wind?"

He dropped his eyes down to his glass. "Um ... a little. It was fine."

She chuckled, but the sound was forced. "Just fine? I expected you to charm the wind until she was eating from the palm of your hand. How disappointing."

He twisted his lips and continued to study his tea. "Maybe we should discuss something else."

"I'm sorry," she said.

The apology caused him to look up. The hope on his face was so fragile she didn't want to break it.

"I'm trying, Wilder. I'm trying to be supportive and happy for all of you, but it's hard." She dropped her eyes again. "I'm sorry I'm so weak."

He took her hand. "You aren't weak, Rose. It's okay to be sad. I ... I just don't want to be the one that hurts you."

"It's not your fault. I know that logically, but ..." She shrugged. "I'm not always the most logical."

He smothered a grin. "I have no idea what you mean. You always seem perfectly rational to me."

She snorted. "I'm sure I'll adjust over time, but for now, it's hard seeing the seven of you together and being the odd one out."

He bit his lip. "I've been thinking about that ... Maybe you aren't the odd one. It doesn't make sense that the Goddess would leave you out. I think maybe she did return your Gift. Maybe it's just taking some time for you to find it again."

She studied his hopeful face and wondered how her emotions could travel so quickly from desire to fury. Her fingers flexed on the table, as if her nails were claws. Her hands shook with rage, and it took everything within her to dig them into the wooden table and not into him.

"I have prayed and begged and pleaded to the Goddess to return my Gift. And you think maybe she returned it and I didn't notice?" He flinched at her low growl, but she continued harshly. "You feel it now, don't you? Even before you use the Gift, before the tears, you can sense the wind flowing around you. Like raw potential waiting to be grasped. I can't feel that anymore. That part of me is empty, Wilder. Cut off. It's an aching wound more painful than the one at my throat." Her voice caught on an angry sob. "It's as if the wind forgot me. As if it is dead. If the wind had returned to me, I would notice."

Wilder reached his hands across the table and whispered, "Rose, I'm so sorry. I just hoped—"

"I don't need your hope," she hissed. "Or your pity."

He pulled his hands back as if slapped. "It's not pity—"

"Stop," she commanded. "Never bring this up again."

He nodded, and his eyes glimmered with unshed tears. "I shouldn't have said—"

"No, you shouldn't." She stood abruptly.

The wolves jumped up as if to follow her out, but her head snapped around. "No. You stay with him." She pointed a harsh finger at them. "Don't let his tears fall until he is somewhere safe, do you hear me?"

The wolves whined softly as Wilder watched Rose walk out the door.

Rose didn't go straight back to the house but wandered around the streets of Delirium once again. The people in this Grotto were more subdued than the ones in Chaos, and it gave her plenty of space to think.

Not that she could do much thinking with her mind flooded with rage. She couldn't believe Wilder had suggested she still had her Gift. He believed it made more sense for the Goddess to bestow her Gifts on the eight of them than it did for the Goddess to forget about her. It was clear to Rose what had happened.

The Goddess had forsaken her, just like Vaylan had said.

She recognized the thought as sacrilegious, but her anger at Wilder swirled together with her anger at the Goddess, and she couldn't identify which was which. They were the same. Wilder had let her down as much as the Goddess had.

She wiped furious tears off her cheeks, angry at their pointlessness. Wilder could summon an underground hurricane with the tears in his eyes, but her tears were common. Just water with no power.

She walked until the tears dried and her face was clear. She would walk into the house calmly, not a weeping mess.

The pity on Wilder's face was bad enough. She couldn't tolerate it from any of the rest.

As she approached the house, she noticed a note stuck to the door. She turned to read it by the crystal's light.

Rose,

It was nice seeing you today. I know it was a lot to take in, but you are strong. I know you can handle it. After you left, the children wouldn't stop talking about the red-haired girl with the wolves. They found you fascinating. I'll be heading to Peculiarity tomorrow, and I bet those children will be equally mesmerized by you. If you pass by the Haven soon, I'd love to talk to you again. It's good talking to someone who understands.

Blessings,

Vaylan

Rose hid the note in her pocket and went inside. The crew was in the middle of a conversation, which abruptly stopped as she entered. She pretended not to notice. Wilder sat on the couch next to Rev and tried to catch Rose's eye.

She pretended not to notice that either.

Her voice was calm as she said, "I think we should travel to Peculiarity tomorrow."

Rev exchanged a look with Wilder. "I don't know ... We probably have more we can learn here ..."

Rose didn't explain but stared at her with hard eyes.

Rev cleared her throat and looked around at the rest of the crew. "Peculiarity next?"

They nodded with various levels of excitement as Rose turned on her heel and went to her room alone.

Peculiarity

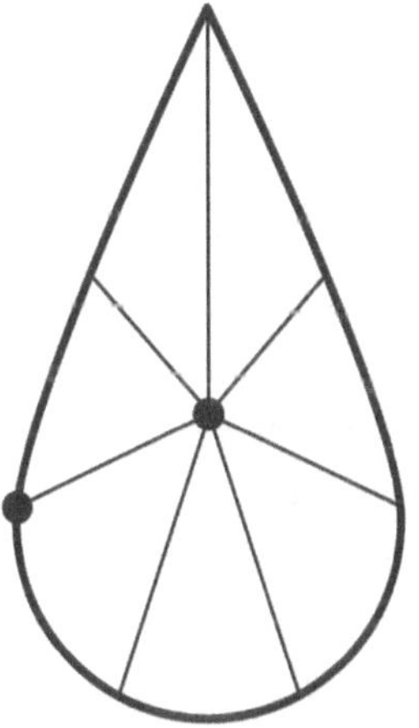

13

———

The journey to Grotto Peculiarity was a quiet one. Usually, they chatted to pass the time on the long walk, but this time, they were subdued. Rose wasn't sure what Wilder had told the crew about their conversation in the tea shop. She wanted to know what he said yet never wanted to speak of it again.

Soon after they arrived in Grotto Peculiarity, Rev charmed her way into a cute little house with enough beds for all of them. Rose claimed a bed for her own, set down her pack, and started to head out again. She passed Wilder in the kitchen.

He sat at the table, writing in the notebook she frequently saw him scribbling in. He closed it calmly but didn't say a word. As she moved past, the wolves at his feet jumped up and fell into step at her heels. His eyes didn't leave her face, and she didn't say a word.

Once she left the house and its seven other inhabitants, her heart felt a little lighter. Peculiarity lived up to its name, and she found all the unusual houses charming. It was nothing like the rows of matching cottages Upstairs, but it was beautiful in its own way.

When she approached the Haven, a woman at the door let her right in. Rose had left her mark visible, and the wolves marked her in their own way. The woman waved her inside, straight into a hallway full of children.

Instead of storytelling, Vaylan counted the children of all ages standing around him. They bounced excitedly, and he laughed as he tried to get their attention. He turned with a start. "Rose! It's so good you are here. We are just about to head out."

"Where are you going?" she asked.

"I promised I'd take them to the circus." At this, the kids cheered, and he laughed again.

"The circus?" She coughed, trying to hide the breathless excitement in her voice.

He grinned. "You've been?"

"No, but I dressed up like a circus performer once." She struggled to keep her lips from curling into a smile. "I was very good at it."

"I bet you were!" He laughed. "You should join us. I'm sure the kids would love it."

Two kids rubbed the bellies of the wolves, who had flopped over on their backs.

Rose rolled her eyes at the squirming wolves. "Ladies, can you try to have some self-respect?" The wolves scooted closer to get a better angle on the scratch.

Vaylan clapped his hands to get everyone's attention. "Okay, everyone! Line up! We are going to the circus!"

A young girl put her hand in Rose's and pulled her to follow Vaylan, the other children, and the scampering wolves out the door.

As they took the winding route to the circus, Rose wondered how she had stumbled into the unusual situation. She had been so distracted by her anger at Wilder that she hadn't thought through why she was going to see Vaylan at all. If she hadn't let herself be pulled into the strange outing, she might have been able to investigate the Haven without him there.

But when they arrived at the giant tent, Rose finally admitted to herself that there was no way she could leave. The last performance she'd watched was the failed Pageant, and she needed a show to erase that memory from her mind. And the idea of the circus was just too intriguing for her to pass up.

An usher met them at the entrance and led them into a special set of box seats in the front. The kids hopped from couch to couch as they figured out which was the best seat. Vaylan whispered something to the usher, then came over to sit by Rose.

"I've been to the circus many times, but I admit, I'm just as excited as the kids are." He looked out at the empty ring in front of them. "These are great seats. The kids will love the show.

She pinched her lips, trying to contain her grin. "I can't believe I'm actually at the circus."

"You won't be watching the show, I'm afraid," he said.

Her forehead wrinkled. "Excuse me?"

"You won't watch it." His eyes twinkled merrily. "You're going to be in it."

As her mouth dropped open, the usher returned with a tray full of popcorn and a woman in a sparkling leotard at his side.

Vaylan stood to address the usher. "The kids get the popcorn." He nodded to the woman. "And Rose is going with you."

The woman in the leotard held out her hand. "Are you ready?"

Rose blinked and obediently took the woman's hand.

After the woman led Rose backstage, things happened

quickly. She threw Rose a leotard covered in sky blue sequins, then shoved her into a dressing room packed with other performers squeezing into sparkly costumes of their own. After Rose dressed, an older woman pushed Rose into a chair and pulled her hair up into a high ponytail, wrapping it in a white ribbon that fluttered in her red locks.

She passed a line of women who doused her with glitter and rouge and then more glitter. A brown-haired girl close to Rose's age summoned her into the wings. The girl wore a leotard with the same sky-blue sequins and a ribbon in her hair.

The girl began climbing a rope ladder, and Rose stuck close on her heels, following her onto a narrow platform high above the ring. Below them were horses and clowns and lions in a wild performance in the middle of the ring. Rose grinned as she watched the show from the best seats in the house.

The platform under her feet shifted as the girl hopped onto a long ladder stretching above the stage. Rose clutched the railing as she suddenly realized how far off the ground they were.

Rose grabbed the girl's arm. "Wait! What are we doing?"

The girl looked at her oddly. "We climb out on this ladder and lower onto those rings suspended over the stage. Then we do whatever fancy tricks we've got."

Rose studied the hanging rings. They looked like the gymnastic rings she had practiced on back in Temple Discipline, but she'd never been so high off the ground.

She swallowed. "Is it safe?"

The girl stared at her, unblinking for several moments. Then she threw her head back and laughed. She patted Rose on the arm before crawling out over the stage.

When Rose had practiced gymnastics in Temple Discipline, she'd had the benefit of the wind on her side. If she had fallen from this height, she could have slowed her fall. But without her Gift?

One wrong move would kill her.

Rose watched the girl crawl along the long ladder, then slide down onto a ring. She flipped herself around until she hung upside down, brown ponytail and ribbon flowing in the wind. The girl had no control over the wind, yet it flowed around her, proclaiming her a star.

Rose rubbed her hands together with determination, then climbed onto the ladder.

She crawled out over the stage, slightly nauseated by the height but exhilarated by the feeling of flying. She took a deep breath as she perched over a suspended ring, then slid down the chain until her feet touched. Once she was situated inside the ring, her training kicked in. She twisted until she hung suspended by one arm and leg, with her red ponytail streaming as the force of her flip spun her around.

The soft wind of the Underneath blew through the tent and streamed around her. It tickled against her bare skin and brushed through her hair. The wind was not in her control. It might try to blow her off the ring, or it might not. It might spin her in a dramatic circle, or it might not. She couldn't control it.

But she wouldn't let it control her either.

She straightened into the splits, the strength of her legs holding her in place, then let go of both hands, twisting her fingers as if she had the wind at her command. The blood rushed to her head, and she laughed at the thrill. She arched her back, and the momentum spun her in reverse. The feel of the wind as it curled in the opposite direction sent a delighted chill across her skin.

When she tired of one move, she transitioned into the next. If she found a position boring, she stretched out an arm or leg until she found the perfect pose. The crowd cheered, but she didn't know if it was for her, the brown-haired girl, or another performer inside the ring. Eventually, she realized it didn't matter if they cheered or not. She would have felt the same thrill even if she were alone.

She would have continued her performance until her body gave out, but before that happened, the lights faded, and the crowd gave their final applause. Her muscles trembled with exertion and euphoria as she climbed the chain and crawled back to the platform.

Her fellow performer's face lit up with a smile. "You really tricked me with your 'new girl' act." She laughed as she squeezed Rose on the arm. "It was fun working with a pro." She headed down the rope ladder, leaving Rose to catch her breath on the platform alone.

By the time she changed out of her leotard and back into her clothes, the kids and wolves were getting restless. She hopped into the box seats with a smile.

Vaylan studied her with serious eyes. "So ... how did you feel?"

She knew the answer he sought, and the contrarian part of her wanted to give any other response. But she couldn't stop the truthful answer from spilling from her lips.

"Free," she said. "I felt free."

14

Rose left Vaylan to get the kids back to the Haven on his own and headed back to the safe house with a smile on her face. After such a fun afternoon, she felt slightly more prepared to handle whatever her seven roommates were doing.

Before she got to the safe house, she found them. She first saw Tayeh and Fitz standing outside a tattoo parlor. She had seen a tattoo parlor Upstairs, but this one seemed like it had been in the same place for a long time. Drawings covered the stone walls with images of what Rose assumed were tattoos this artist had created.

Tayeh looked up as she approached, and Fitz waved her over with an excited grin.

"I didn't expect to find you out," said Rose.

Fitz shrugged. "We got tired of practicing and vomiting, practicing and vomiting."

"I'll have you know I haven't vomited once," said Tayeh proudly.

"Neither has Wilder," said Fitz. "I think it hits each of us differently."

Rose nodded absently as she peeked through the window. "Who's getting the tattoo?"

"Feather," said Tayeh. "She's getting a small feather on her ankle."

Rose rolled her eyes and mumbled, "Original."

She peeked inside the window and found the rest of the crew gathered around Feather. She leaned back in a lounge chair with her ankle propped up so the woman tattoo artist could reach it. Feather's pretty, heart-shaped face twisted in a cute expression of pain as she bit her lip.

Wilder sat at her side, holding her hand.

Rose wasn't sure who growled: her or the wolves at her feet.

Fitz spoke in an apologetic tone. "When the artist first began, Feather started to cry. Wilder thought it best to distract her so she didn't have any errant tears."

Rose's lips thinned into a line. "One of you could have just gone home. Then her tears would have been as useless as mine."

Fitz's mouth opened and closed silently before he said, "I will keep it in mind for next time."

Rose shrugged it off. "It's not a big deal. Wilder's free to hold as many hands as he pleases."

"I'd hope so," said Tayeh drily. "It's not like he's kissing strangers in a nightclub."

Rose didn't even acknowledge the statement before walking into the parlor.

Wilder looked up at her approach. He relaxed his hand as if he might let go before reconsidering and only adjusting his grip.

"You're here!" Feather reached out her other hand to Rose. "I'm so glad you made it!"

Rose hadn't planned to get close, but she relented and took Feather's outstretched hand.

Feather's sweet face lit up with her smile. "Now we are all here." She closed her eyes. "This is the memory I want to remember with this tattoo. All of us here together."

Rose blinked in surprise. She had to admit that she had not been nice to this girl, starting from Rose's typical sharp words at the audition, up to this morning when Rose snapped at her for putting sugar in Rose's coffee. Why would Feather want to keep Rose in her memories?

Wilder's expression said that he knew Rose didn't understand. It was not quite pity but was close enough to rankle.

She went against her natural reaction, just to prove she could. She looked at the tattoo and said, "It looks beautiful, Feather."

Feather's eyes opened and lit up with an expression of joy. "Thank you for saying that! I thought you might think I was silly for getting a feather." She looked down, blinking her long lashes. "But I wasn't sure what else I'd want on my body for the rest of my life, you know?"

Rose remembered saying the same thing to Wilder before learning about his tattoo of the Goddess's symbol on his chest.

He, too, must have remembered the similarity of her words, because his eyes glittered in a silent challenge.

Rose cleared her throat. "It makes perfect sense. A feather is a wise choice."

Feather smiled and leaned her head back against the chair, closing her eyes again.

Wilder's expression settled, as if she'd passed his silent test. The thought of him judging her sent prickles along the back of her neck. What right did he have to judge her? He was the one who was inconsiderate of her.

The tattoo artist sat back to examine her work. "All right, Feather. You're all done. What do you think?"

Feather sat up and examined her ankle awkwardly. She slid out of the seat and hugged the woman around her neck.

"Thank you so much!" said Feather. "It's lovely. I will treasure it forever."

Wilder slipped a stack of coins into the woman's hand. She gave him an appraising look as he turned to go.

The woman must have sensed Rose's disapproving glare, because she turned around. Then she cocked her head to the side and came closer. Rose stepped back as the petite woman stood directly in front of her chest.

"Wow. That's gorgeous," said the woman. "I can see the fingerprint outline. How did the artist manage it?"

Rose quickly covered the mark with her shirt. "I'm not sure I'd call him an artist."

The woman shook her head. "Well, I've seen nothing like it. And now that I've seen it, I'll do my best to recreate it."

Rose imagined the look she received from the men and women in white as she displayed the fingerprint. "I don't recommend that. In some circles, it has a specific meaning. And honestly, I'm not sure it's good."

The woman shrugged. "I'll take your word for it."

Rose turned to leave and found Rev watching her. Her blue eye was unblinking, and Rose squirmed like an animal in a trap.

"Time for a talk," said Rev.

She looped her arm through Rose's and pulled her toward the back of the group as they walked to the house. Rose tried to lean away and walk at a more comfortable distance, but Rev held her close, as if they were best friends out for a stroll.

"Let me guess," said Rose. "A girl talk?" Most of Rev's supposed "girl talks" ended with sweetly phrased threats of violence.

Rev grinned. "You're catching on."

Rose sighed and sagged in Rev's grip. "Fine. Reprimand me quickly, then let me walk the rest of the way on my own."

Rev frowned. "That's just it. You don't need to be on your own."

"That's what this is about?" Rose rolled her eyes. "The only time I leave is when you practice your Gifts, and you don't need me for that. I spend every other moment with you. What else do you want?"

"It's not about you being there physically. It's that you don't truly consider yourself a member of the crew."

Rose rolled her eyes. "I'm *not* one of the crew. And that's okay. I appreciate you letting me spend time with you, but you don't have to pretend like I belong."

"You *are* part of the crew, Rose. Or you would be if you allowed yourself to believe it."

Rose didn't respond, and Rev switched tactics. "Everyone in the crew has their own strengths and responsibilities. My job is to make sure the relationships inside the crew are all healthy. If a problem doesn't get addressed, the entire crew will suffer."

Rose scowled. "This is about me and Wilder."

"No." Rev's voice was firm. "It's about you and the seven of us. Being in a crew means you can rely on the others to have your back. You might not believe this, but I trust you like I trust the rest of the crew. I trust not only your skill, but your commitment to protect those weaker than yourself, including me. I trust you to have my back when it counts. But I don't think you trust us to have yours."

Rose had just started to trust Wilder to have her back like she trusted Caed or Kai. Wilder continued to look out for her, no matter how many times she hurt him. Her heart stirred at the thought, but she pushed it beneath her current anger at him. Even if he had her back in the past, that was before he became one of the Chosen. They were part of a perfect circle of seven, and she would never fit.

Rev sighed. "I don't think I was as inspirational as I hoped." She released Rose's arm and took her hand instead. "Just keep it in mind, okay? You are part of this crew. But it won't feel like it until you believe it."

She gave Rose's hand one last squeeze, then let her walk alone.

15

The next morning, Rev made a big deal about gathering for a crew meeting. Rose didn't put up any resistance. What she said to Rev was the truth: she appreciated being included, even if she wasn't an actual member of the crew.

They had several leads to track down in Peculiarity, so they broke into groups. Rose assumed Rev would assign her to Wilder's group, forcing them into a conversation, but Fitz was her partner. They hadn't spent much time alone since they were no longer roommates, and Rose found it strangely comforting to be in his presence.

"So, who are we meeting today?" she asked.

"Jaida. She cares for some people in Peculiarity who need extra help. It's the way she serves the Goddess." He stopped in front of a house painted bright purple.

"How do you know her?" she asked.

"We used to be ... close." His cheeks turned a faint pink as he knocked on the door.

The door opened to reveal a tall woman with a huge smile. "Fitz!" she squealed. She gathered him into her muscular arms and pressed his slight form to her full chest.

He returned her hug, then pulled himself away. "It's good to see you, Jaida." He looked her up and down with a crooked grin. "You look good."

Jaida flushed under his gaze. "Oh, Fitz. I've missed you." She bit her lip coyly.

Rose stood to the side, completely forgotten. She was glad they didn't notice her, because she knew her face was a picture of shock. She hadn't discussed it with him, but Rose had always assumed Fitz favored men. Rose looked at the tall, womanly form of Jaida and realized how wrong she was.

Eventually, Fitz stopped staring and remembered Rose at his side. "Oh, um ... Jaida, this is Rose. She's a Priest from Temple Discipline. Rose, this is Jaida."

Jaida's cool eyes landed on Rose and sized her up, head to toe. "This is your new girl? She seems a little frail."

Rose huffed in indignation. "Frail?"

Fitz stepped in quickly. "No, Jaida, she's not my girl. We're in the same crew and checking out our contacts while we are here."

Jaida's eyes warmed again as she looked at him. "Honey, you know you can check me out anytime you stop by."

Fitz's cheeks turned pink again, and Rose stayed quiet to avoid drawing Jaida's eye.

"Well, come inside!" Jaida ushered them in.

The house swarmed with life. A group of children ran past them into a back room. Rose noticed a girl with only one arm and a boy on crutches who lagged slightly behind. Jaida ruffled her hands through his dark hair as he passed by with a grin on his face.

Jaida took them through another room, where a couple sat on a couch together, having a silent conversation using their hands. Rose tried to guess what the hand signs might mean but then realized staring at them was probably like eavesdropping, so she followed Jaida into the kitchen.

Jaida offered Rose a seat at the kitchen table while she and Fitz chatted and made some coffee. Rose sat down next to a man with unruly gray hair. He didn't look up and continued writing in a little notebook.

Back when the Priests could heal, there were still people who were born differently or who couldn't be healed. There were healing centers where Priests cared for them, but often, they spent a lot of time alone. She also heard some parents kept their children at home their entire life, terrified what the High Priests would do if they found someone who didn't live up to their ideal of Perfection. Rose couldn't imagine that kind of terror, but Jaida had created a place where people could live without fear.

The man next to her had stopped writing and stared at her.

"Hi," she said politely. "I'm Rose."

He nodded his head while rubbing his chin in thought. "A flower of tremendous beauty, but beware the thorns."

She smiled wryly. "Apparently you've heard of me."

"I can read the story your eyes tell." His smile was kind, and she smiled in return.

"So, you live here with Jaida?" she asked. "Have you been here long?"

"Not long," he said. "A butterfly landed on my shoulder, and she whispered a joke. I laughed for several hours, then I followed her here." He tapped his bottom lip, then opened his notebook. "I should write that down in case I forget again."

Rose blinked, trying to follow his train of thought. She peeked in his notebook.

It was filled with scribbles and random numbers.

"I see you've met Walter." Jaida handed Rose a cup of

coffee. "He arrived just before the Uprising. I'm not sure where he's originally from, but we've enjoyed having him here." She handed him a cup of coffee, and he took it with one hand while writing with the other.

Fitz sipped his coffee, then turned to Jaida with a serious expression. "We've been monitoring a man named Vaylan. He is taking over the Wardens' Dens and filling them with his people who call themselves the Adopted. Have you heard about them?"

"Yes, I've heard." Jaida frowned. "I know two people who joined him. I haven't met him, but they said he was the kindest, most generous person they ever met."

"You believe otherwise?" Fitz asked.

She gave him a shrewd look. "In my experience, if someone seems too good to be true, they likely are."

Rose still didn't trust Vaylan, but she could see how his Adopted could believe he was kind and generous. All his actions seemed above reproach. Her doubts came from his involvement in the death of Brother Owyn and the Priests.

And, of course, Wilder's childhood.

Fitz leaned forward. "Do you think we could talk to them?"

"No. They're gone." Jaida sighed. "They're inside the Heart now."

Rose set her coffee cup down with a thud. "What does that mean?"

Jaida shrugged. "It's where all of Brother Owyn's devoted followers end up. They travel into the Heart of the Grottos and never come back out."

"Why haven't we heard about this before now?" asked Rose.

Jaida gave her a wary look. "How many of Brother Owyn's followers have you met before?"

"I saw Brother Owyn speak at one of the rallies Upstairs,

but other than Vaylan, I never had an actual conversation with anyone there."

"The two people I knew were always both a little … odd." Considering Jaida's home was in Peculiarity, Rose wondered what she might consider odd.

Jaida continued. "They had a lot of unusual ideas and never found a place they fit in. When they heard Brother Owyn speak, something awoke in them, and they talked as if they'd finally found their place. They said they were moving to the Heart to be with fellow believers." Jaida frowned. "The way they packed, it's like they planned to never return."

Rose's eyes widened. "But can they leave if they want? Or is Vaylan holding them hostage? How many others have joined them in the Heart?"

"I don't know," said Jaida. "But if the rest of his followers are odd folks living on the margins of society, their disappearance might not be noticed at all."

Rose's chest felt tight as she considered how many people might be missing without anyone noticing.

Fitz sighed and stood as if to leave. "Thanks, Jaida. You've given us a lot to think about."

Jaida leaned back in her chair and crossed her arms. "Now, Fitz. Aren't you forgetting something?" She cleared her throat and murmured, "A donation?"

"Oh, yes." He blushed slightly. "Of course, Jaida."

Rose considered the house full of people, mostly children or adults who couldn't work. She was still learning how the new economy worked, but it made sense Jaida would need funds to provide for all these people. And since Wilder and the crew always had plenty of money, they could donate some to Jaida.

Jaida nodded her head as if Fitz had chosen wisely. She

led the two of them deeper into the house and stopped at a wall covered in children's drawings. She slid her hand behind a picture of a crudely drawn blue horse. Rose heard a *click*, and part of the wall swung open on hidden hinges.

Two women sat on either side of a long table stacked with piles of silver coins that glittered from the bright crystalline lamps overhead. The women looked up, but after seeing Jaida, they turned back to their work. They studied each coin under a magnifying glass, and when satisfied, they added the coin to a neat little stack.

Jaida walked to the far wall and picked up a small wooden box. She opened it to reveal neat rows of silver coins packed tight enough to prevent any telltale jingling. She handed him the box, and he slipped it into his bag.

"Thanks for the donation," he said with a smile.

She grabbed the front of his shirt with a firm hand and pulled his mouth to hers. When she released him, she stroked her thumb gently across his lips, and he blushed again.

"Come back anytime, Fitz." Jaida blew him a kiss as he led Rose out of the hidden room.

"This is the reason that the crew always has plenty of money?" she hissed.

He winked. "It's one reason."

She wondered if she wanted to know the other reasons.

Before they made it out the front door, Walter stepped into her path. She looked at him expectantly, but he just stared at her.

"Do you need something, Walter?" she asked.

"I remembered what the butterfly told me." He handed her a slip of paper. I think you need it more than I do."

She opened the note to find neat rows of strange little symbols. He had drawn a line of roses along the top, with a butterfly flitting among falling petals. It was beautiful and yet disturbing.

"Thank you, Walter." She tucked the note into her pocket. "That's nice of you."

He bowed his head. "Goddess blessing upon you, Rose."

She answered by rote. "And also upon you, Walter."

16

A fter dinner and practice with their Gifts, the crew decided to go out. Rose didn't think she would be good company, considering she was still disturbed after everything she'd learned at Jaida's. She wondered how many people were missing and exactly what Vaylan was doing with them in the Heart of the Grottos. She couldn't believe people were stupid enough to trust Vaylan and give up everything to follow him.

Although, she had just performed an aerial act in the circus at his request, so perhaps she was just as stupid.

She avoided talking to the crew as they walked toward the giant stone bridge that arched up into Perfection above. The crystal spire lit the Grotto in a constant glow, but the bridge cast a wide shadow. In the darkness beneath the bridge, someone had constructed a candlelit oasis.

Rose was stunned by the beauty. Jars filled with candles hung suspended over a dance floor of brightly painted wood planks. The candles cast a flickering glow unlike anything the crystal spire or crystalline could replicate. Rose had never seen so many candles. Since the City above had easy access to Priests who could shape the stone that controlled crystalline, they were rarely needed.

She closed her eyes and breathed in the sweet scent of the candles and let the music from the string quartet wash over her. Rev was wise to force her to come. She felt her crankiness melt away.

She opened her eyes to find Wilder standing in front of her.

"I'd like to apologize again." His moodiness from the last few days had faded, but he didn't appear to be his usual smug self yet, either. "I know I apologized once, but Rev told me one time isn't enough since I was such an idiot."

Rose arched a single eyebrow. "Sounds like you occasionally receive a 'girl talk' of your own."

His lips curled slightly. "No matter how many sweetly worded threats you have received from Rev, I guarantee I have had more."

She crossed her arms over her chest. "I will listen."

"I should have trusted your years of experience as a Priest. You would know if you had your Gift. I'm sorry for suggesting something so hurtful. Can you forgive me?"

She studied his dark eyes shimmering in the candlelight and considered his question thoughtfully. But she had already forgiven him the moment she opened her eyes and saw him standing before her.

"Yes, I forgive you, Wilder."

He exhaled a deep breath, and she felt the barrier between them melt away into the night.

"I understand why you said it," she said.

"You do?" he asked with wide eyes.

"You don't know why the Goddess didn't return my Gift, so you are grasping for an answer that makes sense." She sighed. "Believe me, I'd welcome any answer if I could just understand her."

He smiled sadly. "I don't understand, but I desperately wish I could." He ducked his head. "There's another reason I suggested what I did, but I'm worried you will make fun of me if I tell you."

Her eyes lit up with amusement. "Now you must tell me. Allowing me to tease you will count as part of your apology."

"I thought that if you had your Gift, it would make sense why I'm ... different." He shuffled awkwardly.

"Different how?" she asked.

"I used my Gift that first night in the amphitheater," he said.

"Yes, I remember."

"The other six weren't there," he said significantly.

Her mouth dropped open. "I didn't consider that."

"Quinn did. He thinks it's because I saw the Goddess face to face." He shrugged. "I guess that makes sense, but I thought if you had the actual Gift of Discipline, my Gift might be ... something different."

"An interesting theory, except that I clearly saw you use Discipline. And like I said, I would have noticed if I had the Gift myself."

"Yes, I realize that now. I was just grasping for something. Trying to make sense of ... her."

Rose sighed. "I understand. Believe me, I understand." The glowing dance floor gave her an idea. "Do you get sick like the others when you use your Gift?"

He shook his head gently.

She smirked. "One more way you are exceptional, I guess." She took his hand and pulled him onto the dance floor.

"What are you planning?" he asked.

Her heartbeat leaped at the anticipation in his voice. "It's time for some training," she said with a smile. "I'm going to ease your mind that your Gift of Discipline works properly. Unless you believe you are so special you don't need any training?"

He gave her a rueful smile. "I knew you would tease me."

She took hold of his hand and rested her other hand on his shoulder. When he didn't move quick enough, she cleared her throat. "Are you going to force me to lead?"

"I thought we were training?" he asked.

"Dancing is the easy part," she said. "Start with that, and we will go from there."

He grinned, then swept her into a turn. Her feet moved in response to his steps, and her whole body felt highly attuned to each subtle move he made. He spun her until she was breathless, then leaned her back into a slow, luxurious dip.

"Is this a good start?" His voice was a low purr against her neck. He pulled her close and raised her back to standing.

"You are an excellent student." Her voice was breathless, but not from exertion. "Now produce a tear so we can continue."

She saw his expression shift, and soon a tear formed on his lashes. She wondered what he thought about to stir his tears. Not that she would ever ask. That was highly inappropriate.

"Good," she said. "Now close your eyes."

He obeyed, and the tear trickled down his cheek.

They hadn't moved from their position on the dance floor, and their bodies were still locked in perfect form. She dropped her voice to a soft whisper that only he could hear.

"The warm wind from the City is flowing down the winding bridge above us. Can you feel it?"

He nodded with eyes shut.

"The Underneath has currents of its own—a colder

wind pulled in through air shafts leading outside the City walls. Can you feel it?"

His head tilted as he considered her question, but then his lips curled in a smile, and he nodded.

"A couple is spinning past us, pulling a cool breeze in the wake of her long skirt. Can you feel it?"

"But how do you know—?" His shoulders curved, and his eyes threatened to open, but she squeezed him tighter until he stood back in proper form with eyes shut.

"I thought you trusted my training?" she said archly. "I might not feel the wind myself, but I know all of her moves."

"Her?" he asked with a grin.

She cleared her throat and continued. "Another couple is passing by. The woman is tossing her long golden hair, and the gentle breeze is floating on the air, striking your neck right ... now. Can you feel it?"

She felt him shiver before he nodded. She leaned in close until her soft whisper was more breath than sound. "And this whisper ... this breath ... can you feel it against your neck?"

He nodded slowly.

Her quiet voice was precise, as if the breath of each word was the lesson. "You can't grab hold of this breath like you would a windstorm. If you move too fast, the wind stirred by your grasp will blow the breath away. You must sneak up on it slowly, carefully. And instead of forcing it to your will, you must coax it. Convince the wind that its will is your own. Then do with it as you please." She leaned even closer, then exhaled gently on the soft place directly under his ear.

His breath caught in his lungs, and she felt a wicked pleasure that she could move him so. But before she could gloat, she felt an answering breath on her neck.

His eyes were closed, and he bit his lip in concentration. The warm breath of air lingered underneath her ear, then trickled up her jaw before caressing her cheekbone. She held her breath and leaned into the touch, despite her attempt at restraint. The breath broke into smaller pieces that combed through her hair like soft fingertips, fluttering through the length of her hair before scattering back into the night.

Wilder opened his eyes.

"You definitely have the Gift," she said breathlessly. He lowered his head and pulled her into a kiss.

Even without her Gift, she could feel the wind flow around them. The warm breeze rushed through her hair and tickled her bare legs. The cool air was gone, replaced by a whirlwind of warmth swirling down from the City above. She pulled him closer, savoring the feel of his lips on hers. Wind whipped her hair into a frenzy and tugged at her clothes, but she refused to pull away from the kiss, even though she stood directly in the center of a sweltering tornado.

"Sorry to interrupt, but you've created a bit of a storm." Quinn's voice broke through the sound of the rushing wind.

She blinked her eyes open at the same time as Wilder, and the tornado shuddered, then dissipated. Quinn's hair was even more disheveled than usual, and the people on the dance floor stared up at the bridge, wondering where the sudden windstorm had come from. But instead of the candles being blown out, they blazed even brighter than before.

Quinn noticed her staring at the candles. "Fire uses air to burn hotter. It appears Wilder's windstorm stoked the fire like a blacksmith's bellows." He looked at Rose. "Does that happen often when Discipline Priests use their Gift?"

"We rarely used candlelight in the City since we always had plenty of crystalline lamps." She considered the blazing candles as they began to settle back into a normal glow.

"Although maybe this is why we never used candles. I can imagine it getting out of hand rather quickly."

The people on the dance floor finished straightening their windblown hair and clothes and looked around for anything to explain the sudden windstorm.

"We should get out of here," said Wilder. "We don't want anyone to think too much about what just occurred."

They gathered up the rest of the crew and left before anyone could ask questions.

17

A t breakfast the next morning, Rev had a few things to say.

"I suggested you leave the house for a while. See something pretty. I didn't say create a windstorm in a public place so the entire Grotto could see!"

Wilder and Rose sat at the kitchen table, staring into their coffee cups. Neither looked up as Rev paced behind them.

"We've been so careful to use our Gifts privately. Or at least we have been." Rev tapped the table with a long nail. "But I guess we can't leave the two of you alone in public. Not if you lack common sense and self-control."

Rose wanted to protest that she wasn't the one who lacked self-control. It was Wilder who'd called the storm. Although, she had to admit with pride, her "training" may have been a bit too good.

"I'm sorry, Rev," said Wilder. "I should have been more careful. I won't try that in public again."

Rose imagined trying that with him in private. She took a sip of coffee to hide the color of her cheeks.

Rev crossed her arms and considered them both with a

frown. "I hoped we could stay in this Grotto for a few more days, but I think we should move out today."

Rose tried to hide her disappointment. She would have liked another day with the circus.

"I'd like to talk to Vaylan again before we leave," said Rose.

Rev shot her an irritated look. "Do you need to ask him for permission?"

"No!" said Rose with a huff. "I want to know what he's doing in the Heart. We should find out how many people are missing."

Rev sighed dramatically. "Fine. Take the wolves. And we should try to gather information from one of his Adopted. They might speak freer than Vaylan himself. Take someone else with you to see what they can learn."

Rose invited Wilder with a glance.

"Take anyone but Wilder," growled Rev.

Rose attempted not to sulk.

She talked Quinn into going with her. It wasn't hard to convince him since he was so easygoing. And because of his fascination with the windstorm Wilder created, they had plenty to discuss.

"I think it was an intriguing experiment!" His blue eyes sparkled behind his dark-rimmed glasses. "Wilder has been reluctant to test out the full range of his Gift when we practice together. It was amazing to see it in action."

"The seven of you have practiced in living rooms so far. It's hard to summon a hurricane when you are worried about breaking furniture."

"That's a good point. We should find a practice space." As they drew nearer to the Haven, he asked, "So what am I hoping to learn from these Adopted? Should I ask about anything specific?"

"Do you believe in prophecies?" she asked.

His face lit up. "Fascinating question! Why do you ask?"

"There are rumors that Brother Owyn was a prophet. Vaylan believes Brother Owyn said things that came true and that he even predicted his own death."

Quinn considered the question thoughtfully. "If you asked me last year, I would have said Brother Owyn was like the fortune tellers who give vague predictions that you can interpret as coming true after the fact. But after meeting Ylena, I'm not so sure."

"What does Ylena have to do with Brother Owyn?" Even though the girl had left the City, she still came up in too many conversations.

"Only that we know some people have a Spark. Like Vaylan can manipulate crystalline."

She stared at him as she pieced together his logic. "So, it's possible that Brother Owyn had a Spark of prophecy?"

Quinn shrugged. "I don't know. I'm curious if these prophecies are legitimate glimpses of the future or simply good guesses."

"We need to get our hands on some of these prophecies."

Quinn nodded. "Let's split up and see who will talk."

He went to talk to some of the Adopted who lingered outside the Haven while she and the wolves passed through the doors thanks to her mark. She didn't see Vaylan, but she found plenty of people in white serving meals to children and tired women.

A young man in white approached her with a kind smile, as if he might point her to the serving line. At the sight of her mark, he gave her a quick bow.

"Marked One," he said. "How may I assist?"

"It's just Rose," she said. "Is Vaylan available?"

"He is making preparations before he leaves for the next Grotto tomorrow."

"Ah, then I guess I will see him there." She studied the young man, realizing she was usually accompanied by Vaylan but could now ask questions on her own. "Have you been an Adopted long?"

"Not long, Marked One. I am originally from Perfection Diocese."

"You're from Upstairs?"

"Yes!" His smile was bright, and he seemed genuinely excited to speak to her. "I heard Brother Owyn speak at an event in Perfection. He said after hearing him speak, my life would never be the same. He was right."

She had heard Brother Owyn speak, and it had affected her, too. Although she didn't feel as cheerful about it as this young man appeared. But it was a good opening.

"You've heard Brother Owyn was a prophet?" she asked.

"Well, of course." He looked at her like she was strange to ask. "To become one of the Adopted, we must study his prophecies."

Her eyes widened. "You've read all his prophecies?"

He chuckled. "No, I'm too new for that. I only know the basic prophecies they teach the new initiates. The ones about what it means to be the Adopted. And, of course, the one about you and the Chosen."

She nearly choked. "Excuse me?"

He gave her a shy smile. "Obviously, they would teach us that one first so we would know how important you are. We should always let you in to see Vaylan, because you are the one who will deliver the Chosen into his hands."

She couldn't breathe but choked out, "I will deliver the Chosen to him?"

His face turned thoughtful. "I know it's tied to the prophecy about the Seven, but I don't understand how they fit together yet." He sighed in happy resignation. "There's so much to learn!"

"I completely agree," she said neutrally. "I really want to read all of Brother Owyn's prophecies myself."

He shook his head and looked at her strangely. "I thought you had access to all his prophecies. Since you are the Marked One?"

Her thoughts snagged on the title, and she couldn't come up with an easy way to deflect the question.

He bit his lip, and his eyes grew wary. "I thought I was allowed to discuss the prophecies with you, but maybe I shouldn't ..."

She forced a laugh, then leaned in for a conspiratorial whisper. "Some people say it's bad manners to discuss prophecies with the people they are referencing."

His eyes widened in fear.

"Don't worry." She forced her voice to sound light-hearted. "I won't tell anyone about your little social blunder. It can be our secret."

He gave a relieved sigh and bowed his head. "You are truly blessed, Marked One."

She gave him a small bow in return, then forced her legs to walk slowly from the room.

Indulgence

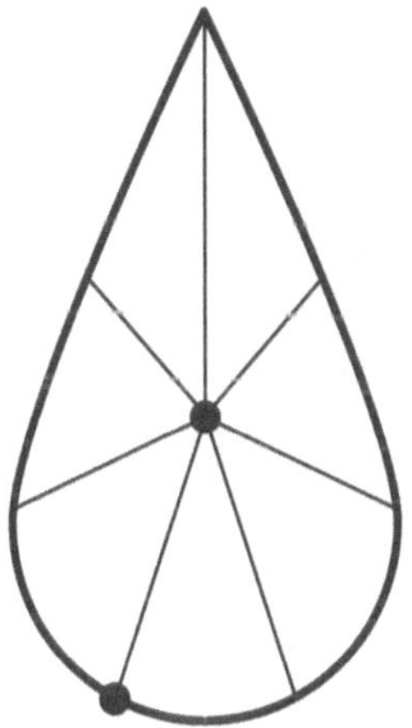

18

———

Rose was still reeling from the prophecies by the time they arrived in Indulgence. She talked little on the walk as she replayed her conversation with the young Adopted, trying to remember his exact words.

Quinn had been less successful in discovering any prophecies. The two Adopted he'd spoken to were more interested in converting him to their cause. They had a lot to say about how kind and generous Vaylan was and the good work they were doing in the Havens. Quinn suggested perhaps he let the Adopted "convert" him so he could investigate from the inside.

Rose thought that felt too close to delivering him into Vaylan's hands. The rest of the crew agreed.

Even if the prophecy wasn't true, Vaylan and the Adopted believed that it was. And that meant that the seven of them were in danger. Rose couldn't shake the fear lingering in the pit of her stomach. What if she did something accidentally to deliver them to Vaylan? If Brother Owyn had a Spark, did that mean she was destined to deliver them?

They arrived at a cute gray house with a red door. Tayeh unlocked the door and let them inside.

"No Gifts inside the house." Tayeh's voice was stern, and the other six nodded in understanding.

"This is your house?" Rose looked around the living room in surprise. The walls were pale blue with decorative navy swirls highlighting door frames and artwork. Colorful pillows lined a gray couch and matching chairs.

Tayeh crossed her arms. "Yeah, it's my home. Would you like to comment on it?"

Rose could see in the young woman's eyes that any joke about how the luxurious home didn't match Tayeh's stark attitude would be unwelcome.

"It's lovely." Rose said the two words, then kept her mouth firmly closed.

Tayeh raised an eyebrow but didn't murder her. Rose thought that was a good sign.

"Tayeh!" Fitz stood in front of a wall of shelves displaying a collection of fine pottery. "This is stunning. You have an amazing eye for design."

Tayeh ducked her head and couldn't meet his eyes. "Thanks, Fitz. That's nice of you to say."

Rose stared at her in surprise. Was Tayeh embarrassed by the compliment?

Rev cleared her throat. "Wilder, you can take Rose, Kieran, and Feather with you to find a training studio close by. Tayeh, Fitz, Quinn, and I will start asking around to see if we can get our hands on any of Brother Owyn's prophecies."

Wilder elbowed Rose and whispered, "Why do I get the feeling Rev assigned us chaperones?"

Rose chuckled as they headed back into Indulgence.

They finally found a training space that met their needs: a large open room, stone walls, no windows, and access to running water. Feather would have to bring in her own plants, and she assumed Tayeh could always find some injury to heal. If not, she had multiple ways to cause one. She wasn't sure what Kieran would do. He still wasn't interested in sharing his Gift of Knowledge with anyone. She didn't blame him. The thought of sharing a private thought or a memory with someone else wasn't appealing to her, either.

The four of them examined the space to see what else they might need. Feather walked around with her usual bright-eyed wonder, while Kieran's face was the picture of disinterest.

"Did you ever train in a gym like this before, Feather?" asked Wilder kindly.

She shook her head. "We didn't have many gyms in Perfection Diocese. But I took a few dance classes. The mirrors remind me of that." She looked at Wilder's reflection in the wall of mirrors and smiled shyly.

Rose knew Wilder wouldn't appreciate it if she rolled her eyes at the girl, so instead she said, "Kieran, what about you?'

He arched an eyebrow and gave her a fake smile. "I'm from Rivalry. I was basically born in a gym."

At that, Rose did roll her eyes.

"This will be fun," said Wilder drily.

"I'm going to train on the equipment for a while," said Kieran. He gave them all a pointed look. "Alone."

None of them put up a fight as he walked over to the training equipment on the right side of the room.

Wilder caught Feather's eye. "If you want to practice dancing, Rose and I will let you take all the mirrors. We'll go spar over there." He jerked his head to the far-left side of the room.

Feather's face lit up. "You're so nice! Yes, I would love some time to dance. I need to prepare for the role of Goddess, of course!" She gave him the same shy smile and ran to the center of the room.

As he walked with Rose to their side of the room, he whispered, "I'm afraid this is as private as Rev will allow us to be. She doesn't trust us not to flatten the Grotto with a storm."

She crossed her arms sternly, but her lips twitched at the corners. "You're the one who did it. Don't blame me for your lack of control."

He put his hands on her waist and pulled her close. "I blame your training. You were entirely too thorough."

She laughed. "That was only the first lesson! You still have a long way to go."

"Oh, really?" He grinned and pulled her closer. "What's the next lesson?"

She cleared her throat primly. "Okay, *student*." She separated herself from his arms. "Watch me closely."

He raised his eyebrows. "I always do."

"Last night, you learned how to detect existing currents and use them to your advantage. But sometimes, the wind needs extra motivation to go where you want it to." She rolled her shoulders in a stretch and bounced on her toes. "Obviously, I don't have the Gift, so all I can do is stir up little boring air currents, but if you pay attention, you'll see what I mean."

He blinked a tear, then watched her with focused determination.

Rose closed her eyes and tried to remember what it was like to use her Gift. She had been without it for weeks now, but it felt like years. She traveled back to when she was a girl practicing in the gym with Caed and Kai. They were both bigger and stronger than her, so she'd had to learn to beat them in other ways. She learned to be fast and use her lighter weight to her advantage.

She struck out with a quick hand, her palm pushing a current right at Wilder's midsection. It was a puny current, but she couldn't see it. She bent her knees, then leaped into the air, twisting her body with her leg swinging around in a wide arc. If her first shot bent him over, the current would swing around to hit his head. She landed in a crouch, using the momentum to punch an air current from her elbow directly into his groin.

She straightened and gave him a ceremonial bow. Not even the softest trickle of air had touched him, but his eyes unfocused as he thought through each move.

"Do you understand?"

"Ouch," he said simply.

She nodded. "Good. Now you try." She settled into a fighting stance and waved him forward.

He made a show of examining her form for weaknesses, but the evaluation was more salacious than technical. She grinned, then prepared for his attack.

However, when the wind hit her, she was not prepared.

He pushed his flat palm forward in the same move she had demonstrated. She didn't even have time to block before the wind lifted her and threw her backward. She threw her hands out by reflex, and when she crashed onto her backside, she landed hard on her wrist.

She rolled onto her back, cradling her wrist against her chest. Wilder skidded to a stop at her side and reached for her.

"Oh my Goddess, I'm so sorry. Are you okay? Your wrist. Oh my Goddess, I'm so sorry." The words bubbled out of him without coherent thought, and he alternated between reaching for her and trying not to touch her.

"It's fine," she said through clenched teeth. "I've had a broken wrist before. I know better than to land like that. It was my fault."

"I shouldn't have hit that hard. I didn't know ..." He reached a slow hand to her wrist. "Let me help—"

She shoved him away with her other hand. "Don't," she snapped. She took a shaking breath in. "Help me stand. I can walk back to the house to wait for Tayeh."

Wilder bit his lips, but he lifted her under the shoulder until she was on her feet.

Rose blinked tears out of her eyes and realized Kieran and Feather were both staring at her. Feather's lips puckered into a terrified little pout, and Kieran looked at her wrist as if he was familiar with the pain.

"I'll carry you," said Wilder.

"Goddess-dammit, Wilder, stop coddling me!" she yelled.

He flinched, then slowly released his grip on her arm.

She tried to hold her wrist steady as she wiped the embarrassing tears from her eyes using her other arm. She ground her teeth together to keep from making any humiliating sounds of pain as she turned to leave.

Wilder hurried ahead of her and opened the gym door. She didn't acknowledge him as he ordered the other two to lock the door before heading back.

He walked by her side the whole way to Tayeh's. She knew he wanted to apologize more. He wanted her to say something, but she couldn't. Not because of the pain.

Because of the shame.

Her brothers had knocked her on her backside many times while fighting with the wind. In fact, fighting with them caused her previous broken wrist.

And she had practiced fighting Wilder without the wind before. She didn't like it, but she was learning to adapt. She knew how to react in a fight when she was on equal ground as her opponent. No wind. No Gifts. Just fighting skill.

But this was the first time she'd fought a Gifted opponent without a Gift of her own. She wasn't prepared for how off balance she would feel, both physically and emotionally. When they had fought one on one without the wind, she knew Wilder was stronger and a better fighter. But with the wind on his side, she was nothing.

He opened the door to let her inside Tayeh's house. As she sat down on the couch to wait, she kept her head bowed over her wrist. She knew her hunched posture made her seem weak from the pain when that wasn't it at all. She couldn't tell him that the overwhelming strength of his Gift not only broke her wrist, but broke a piece of her spirit as well.

19

Rose sat at the bar, sober and miserable. Her wrist tingled painfully. Tayeh hadn't been able to heal it completely, though she had tried. Rose was glad to keep a little of the physical pain. It was a fitting companion for her agonizing thoughts.

Tayeh was nearby, though the focus of her quiet conversation was Fitz. Her body leaned against the bar as she slumped over her glass of water. She didn't vomit after healing Rose, but she still wasn't well. Tayeh didn't want to miss a chance to go out with the crew, so she'd stumbled to her feet, shaming Rose into also joining the trip.

Wilder watched Rose silently from his position at the other end of the bar. He didn't approach her, not after she had yelled at him. Rev, Quinn, and Kieran surrounded him as they bought the next round of drinks, putting yet another drink into Feather's outstretched hand. They joked and laughed, but Wilder's eyes were mournful and out of place.

Rose watched Feather do another shot that led to coughing and giggles. There was a part of Rose that wanted to drink and lose herself in the oblivion that would eventually come. But before the oblivion came the euphoric burn of the alcohol and the feeling of invincibility that followed. She couldn't be trusted with that kind of bliss.

And she didn't deserve it.

She watched as Kieran's eyes took on a predatory glint that she found familiar in a bar. He circled both Feather and Quinn with eager glee. Rose wondered if Wilder would step in to protect them like he'd protected others before. Not that Feather or Quinn were helpless. They were both Gifted.

Rose was the only helpless one in the group.

Her melancholy thoughts were irritating, even to herself. Caed was the moody one. Kai would tease her mercilessly if he saw her like this. She used to believe she was strong. She should at least fake strength and not be so pathetic.

She slid away from the bar, unnoticed by Tayeh and Fitz, and walked outside. She still found the constant night of the Underneath disorienting. The only real clue to the time was the top of the bridge in the distance. Currently, it was dark, not sunny.

She faced the crystal spire and traced it up to where it met the roof of the cave. The other side of the crystal shot through the middle of Temple Discipline. Her home.

She wondered if she would ever live there again.

"Rose ..." Wilder's voice was soft, hesitant.

"I don't want to talk about it," she whispered.

He followed her gaze up to the crystal but didn't speak. He knew her well enough to not ask what any other fool would have. *Are you thinking about home?*

She was grateful he didn't ask, so she answered a different question. "I miss Kai."

He turned to her with a sincere smile. "I like Kai."

"Everyone likes Kai," she said with mock exasperation.

"What do you think he's doing?" he asked.

"Still working with kids in the temple, I guess. I'm not sure how things have changed since we left."

"I've heard there is still a lot of anti-Priest sentiment among some factions. No one is sure which group is going to come out on top."

She nodded absently. She should have guessed Wilder had gathered information about Upstairs. He always had information but rarely told her everything unless she dragged it out of him.

"They probably need you back inside," she said. "Kieran was sizing up Feather and Quinn, just waiting to see which one of them loses their good sense first."

"Rev was already handling that when I stepped out." He smirked. "Some 'girl talk,' you know."

"Good." Rose's smile was faint but vicious. "I hope she leaves a mark." Wilder's face grew serious, and she prepared for the words she knew he would say.

"I retract my apology."

She blinked. That was not what she guessed.

Wilder took a deep breath. "I apologized for hurting you, and I take that back. Even though I hate seeing you get hurt, I shouldn't have made such a big deal about it. You're strong and have handled worse. I've seen you fight with broken ribs. A broken wrist is painful, but it's nothing compared to your strength. I overreacted. I'm sorry."

She wanted to continue sulking, but her lips twitched despite herself. "Are you apologizing ... for apologizing?"

The corner of his lip curled in response. "I guess I am."

She shook her head with a wry smile. "I'm trying to wallow in self-pity, and then you hit me with some sort of reverse apology. I'm not sure if you are very good at apologizing or very bad."

"I'm not sure either, but I'm glad I could distract you from your self-pity." He grew serious again. "Instead of apologizing for hurting you, I should have thanked you for training me. I know it's not easy for you." He gestured inside at the rest of the crew. "All of us … It's a lot for you to handle. And yet, you decided to train me, despite how difficult that must be for you. Thank you for doing that for me."

She looked at the crystal spire again, unable to meet his eyes. "It hurts, Wilder. Worse than a broken wrist. Worse than broken ribs. I know I should probably just grieve the loss of my Gift and move on, but I can't. The wind still haunts me at every turn. So yes, it's painful for me to train you, for me to remember what I've lost. But it's also painful to think of all my years of training as a waste. I need it to count for something. I need my devotion to the Goddess to have not been in vain."

"Your devotion wasn't in vain, Rose." His voice was soft but fierce. "I don't know how this will all end, but it will not be in vain."

"It's comforting to know at least one of us believes." She wiped away a wandering tear and cleared her throat. "I owe you an apology as well. I shouldn't have yelled at you."

"I understand. You were in pain—"

"I yelled because I was angry, not because I was in pain. And despite my anger, I knew you overreacted because you care about me."

"I'm glad you know that," he said with a soft smile.

She ducked her head, unsure what to do with the fragile moment between them.

He glanced inside toward the crew. "I should get back in there. Earlier, Quinn was feeding the wolves treats from the bar. If he sheds a tear to have a conversation with them, it will be a long walk carrying him home."

She chuckled, and he turned to go.

"Wilder?"

He stilled in the doorway at her soft call.

"Is this how it will always be with us? Doing something stupid, then apologizing, over and over for all time?"

Her question was playful, but his eyes locked on hers with such intensity she held her breath.

"I sincerely hope so." He held her gaze for a long moment before ducking his head and leaving her alone, struggling to regain her breath.

20

———

The wolves were missing the next morning, so Rose walked to the Haven alone. Quinn couldn't remember *talking* to the wolves the night before, but he admitted to drinking a lot, and it was possible he gave them instructions he couldn't remember. She didn't mind going on her own. She didn't think Vaylan wanted to hurt her.

What he wanted to do to the seven Chosen was still unclear.

He knew the Goddess had returned the Gifts. He had used that fact to remind her she was not one of the Chosen. Beyond that discussion, he hadn't mentioned the crew again. He had focused all his conversations on her. Did he truly believe that she would ever trust him enough to bring her friends to him?

Her mark was visible, and the Adopted at the door waved her inside. She tried to school her expression and act like she had never heard that prophecy. She wanted to see if it was something Vaylan would admit on his own. When she told Wilder her plan to pretend like she didn't know and just act casual, he covered his mouth with his hand to hide his grin.

"You're going to 'act casual' when you're furious with him?" asked Wilder. "He's going to know something is up within five minutes of you walking through the door."

"Then why are you letting me go?" she had asked.

He snorted. "I'm smart enough to know that I don't 'let' you do anything. And besides, when you lose your temper and force him to admit he believes in the prophecy, maybe he will reveal more about his motives."

She had huffed loudly and left the room. And now she was determined to prove him wrong.

Vaylan wasn't in the common room, so an Adopted led her up a set of stairs to where he stood talking to a group of people in white.

"These rooms are in rough shape, so it will take a lot of cleaning to get them looking good enough for our guests," said Vaylan. "Thank you for your hard work turning this Haven into a place of refuge."

The group chatted happily as they picked up their mops and cleaning supplies and split up into the small rooms off the hallway. Rose watched them with interest, trying to think of questions to ask him about what was happening. Anything to distract herself from the burning questions about prophecy that would trigger her anger.

"Good morning, Rose! It's good to see you!" His eyes twinkled. "Did you come to join the cleaning crew?"

She snorted. "I wasn't planning on it." She peeked into a small room where two Adopted scrubbed the floor. "What are they doing?"

"I'm creating a safe place for people to stay and receive the help they need." He stared into the room as if imagining someone inside. "I can't help but think how different the

Underneath would have been if we could have had healing centers of our own."

She shook her head. "But there are no more Priests to heal."

"No, but there are apothecaries with remedies and people skilled at caring for those who need help. We won't be able to offer healing, but we can provide care and support."

She imagined the people staying with Jaida in the middle of her counterfeiting enterprise. Vaylan's clean room lit with bright crystalline reminded her of the healing centers Upstairs. Maybe a place like this would be a better place for someone like Walter to live.

"I admit I'm surprised, Vaylan. I didn't think creating Havens like this would be top on your list of strategies to take over the City."

He smirked. "Did you think I would start by killing everyone who opposed me?"

She shrugged. "Honestly, yes."

He chuckled. "Well, it turns out I don't have many opponents. Few people are stepping forward to challenge me. After the show I made in Grotto Chaos, the bad people who had set up shop in the other Dens fled before I arrived. Haven't you noticed how calm the factions are down here?"

She thought back to her time Upstairs and realized there had been protests and rallies almost every night. She had seen nothing like that in the Underneath.

He waved a hand to encompass the line of rooms. "There's a reason for that. I'm providing a valuable service to the Underneath, something they've never had before. No one is opposing me, because they need me."

"Is that all this is to you? A means to an end?"

"If the end is a better City for all, then yes. Imagine how different the Underneath would be now if I had led it these last fourteen years. What if these had been Havens instead of Dens this whole time? Imagine how different Wilder's life would have been."

She sucked in her breath in a hiss. "What does Wilder have to do with this?"

"His mother." Vaylan spoke out loud, but his eyes unfocused as if replaying the past. "What if she'd had somewhere to go back then? Somewhere to receive help? And if she refused help, Wilder could have come to a Haven on his own. He would have been fed and cared for in these walls instead of having to find his way alone through the Grottos."

She had started to relax, but now her distrust of Vaylan snapped back into place. "How do you know what Wilder went through? He never told you."

Vaylan sighed as if he carried a heavy burden. "I imagined what he went through every night as I sat alone in my cell. I knew his mother would hurt him without me there. She always lashed out when she was out of control. If she believed I abandoned her, I knew her rage would end in violence toward Wilder. I imagined the scenes in detail every day."

Rose again looked in one of the bright rooms. She tried to picture a small version of Wilder sitting inside. He sat on the floor, scribbling in a little notebook like the adult Wilder did. She liked the way the adult Wilder had turned out, but she had to admit, she wished he could have fewer scars inside and out to deal with.

"I assume you stopped by to discuss prophecy with me."

She immediately snapped out of her musing. "Why do you say that?"

"One of my young Adopted said he'd discussed some of Brother Owyn's prophecies with you. He came to ask my forgiveness in case he spoke out of place." He gave a paternal grin. "I forget how enthusiastic young people can be."

Rose bit her lip to keep from scowling. So much for asking the young man to keep their conversation secret. However, she felt a slight twinge of pleasure that Vaylan brought it up on his own. She would enjoy flaunting her success to Wilder.

"I found his ideas on prophecy fascinating." She tried to keep her voice as neutral as possible. "He believed that everything Brother Owyn said would come true."

"Yes, of course it will." Vaylan's voice was matter-of-fact. "Many things already have."

"You can't honestly believe everything he said will come true." She spoke in an offhand matter. "It's not like you wrote down everything he ever said."

He raised an eyebrow. "Of course I did."

She nearly choked. "You did? Why?"

"Every word Brother Owyn spoke is precious to me and his other followers. His words have power, and the one who knows his words best knows the future."

"And that's you?"

"I spent over a decade in prison with Brother Owyn, listening to his prophecies. I memorized every word he said and wrote it all down in painstaking detail."

She crossed her arms over her chest. "What's to stop you from writing down whatever you want and claiming it came from Brother Owyn?"

He gave her the look that said she was an ignorant child. "His words are proven every time a prophecy comes true."

He noticed the skepticism in her eyes and pulled a sheet of paper out of his pocket.

"Here are the prophecies the young Adopted spoke of. This copy is yours."

She narrowed her eyes and didn't take the paper.

"There's not a catch, Rose." He shook his head. "It's not a secret. Anyone who agrees to work in one of the Havens is handed these prophecies. I know you aren't officially one of the Adopted, but consider it your reward for assisting me with the children at the circus."

She tried to hold her scowl, but her heart cheered at the memory.

He clasped the paper between his palms in reverence. "These words are sacred to me. They are more valuable, more holy, than any liturgy of the Goddess. Because these can be proven. They have and will continue to come true." He held it out again on an open palm.

She took the paper with a skeptical glance, but a word from the first prophecy caught her eye. "*True power lies in the heart* ..." She looked up at him and tried to keep her voice calm. "Is this about the Heart of the Grottos? I haven't been. What's it like?"

His eyes twinkled as he clearly saw through her question. "I'm surprised it took you so long to ask. As the Marked One, you are welcome there anytime." He tapped his lip as if a thought just occurred to him. "In fact, bring Wilder and the whole crew with you! It will be fun."

Her breath caught in her lungs. "Um ... I don't think so."

He shrugged lightly. "Perhaps another day."

The page of prophecies felt like a dangerous fire burning between her fingers. She had the sudden irrational fear that just by reading the words, they would come true. She tried to hand the paper back to Vaylan, but he shook his head.

"Take it with you," he said. "Study the words. I guarantee you will believe as I do someday."

"In case you haven't noticed, I'm pretty stubborn about what I believe."

He gave her a knowing grin. "I know you will believe,

Rose. It's been foretold, and you can't escape prophecy. No matter how hard you try."

She walked out of the Haven with the prophecies shoved in her pocket, trying to shake off the ominous echo of his words.

21

After the end, the Seven will return, a gift only for those she favors.

The Marked will deliver the Chosen into your hands, and you will understand the truth.

True power lies in the heart. Hide your treasure within, and never let it go.

You will stand with the Marked and cast the City into darkness, because death must come before life.

So, seek the light, for the light will be a sign of the City reborn.

Rose stared at the prophecies, trying to make sense of the words. Familiar phrases jumped out to her as she recalled the words of Vaylan and the Adopted. She sensed power thrumming through the words, as if they lived and breathed, and that power terrified her. She'd read the words immediately after leaving the Haven and then again when she showed the page to the crew. She continued reading even though the crew had forced her to join them at another bar.

This bar differed from the others she had seen. She sat at a table outside—outside being relative in the Underneath. The outdoor bar was under a wood pergola draped with a few fake vines. Most of the crew was dancing, but Wilder took the seat across from her, setting down two beers.

Rose looked around the dimly lit space. "This is a beer garden? It doesn't seem very garden-y."

He chuckled. "Gardens are in short supply in the Underneath, so the emphasis is on the beer."

She took a sip of beer and frowned. It didn't have the same kick as a fiery shot.

Wilder looked at the prophecies in her hand. "I think you should put that away for a while. You won't unlock the mysteries of what Vaylan believes in one night."

"I won't figure it out by drinking this pathetic stuff either," she said with a glare at her glass.

"No, but you might enjoy your evening if you look up from the page. You might find something else more pleasing to the eye right in front of you." He gave her a smug smile.

She looked behind him. "Oh, is Quinn close by?" she asked innocently.

He laughed. "You're so feisty. Good thing I love that about you."

Her heart slammed to a stop in her chest. She replayed his words a dozen times in a split second, trying to interpret the depth of his comment.

Before she could respond, he broke eye contact and tilted his head as if he heard something.

She couldn't see anything unusual, but then she heard it. A faint yip and the scrabbling of claws against wood planks. One wolf slid to a stop at the other end of the bar, then gave a sharp huff over her shoulder in impatience. The second wolf joined the first.

Followed by Kai.

Rose's eyes widened in surprise. He looked different,

wearing a gray shirt instead of his usual black, but her heart clenched seeing his familiar face. She ran and grabbed him in a fierce embrace.

"Kai! It's so good to see you! What are you doing here?" she asked.

He sagged in her arms. "Thank the Goddess, you are safe. I looked for you at Temple Order days ago, and when you weren't there, I feared you were one of the many people who have gone missing. Why didn't you tell someone where you were going?"

He looked like he'd been crying, and she felt the sharp sting of guilt. She realized she hadn't considered what he or anyone else would think when she left. "We had to run away suddenly. Vaylan threatened the Priests if I didn't leave."

His eyes widened in fear. "He threatened you?" He looked around the beer garden. "Should you be somewhere so public?"

She opened her mouth to explain that she spoke to Vaylan today inside the Haven, but instead she said, "It's complicated."

He leaned closer and whispered, "I've had some complications of my own. But I'd rather not say it here."

"Sure. We can go to Tayeh's and talk privately." She turned around to look for Wilder and found him at her back.

"I'm glad to see you, Kai," he said. "Rose has missed you."

"I missed her, too," he said. "I have something to talk to her about, so can we …?"

Rose turned to lead him out when Quinn ran up.

"Hello, Kai! It's good to see you!"

"When did you meet Kai?" asked Rose. She had introduced Kai to Wilder and Fitz at dinner during the auditions but couldn't remember introducing Kai to any of the others.

Quinn answered cheerfully, "I found him that night you were completely drunk in Discipline." He laughed. "He had to carry you home, kicking and screaming. I couldn't have managed it on my own, but luckily, he's very strong."

Kai's normally playful voice was shy. "Thanks, Quinn. It's good to see you, too."

Rose stood close enough to see a faint blush on his cheeks. Her mouth dropped open. Her cocky brother was blushing?

Kai cleared his throat awkwardly. "Can we go now, Rose? We need to talk."

She closed her mouth. "Yes, of course."

But then the rest of the crew wandered over, trapping them in place.

Rev was the first to pounce. She stepped close to Kai and gave him an approving glance up and down. "Why hasn't anyone introduced me to our charming guest?"

"Rev, this is Kai. My brother." Rose expected this introduction to lead to teasing and enough flirting to make her sick, but surprisingly, Rev took a polite step back.

"Ah, Kai!" said Rev. "I've heard a lot about you. I'm glad you found us."

He looked at the wolves, now seated at Wilder's feet. "I had help."

From the rips and bite marks on his pants, Rose wasn't sure if he'd had much choice in the matter.

The rest of the crew went through the formalities of introductions, and by the end, Kai's hand was clenched on Rose's arm. He was like an animal, straining for escape.

"Kai and I are heading back to Tayeh's," said Rose. "The rest of you should stay and enjoy yourselves." The crew ran back out to the dance floor, with Kai giving one last glance at Quinn, who was already dancing with Feather.

She was about to mention the blush from earlier when Kai pulled her around the corner out of eyesight of the crew.

"Please tell me I'm not alone," he whispered frantically. "I can't handle this if I'm all alone."

"What are you talking about?" she asked.

He rubbed a hand through his hair, making it even more chaotic than usual. "I tried asking the other Priests, but they thought I was crazy. They didn't say it out loud, but I could see it in their eyes. They thought I snapped. But I know I haven't!"

She caught him by the arms and looked into his eyes. "Kai, I don't think you are crazy. But I need you to tell me what happened."

"It's back," he whispered. "My Gift is back."

She staggered backward a step, coming up hard against the wall.

His shoulders slumped. "I hoped you would say that your Gift was back, too, but guessing by your face, I see the answer is no."

She shook her head, unable to speak.

He ran angry fingers through his hair. "Maybe I am crazy. It's not like I have any proof. I haven't been able to use my Gift, no matter how hard I try. But I can feel the wind again, you know?" He shook his head. "Of course you know. I hoped you would say the same thing happened to you." He started pacing. "The night you disappeared, I heard a strange sound, and I woke up next to the crystal spire. Then I realized I could feel the wind again. I ran all the way to Temple Order, but by the time I arrived, you were long gone. I've been going mad keeping this to myself. I've only hinted to other Priests, but even that was enough for them to look at me strangely." His voice broke. "I can't do this alone, Rose."

Her own heart was shattered, but the sight of her strong

brother crying was enough to make her put that aside. She gathered him into her arms and held tightly.

"Kai, you aren't alone, and you aren't crazy. I believe you. And you are going to be okay."

He took a few shaking breaths before his breathing steadied. Once he seemed calm, she slowly released him.

"Thanks, Rose," he said. "I knew you would believe me. That's why I followed the wolves. I hoped they would lead me to you."

She gave him a comforting smile. "You are exactly where you need to be." They were still close enough that she could hear the crew laughing, and she realized he belonged with them even more than she did.

"I just don't understand how my Gift can be back if I can't use it. This doesn't make any sense." He started pacing again.

"Kai, it will make sense now that you are with us. You will have no problem using your Gift." She tried to keep her voice calm, but seeing Kai so anxious was putting her on edge.

"But I do have a problem!" he said, voice frantic. "I've tried over and over. I reach for the storm, but it won't respond!" He lifted his arms to the sky with a roar, then flung his arms down to his sides.

Rose's eyes widened, and she lunged for him, but it was too late.

A rushing wind gathered at the top of the cavern and whipped into a frenzy. It twisted into a whirlwind that crashed down around the beer garden. Rose gripped the side of the building to stay standing in the middle of the sudden storm.

Kai stood unmoving, staring at his hands in wonder. He began laughing, almost maniacally, and more tears formed in his eyes.

She lunged for him, this time catching him. She used her sleeve to wipe his eyes and spoke soothing words as if he were a tiny baby Priest.

"Kai, I need you to calm down. I believe you. You aren't alone. Please stop. I will explain everything, but please let the wind go."

Her words eventually sank in, and his eyes widened in understanding. The wind dissipated into a gentle breeze, sliding calmly through the streets.

Wilder and the crew ran around the corner to find Rose still wiping Kai's face. Rose couldn't see the full extent of the damage the storm had caused, but she could guess by the look on their faces. The look on Wilder's face was different, though. Before his face dropped in disappointment, she had seen the hopeful look blazing in his eyes.

It only took Rose a heartbeat to interpret. When the windstorm struck, Wilder had thought she was the one who called it.

But no, the Goddess had passed her over again.

22

———

The arguing began as soon as they were safely inside Tayeh's house.

"We need to leave," said Rev. "Unusual activity like that is going to draw attention, and we don't want to draw the wrong sort of attention. That's the second windstorm our crew has caused, and we need to move on and lie low for a while."

Wilder drawled, "We aren't the best at lying low, Rev."

"Why does it matter?" said Kieran. "From what Rose says, Vaylan already knows we have Gifts, and we've been trailing him around the Underneath. If we aren't hiding from him, who are we hiding from?"

Tayeh gave him a look that said he was an idiot. "Vaylan isn't the only person with questionable motives in the Underneath."

Kieran shrugged. "Sure. But we have Gifts, so who cares if they come after us? We're not exactly helpless."

Rev crossed her arms. "You wouldn't know this since you have been too scared to use your Gift, but for the rest of us, using our Gift isn't very pleasant. It's hard to protect yourself when you are vomiting your guts out."

At this reminder, Rose turned to look at Kai sitting next to her on the couch. He was hunched over and seemed dazed, only partially following the conversation.

"How do you feel?" asked Rose.

His eyes fluttered as he thought about her question. "Fine. Strange. Back to normal." He shook his head as if he wasn't sure which answer was correct.

"Do you mean 'fine' in a tough guy way? Like you want to vomit but are faking it?" she asked.

"What?" His eyes finally focused on her. "I'm not sick. But it feels strange to have my Gift back."

The crew exchanged meaningful glances, trying to interpret his words.

"Tayeh and Wilder don't get sick," said Fitz. "Maybe he's just as strong as they are."

"I've never vomited, but I still feel awful," said Tayeh. "He doesn't look sick."

"So, he's like Wilder?" asked Quinn.

Rose looked at Wilder across the room. He wouldn't meet her eyes and didn't respond.

"Maybe we got sick before because he wasn't with us," said Feather.

Everyone's attention snapped to her. She sat on the floor with her legs neatly tucked beneath her, and she seemed startled by their attention.

"Explain your theory," said Quinn helpfully.

"Well, we can't do anything when we are separated, right?" Her voice was hesitant, but when Quinn nodded, she continued. "Maybe because we were missing one, we couldn't use our Gifts all the way. I could try to use my Gift and see what happens, if that's helpful?"

Tayeh growled, "No using Gifts in my house."

Feather's plants often grew out of control, and she bowed her head in acknowledgment.

Quinn's face lit up at the thought of an experiment. "Tayeh, I can talk to the wolves without making a mess. I promise."

She gave him a fierce look, but it didn't hold up under the weight of his smile. She sighed. "Fine."

He grinned while shedding a tear at the same time. He looked at the wolves at Wilder's feet, and their heads perked up. His face shifted through expressions, as if he were talking to them, but he remained silent.

They stood up and stalked over to Kai, who blinked his eyes in surprise. Even though he had followed them to the Underneath, they appeared quite intimidating up close. From his position on the couch near Rose, the wolves were almost at eye level. They stared at him a moment, and Rose held her breath, waiting to see what they would do.

They plopped down on the floor in front of him, bellies up. He looked around in confusion, and at Quinn's encouraging nod, Kai shrugged as if he had no choice.

He rubbed their bellies.

The crew let out sighs of relief, and Feather cooed at the adorableness.

"You told them to do that?" asked Rose.

Quinn smiled. "I *asked* them to do that. They like Kai enough to agree to it. I thought petting the wolves might make him feel better."

Kai ducked his head and continued to pet the wolves, a slight blush on his cheeks again.

Rev asked, "So how do you feel?"

Rose's attention snapped from Kai to Quinn, waiting for a response.

Quinn's eyes unfocused as if he were monitoring his internal organs. "I think I'm fine."

Tayeh crossed her arms. "If not, you better run to the bathroom quick. Because if you get sick on my floors ..."

Quinn's smile didn't budge, despite her rough voice. "I'm fine. I would have felt it by now. Feather's theory must be correct. We got sick because we weren't operating at our full capacity. Now that Kai is here, our number is complete." He sat back in his chair and smiled at Kai.

Rose was too upset to let Kai's unusual shyness distract her. "Your number is complete?" she repeated. "There are eight of you. That's a strange number."

Fitz nodded. "True. The Goddess's religion is built around the number seven, so eight seems strange." He shrugged. "But maybe eight is not the final number. Maybe there are more of us out there."

The tension that had been building in Rose's chest squeezed so hard she could hardly breathe. She stood abruptly, and all eyes turned to her.

"I'm fine." Her voice sounded choked, and it embarrassed her. "Continue your discussion." She walked as calmly as she could from the room.

When she made it into the dark hallway and away from their eyes, she sagged against the wall, closed her eyes, and drew in several shaking breaths as she tried to calm herself.

There were more Chosen than just seven. It was bad enough that the Goddess hadn't picked her to be one of seven, but now there were an unknown number of people ahead of her in the Goddess's eyes. Rose thought perhaps the Goddess didn't give her a Gift because she was a Priest and had already had her turn. But seeing Kai with a Gift forced her to abandon that idea. She remained unchosen, and her gut churned.

She opened her eyes to find Wilder quietly waiting at her side. She once again appreciated his ability to not ask the stupid question that most would ask first.

Are you okay?

The answer to that question was the same as it had been since the night the Goddess failed to choose Rose.

No. She was not okay.

That answer was obvious to him, thanks to her shallow breathing and trembling hands. Rose gathered her strength and gave him a different answer.

"I'm glad Kai found us," she said.

His smile was gentle. "Me too. He's a good addition to the crew."

"Are we moving on?"

"I think so," he said. "I'm looking forward to it."

She considered the next Grotto's location. "Rivalry." She smiled. "Your home."

"The closest I ever had, yes." His eyes were thoughtful. "I think you'll like it there."

The more they talked, the calmer she became, and as a result, she felt her feistiness return. "Are you accusing me of worshiping the Vice of Rivalry?" She crossed her arms and raised an imperious eyebrow.

He took a step closer and dropped his voice to a sultry whisper, "Rivalry is in your blood. The only worthy adversary is one with the potential to beat you, and you like to test your strength against mine any chance you get." Their closeness in the dark hallway caused her to sag against the wall in a different way. He looked her up and down, noting her hands clinging to the wall for support, then leaned closer without touching her. "It appears I've won this round."

He took a step back, and a smug smile curled his lips. She opened her mouth to protest, but she had no air left in her lungs.

Rev called to him from the other room. He winked and made his escape before she could retaliate. She watched him swagger away and began plotting her attack.

RIVALRY

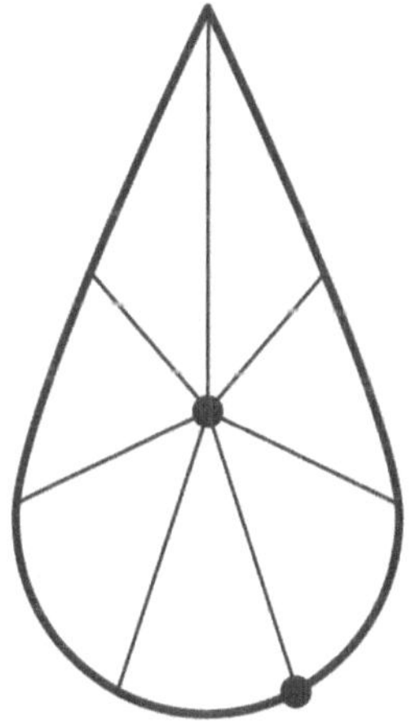

23

Of all the Grottos, Rivalry made the most sense to Rose. As their large crew walked through the streets, they passed boxing gyms and dojos and specialty training studios of every type. The smell of sweat and blood filled the streets, and she smiled at the familiarity. Even though Temple Harmony stood above Rivalry, she felt this Grotto had the most in common with Temple Discipline. Even without her Gift, she couldn't wait to get into a gym with Kai. The world would feel almost normal.

The rest of the crew had mixed feelings about Rivalry. Except for Kai and Feather, the others had spent their childhood here. They spoke about the performing arts school with both nostalgia and dread. Kieran was one of the bullies they had grown up with, but since they were already stuck with him, she wasn't sure how much worse the school itself could be.

She found out once they arrived.

The current students met them in the common room with smiles and giggles and kisses and eyes sharp enough to cut. Rose felt every girl and guy in the room sizing up the crew, looking for weakness, searching for the strongest to follow. She sensed battle lines being drawn with every word. Just the few minutes of introductions were exhausting.

After the initial skirmish, two distinct groups appeared to form. Some were behind Kieran, with the rest, along with the crew, behind Wilder. Rose wasn't sure who the students allied with when Wilder and Kieran were gone, but for now, the two of them rose to the top. Even though Wilder enjoyed his verbal sparring with Rose, he didn't appear to want the honor of being a commander in this battle. But in this war, he didn't get a choice.

"So Wilder," drawled one of Kieran's minions. "Who's your new friend?"

Rose's eyebrow twitched when she realized he was talking about her.

"Her name is Rose," said Wilder calmly. "I expect you to treat her with respect."

A girl with long black braids giggled from her position at Kieran's side. "Oh, you 'expect' that, Wilder? Did you forget what it's like here?" Kieran's squad laughed, and so did a few of the people beside Wilder.

Kieran smiled at the girl and flipped his blond hair. "Now, Lark, don't be too hard on Rose. She's spent weeks sitting beside Wilder, listening to his boring stories and enduring his tedious explanations. It's not her fault that he's made her odd."

Rose shook her head as if she had misheard. "Odd?"

Wilder's face was still calm, unwilling to rise to Kieran's challenge. "Rose won't fall for your blatant attempts to upset her." He glanced at Rose, and she knew he directed those words to her.

Lark nodded knowingly. "Because she's too slow to keep up. You seem to bring a lot of strange girls here, Wilder. That last one was a real freak."

Anger roared to life in her chest. She wasn't sure what

caused it: the girl calling her 'too slow' or that Wilder only scowled after the girl referenced Ylena.

Rose opened her mouth to begin a tirade when Wilder firmly clasped her hand. It startled her, and Wilder jumped into the silence. "It's good to see you are back among friends, Kieran. We'll leave you to catch up." He tried to pull Rose with him to leave, but she kept her feet locked firmly in place.

"Yes, Wilder," said Kieran. "It's good to be back. While we are here, I'd love to sing with you again. Perhaps we can reenact our last competition, except with no cheating this time." He waggled his finger in Wilder's face.

Wilder spoke between clenched teeth. "I didn't cheat."

"Of course you didn't." He gave a large dramatic wink, like he was in on the joke.

Wilder didn't respond, so Rose spoke for him. "There's no need for Wilder to cheat. I've heard both of you sing. There's no competition. Wilder would win every time."

Both Wilder and Kieran's groups murmured at her statement. Wilder gripped her hand harder, but she ignored it.

Kieran sized her up with his predator's eyes. "A skilled performance is a matter of taste. Perhaps you need to take a bigger bite."

"I'll show you a bigger bite—" She bared her teeth, prepared to rip his throat out. Wilder's hand crushing hers was a mild distraction.

"We're going to find the headmaster now," said Wilder. "Right, Rose?"

Lark put a dramatic hand to her chest. "Oh, that's so sad! He's scared to sing, Kieran. I wonder what that other girl did to make him give up singing?"

Rose yanked her hand away from Wilder and pointed a finger at the girl. "Wilder has not given up singing, especially not for some silly girl!" She turned on Kieran. "He will sing. Name the time and place. Prepare to be embarrassed, because everyone will see how much better he is than you."

Kieran's lips curled in triumph, and Wilder heaved a sigh. She thought she scored a point for Wilder, but they both acted like she fell into a trap.

"Terrific," said Kieran. He turned to Wilder as if Rose were irrelevant now. "Tomorrow night. I can't wait to give you everything I've got." He winked, then summoned his troops to follow him.

Rose turned around to find Wilder rubbing his forehead, and the rest of the crew scattering.

"What's the problem?" she asked. "All you have to do is sing. You'll obviously win. I can't believe you are making a big deal about this."

"It's never as simple as that, Rose. You just got me stuck in the middle of something that has consequences for every other time I come back here. You don't understand how seriously they take this."

She crossed her arms. "So what? You'll win. It will make your life easier once everyone knows how much better you are."

"Kieran and I lived here our entire childhood. Everyone knows what we sound like. The competition is a strategy match. Did you hear him accuse me of cheating? That's one of his strategies to discredit me."

"It's ridiculous. How would you cheat at a singing competition?"

He laughed. "I could lace his tea with something to dry out his vocal cords. Or I could sprinkle his food with a lesser variety of the Sentinels' poison dust so his lungs seize up for an hour or two. I could break his ribs, and you know from personal experience how hard it is to take a full breath with broken ribs. There are many ways to make sure your opponent isn't in prime condition."

She stared at him. "You sound like you've tried those before."

He didn't respond.

Her mouth dropped open. "Is he telling the truth? Did you actually cheat?"

He shrugged. "Everyone cheats in Rivalry. In fact, the poison dust is one surprise he left for me that day. It's just part of the competition. I guess I won't be eating or drinking anything for the next two days." He sighed. "This is not how I planned to spend my time here."

"What were you planning?" she asked.

"Normal stuff like training, hanging out in the fight clubs, picking up some new weapons." He frowned. "Now it's all ruined."

She raised her eyebrow. "You mean *I* ruined it."

He struggled to hide a playful grin. "I'm not saying that you owe me, but ..." He shrugged.

"What I *owe* you is some proper training." She tapped his muscular chest with her finger. "I will make sure you are in prime condition for this competition. I know how to whip competitors into shape, and I have no problem doing the same to you." He gave a wicked grin, but she continued tapping him with her finger. "I put my reputation on the line, too, and you will not ruin that by eating poison. I will watch your every move, so don't even think about getting out of it."

"Why would I try to escape such a lovely offer?" He reached out to take her by the waist, but she slipped out of his grip.

"None of that." She smacked his wrist. "You need to be focused. No distractions."

He crossed his arms with a smug grin. "You think I'm the one who gets distracted?"

She stepped closer and squared her shoulders to face

him head-to-head. "You will not lay a single finger on me until you win this competition. I will have no problems with you distracting me, because I trust in Discipline. And I have much more Discipline than you."

His whisper was low and sultry. "You're challenging me to a battle of Discipline?"

She leaned even closer, and her whisper was fierce. "Yes. And I will win."

He crossed his arms over his chest and gave her an approving look. "Welcome to Rivalry, Rose."

24

Rose didn't stay for training with the crew the next morning. Their training sessions often meant Wilder was shirtless, and despite her claims, she didn't trust her Discipline enough not to stare. She made the excuse that she would find out what Vaylan was up to in this Grotto. When Quinn gave the quiet command for the wolves to follow her, he didn't appear nauseous at all.

Her mark granted her access through the Haven's door, but she stopped dead the moment she walked in. The long hallway was filled with Sentinels.

"Rose! How wonderful to have you join us!" Vaylan approached her with open arms, the crowd of Sentinels parting before him.

Rose shook her head to clear away her fear. "I expected you to be reading stories to children. This is … unusual."

He sighed dramatically. "I wish I could spend all day taking kids to the circus, but unfortunately, there is so much more to this job."

"Your job of ruling the entire City?"

He grinned, revealing his dimple. "Of course. I told you I would prove to you I am the one most suited to the job, and today you will get to see another reason why." He nodded at the blade at her waist. "And luckily, you are armed."

She crossed her arms over her chest. "I'm not your weapon to command."

His lips twitched with a barely hidden smug smile. "No command here. But I guarantee you will find it a worthy cause. Walk with me, and you'll see."

She gave him a skeptical look but nodded.

Vaylan turned to face the room of Sentinels. "You know the stakes. Let's bring justice to this Grotto as we planned."

Soldiers straightened shoulders and saluted him with a fist to the chest. They filed out the door and split into groups, stalking silently through the streets.

Vaylan offered Rose an arm like they would follow the Sentinels on a leisurely stroll. At her incredulous look, he dropped his arm with a quiet chuckle and ushered her out the door.

The wolves trotted calmly at her side as they walked. The Sentinels had dispersed so thoroughly that she saw none as they approached the giant structure in the middle of the Grotto.

"Have you been to the arena, Rose?" At her head shake, he continued, "The concept is something you would appreciate: competitors battling it out in front of a crowd of cheering spectators. In theory, it sounds thrilling. But in reality, it's something quite different."

A crowd poured through the wide doors, and Rose and Vaylan followed them inside. The wolves caused a few surprised looks, but otherwise, no one paid them any attention. The crowd pressed forward to stairs leading up to the seating area, but Vaylan pulled away from the group, and Rose followed as he slipped down a hallway.

He walked with purpose past several doors until finally opening one slowly, then ushering her inside. They stood in a small room with a window that overlooked a training room full of children. Inside a ring, a couple of teenagers sparred with blades, and Rose nodded in appreciation of their skill. On the floor next to them, a circle of young children were punching heavy training bags. The children's shoulders drooped with exhaustion, but a grizzled man walked among them, smacking any child with bad posture.

The wolves echoed the growl rising in Rose's throat.

"Is this similar to your training in Discipline?" asked Vaylan.

Rose flinched. She had forgotten he was there.

She cleared her throat. "We train hard, but no one abuses children."

"No one?" His expression was grave, and it unsettled her.

"If so, they will face the consequences, just as the High Priest of Purpose did." Her anger flared at the thought of him. "One reason I've trained so hard is so I could defeat people like him."

Vaylan nodded as he watched the grizzled man drag a child across the room. "I know that about you, Rose. That's why I am glad to see you're armed."

The man pulled the young boy to a square on the floor marked off by tape and stalked off, calling for someone else. The boy stood alone in the square with hunched shoulders and head bowed. Rose couldn't take her eyes off him.

He looked like a young Kai.

His black hair was disheveled, and his dark eyes were wide with fear. He crossed and uncrossed his arms, as if unsure what to do with them. The movement reminded her of Kai's gangly arms before he grew into his now muscular form. Even the boy's pale gold skin was the same as Kai's, but as the man approached, he grew even paler.

The man pulled a girl several years older than the boy into the ring. Her blond curls fluttered as he pushed her directly in front of the boy. Rose couldn't hear through the glass, but the man yelled at the girl, and she nodded with eyes wide. He pointed at the boy, then backed out of the tape square and crossed his arms to watch.

The girl visibly swallowed, then fell into a fighting stance. The move looked practiced, and she was clearly more trained than the boy who stood unmoving. Though she was still young, she was at least a foot taller than him. She looked guilty as she threw her first punch.

The boy stumbled backward, and his foot stepped outside of the tape. The man shoved the boy back into the ring with a yell at the girl. She nodded and threw another guilty punch.

Rose's hands dug into the window frame, and her whole body shook with rage. Her eyes shot around the room, considering the other entrances but deciding against them. Her fist pulled back to punch through the glass, but Vaylan caught her arm.

"That's exactly the enthusiasm I was hoping for," he said.

Rose pulled her arm free from his grip and considered turning her fist on his grinning face instead.

"Unlike you, Rose, I have a plan. However, you're more than welcome to do with that man what you see fit." He stepped to the right side of the window and pointed inward. "But please note, there are also two men guarding that door."

She startled and looked where he pointed. She hadn't noticed the guards at all.

His normally soothing voice rang with a sharp edge. "There aren't any guards outside the door, just inside. They aren't worried about anyone getting in, just getting out." He took a deep breath, and his voice was calm again. "I'll create a distraction, then you can run in and do as you please." His lips turned up in a grin. "But consider walking through the door instead of injuring yourself busting a window before you get to fight."

She bit her lips on a retort, because she knew he was right. "Fine. What's the distraction?"

He raised his hand overhead, and his smug grin and dimple returned. "You've got thirty seconds." His hand closed into a fist.

The room plunged into darkness.

Rose blinked her eyes in the complete dark, trying to understand what happened. There was no light in the viewing room or training room beyond. All the crystalline was gone. Terror rose in her throat at the consuming darkness, and she held her breath to hold back a scream.

Vaylan's voice was a quiet whisper at her side. "Twenty-five seconds, Rose."

She sucked in a breath and stumbled to the door that led into the hallway. When it opened, she heard screams ringing from every level. Vaylan had not just manipulated the crystalline in these two rooms, but had removed it from the entire arena. She ignored the sounds of people running and stumbling down the stairs and focused on her targets.

The grizzled man and two guards in the next room.

She felt her way the few steps down the hallway and slowly cracked opened the training room door. Inside, she heard children screaming and crying. She didn't move further into the room, but counted out the last few seconds.

Three ... Two ... One ...

Unlike the guards, she wasn't surprised when the crystalline returned. She flung the door wide and aimed a kick to the knees of one guard, then knocked him out as he bent over in pain. The second guard recovered enough from his shock to punch her squarely in the ribs. She was grateful for Tayeh healing her, or else the painful punch would have taken her out. She fell back into her fighting stance with a grunt.

The guard was more brute than skilled fighter, and he was soon bleeding from multiple cuts and wolf bites. Fury sang through Rose's veins, and when she slashed out again and cut his thigh, he turned and ran out the door. Apparently, he was prepared to fight children but not an actual adult.

She turned around to look for the grizzled old man and was surprised to find him on the ground. A teenage girl had a knee pressed into his shoulders while two smaller children wrapped leather straps around his wrists. Rose watched them with a vicious grin. Perhaps the man shouldn't have trained them so well.

Most of the other children stood with dazed expressions on their faces, but the young boy who looked like Kai stumbled in shock and sank down to the floor. Rose ran to his side, but he pulled back in fear. She stopped her forward movement and kneeled at his eye level instead.

"Are you okay?" she asked.

He didn't answer and continued to stare at her with wide eyes.

"Don't worry. We'll return you to your parents. This is over," she said.

"They don't have parents, Rose." Vaylan's voice was sad. He stood in the doorway, looking at each child. "They're orphans, or their parents sold them to the arena. Everyone abandoned them, but not me." His eyes studied each child with a fierce protectiveness. "Now they are my responsibility."

"You are taking them back with you to the Haven?" she asked.

"I won't force them." His words were as much for the children as for her. "But I offer them hot meals and my protection. Even if they wander off on their own for a while, they always know they have a home at the Haven."

She gave him a suspicious look. "Why do you want children?"

His cheerful eyes turned cold. "Just because Priests have vile plans for children doesn't mean I do. My values are much different from the Goddess's."

"The actions of the High Priests weren't the Goddess's fault!" she replied hotly.

"She overlooked it for centuries, so yes, she is to blame." Vaylan waved off her next rebuttal and held out a hand for the little boy who looked like Kai. The boy hesitated, but Vaylan's smile convinced him to take his hand.

Rose sat stunned on the floor, watching him walk to the door with the other children following behind. Vaylan turned and looked at her with pity. "I know it's hard for you right now, Rose. You don't believe my motivations, and you are still expecting me to be as evil as the Goddess's High Priests. But I'm dedicated to the prophecies above all else. Brother Owyn said that I would devote myself to the powerless, and that's what I'm trying to do. He also said one day you and I would stand side by side and watch the City go dark. So, I'm not worried. One day, you will believe."

He nodded his head in a slight bow and led the children out of the arena.

25

A s Rose left the arena, she realized her battle had not been an isolated incident. The Sentinels had occupied every level of the arena with a calm efficiency. They had attacked the brutes standing guard, then loaded food out of storerooms to take back to the Haven. Whoever owned the arena had been overthrown, but considering their treatment of the children, Rose didn't care if they'd survived the takeover. Based on the wolves' cheerful licking of their chops, Rose thought they were equally pleased with the results.

Rose found the crew in their practice space across from the performing arts school. She thought Kieran might have given up on the crew to spend time with his own squad, but instead, he had discovered a compromise. He stood outside the practice space, laughing at passersby with his friends at his side. He was close enough to let the others use their Gifts, but he could still act like he didn't care at all.

As Rose approached, Lark whispered something to Kieran. They both laughed loudly as they watched Rose go inside.

Rose wondered if the others could use their Gifts if she

knocked Kieran unconscious.

Inside, Fitz and Feather worked together to shape something out of vines and stone. Feather's pouty lips pinched in concentration, and Fitz cocked his head as he twisted his fingers in experimental patterns. A thin rope of stone looped around a vine that raced along the floor and slid around Quinn's ankle. He leaned down to study it with curious eyes while Tayeh stood over Fitz and Feather's shoulder, giving quiet directions. Feather clasped her fingers into a fist, and the vine tightened on his ankle, pulling Quinn off his feet. He hit the floor with a thud, then clapped his hands in delight.

"That was amazing!" he said. The stone and vine withdrew, and he stood back up. "Try it again."

Rose found their collaborations intriguing. Priests rarely had reasons to work together in such ways, so their experiments were new to her. She chose not to mention that using a Gift of the Goddess as a weapon was heresy. Mainly because she didn't want to explain the nuances of why it was okay to use Discipline so the wind could assist in a fight. She knew there was a theological explanation that made it okay, but she couldn't quite remember what that was.

Instead, she walked over to Rev, who stood watching Wilder and Kai fight. Rose was pleased that Kai could properly train Wilder to use his Gift but also disappointed that she couldn't participate. They both swung blades that moved supernaturally fast thanks to the wind obeying their commands.

As she approached, Wilder looked her way. Even though his glance was quick, it communicated a lot. *Good to see you,* said the smug glance. *And you're obviously glad to see me.*

She wiped the appreciative expression off her face. Just because he was shirtless and muscular and perfect didn't mean she needed to let her face clearly reveal that fact.

Rev had no issues revealing her feelings. Her single blue eye tracked their every move, and she bit her finger as she watched in mindless fascination.

"Enjoying yourself?" Rose asked drily.

"You have no idea," she breathed. "I know Kai is your brother, but you must admit, they really are a striking pair."

Rose rolled her eyes. "I'm surprised you haven't spent more time throwing yourself at Kai. It's unlike you."

Rev shrugged but continued watching them fight. "I didn't think it was appropriate, considering his preferences." She gave an evil grin. "But it doesn't mean I don't appreciate a good show."

Rose snorted. "Kai is already cocky enough and doesn't need any encouragement from you. And Goddess knows it's the last thing Wilder needs." She shook her head as she watched them circle each other. She could practically feel the self-satisfaction pouring off Wilder's muscular back.

"He's hiding something," said Rev.

Rose's head snapped around, but Rev was still watching the fight. Her expression had turned from lecherous to analytical.

"What do you mean?" asked Rose. "Hiding what?"

"I'm not sure." She narrowed her eye and followed him around the ring. "There is something he wants to confess, but he's too afraid."

Rose watched him fight with the same fluid grace as her brother. "How can you tell?"

"Honey, it's my job to hear confessions, remember? I've heard some pretty dark and shameful things. Wilder knows that. If it's something he won't confess to me, it's tearing him up inside."

Rose looked at Wilder and tried to imagine what shameful secret lurked below his cocky exterior. "Why are you telling me this?"

Rev finally tore her attention away from the fight to look at Rose. "You and Wilder are getting close. I hope that means he will tell you, even if he doesn't tell me." Her voice dropped to a low growl. "And if he does, you better not muck it up."

Rose's response was interrupted by Kai's sudden sweaty hug.

"Eww!" said Rose. "Kai! You know I hate it when you're all sweaty." She pushed him away and tried to wipe off the sweat.

Kai brushed his black hair back with a laugh and nodded at Wilder. "I bet you wouldn't mind so much if he was the one hugging you."

Wilder's smug grin grew even wider, but Rose kept her expression cool. "I don't think either of you earned any celebratory hugs," she said. "Your footwork seemed pretty sloppy to me."

Kai crossed his arms over his chest. "Sloppy?" He turned to Wilder, who chuckled softly. "Wilder and I are two prime specimens of manhood here, and I think you should appreciate our brilliant demonstration."

Rose groaned and looked at Rev. "See what you did? They were already insufferable, and you've made it worse."

Rev eyed both guys with a wicked grin, and they punched each other playfully and preened under her attention.

"I think they looked great!" Quinn's cheerful voice caused Rose to spin around. He was smiling at Kai. "I enjoy watching you fight."

She turned back around to find Kai surprisingly off-kilter. He brushed his hair back again, but it seemed less confident than before. "Thanks, Quinn."

Quinn turned to Rev. "Feather and I could use your help on a project. Will you join us?"

The two of them walked off together while Kai put his shirt back on with a glance over his shoulder. Rose wasn't always the most observant of other people's feelings, but it appeared Quinn was even more oblivious than she was. She sighed and wondered if he would break her brother's heart.

Wilder woke her out of her musings. "So, what was Vaylan up to today?"

"His Sentinels broke into the arena, rescued the child fighters, and stole all their food."

Wilder's eyebrows raised in surprise. "That's not what I expected."

She shrugged. "I don't know what to expect from him anymore. Everything Vaylan does is based on his belief in the prophecies. I don't understand what his motivation is in all this."

"He's already told us, Rose. He wants to rule the City."

"Yes, but why choose this way? He has a Spark, and I know from experience that he can use it to wound. Why isn't he just threatening his way into controlling the City?"

Wilder laughed darkly. "He's taking inspiration from the High Priests. That's why they had Sentinels, so they never had to use their Gifts to harm. It helped them keep their delusions of righteousness."

Rose rubbed her forehead as she considered the dark thought. Righteous delusions definitely sounded like Vaylan. "But he really believes in those prophecies. What if they are actually true?"

"They only come true because Vaylan is actively making them come true. Those prophecies aren't destined to happen."

Rose bit her lip and dropped her voice to a whisper. "But what if they do? What if I actually betray you?"

"Rose—" Wilder started, but she cut him off.

"Vaylan said I will deliver the Chosen into his hands.

That must be about anyone with a Gift. What if he forces me to turn you in? What if I'm destined to betray you because of the prophecy?"

Wilder looked at her with fierce eyes. "Rose, no one can force you to do anything you don't want to do. Not Vaylan and not a prophecy." A small grin curved his mouth. "You're so stubborn you would fight destiny itself."

She ducked her head. From his lips, the rebuke felt like a compliment.

He pulled her closer with a grin. "That's enough prophecy talk. I think we have more interesting things to discuss."

She smacked his hands away. "Have you rehearsed your singing? Tonight is your vocal battle with Kieran, and I told you no distractions."

He pouted playfully. "You're so strict. Don't you trust me to win without practice?"

She took a slow step toward him, careful not to touch his bare chest, and not just because of any lingering sweat. "Oh, you will definitely win," she purred. "But I expect more than that. I expect you to sing so Goddess-damn beautifully that Kieran never challenges you again. Your voice will seduce the entire crowd so thoroughly that even Rev blushes. You will use your talent, your Gift, or even cheat to convince me and everyone else that your voice rivals that of the Companion himself."

Wilder leaned close enough that his whisper was a soft breeze against her cheek. "Rose, I will steal the very breath from your lungs, and I won't need my Gift to do it."

He had already accomplished the task, but she straightened with a small cough to hide the fact. "Good," she said. "Then you better start practicing."

She left quickly so he wouldn't see her draw in a shaking breath.

26

Rose stared at the entrance to the dark tunnel, but her feet refused to move. "I thought your competition would be at the school," she said. "Why do you have to come all the way out here?"

The rest of the crew had already walked into the narrow crack in the cave's wall, so dark that she couldn't see where they had gone. Wilder remained at her side; otherwise, she would have considered walking back to the school alone.

"It's tradition," he said. "Formal competitions happen at the school, but secret battles like this require a more intriguing location."

"But why can't that location be a well-lit building? Maybe we can find a lovely, abandoned warehouse?"

He chuckled. "I'll keep that in mind for next time. But for now ..." He held out his hand. "I'll be right beside you."

She took a deep breath and took his hand. "Fine. Let's get on with this show choir fight club."

He smiled and pulled her into the tunnel.

The tunnel was so narrow that she had to walk directly behind him. The darkness was so complete she couldn't even see his broad shoulders right in front of her. She clung

167

to his hand, using the warmth of his body as a comforting presence. The tunnel made a sharp turn, then suddenly she could see a sliver of flickering light ahead.

It opened into a small cavern that was still too narrow for her taste, but at least the ceilings were high and curved like a proper vaulted ceiling in a performance hall. An icy breeze brushed past the wound on her neck, and she zipped the collar of her mauve jacket closed.

Wilder followed her gaze up to the ceiling. "Up there is a vent that leads outside the City and sends fresh air in. A few decades ago, a clever kid discovered the amazing acoustics, and students have been coming here to sing ever since."

Over two dozen students were gathered in the room already. Kieran stood on one side with Lark and the rest of his squad, while Wilder walked over to join the crew. A few students lingered in the middle, waiting to see who the winner would be before declaring a side.

Rose moved closer to Rev, who sat on a large boulder with a lantern at her side. The flame flickered with the occasional gust of cold air that blew through the cavern, but Rose found its inconsistent light comforting. Crystalline light was better than the alternative of darkness, but her mark still throbbed, so crystalline wasn't as comforting as it used to be.

Quinn talked to Wilder in a quiet voice, giving him what Rose assumed were last-minute strategies. She was glad Wilder hadn't ingested any poison or had any unforeseen "accidents" before arriving at the competition. Even though she had grown up in a City that performed a Pageant with life and death stakes, she thought this Grotto took their musical performances a bit too seriously.

Lark strolled into the center of the cavern, drawing all eyes to her. "Welcome to a night filled with a little a cappella warfare." The crowd murmured with excitement. "Kieran has graciously agreed to let Wilder have the first song. They will take turns singing until the group decides the winner or one of them falls. Whichever comes first."

Everyone kept referencing battle and fight clubs, but Rose hadn't considered until that moment that the night really might end with bloodshed.

Lark spun in a circle to draw everyone's eye to her. "They each sing alone. Harmonizing with one of the competitors is a serious offense and will be severely punished."

Everyone nodded as if this made complete sense. Rose caught Kai's attention, and he shrugged. At least she wasn't the only one who found the situation strange.

Lark bowed toward Wilder. "The stage is yours."

Rose caught Wilder's hand before he could move to the center of the cave. Her whisper was quiet but urgent. "I know I told you to use your Gift to win, but considering we are in a little cave filled with open flame, I don't think that's a good idea."

He raised an eyebrow. "Are you doubting my control, Rose?"

She didn't allow his sultry whisper to rattle her. "Yes, I am. You're still too new at using your Gift, and singing with the wind requires precision. If you call down a whirlwind that sets this cave ablaze, I will curse your name as I trample everyone to escape this Goddess-forsaken hole in the ground."

He bit his lip, but it didn't hide his smile. "Noted. I'll be sure the storm only comes for you."

"Wilder, I'm serious!" She tried to pull him back, but he winked and swaggered to the center of the cavern.

She sighed and moved closer to the exit. She didn't really want to be the first one to escape into the dark tunnel, but she definitely didn't want to be the last.

The rest of the crew had settled into position nearby,

sitting on boulders or leaning against the cave wall. Everyone stopped their murmuring and turned their full attention to Wilder.

All eyes on Wilder was exactly the sort of thing he lived for.

He stood with head bowed and hands clasped in front of him. Rose thought she saw a tear sparkling on his lashes, and she muttered a string of curses under her breath.

Until his first note. After that, she had no breath left.

She had only heard him sing a few times since the night of the Pageant, but each time, his voice was more stunning than the last. His voice reminded her of summer sunrises and sweet caramel and warmed her from the inside out. The sound resonated in the open cavern, the low notes a slow thrum in her bones and the high notes a sharp blast through her veins.

The pure, clear sound was so entrancing it took her a moment to actually listen to the words. She had never heard the song before, but the beautifully crafted lyrics were a powerful ode to desire. Some lines were familiar, as if it was a song she knew but had forgotten. She closed her eyes and concentrated on each word, trying to see if she could recall where she heard it.

A lyric wrapped in a warm breeze trickled past her ear.

"Wind's heartbeat racing through scarlet locks..."

Her eyes popped open to find Wilder looking right at her. He'd written the song. It was familiar because he wrote it.

For her.

Once she realized it, she couldn't unhear the lyrics. Each word was for her. Wilder sang in a room filled with friends and enemies, yet he sang a song he wrote for her. Rose took pride in never blushing, but the thought of his innermost thoughts about her laid bare before the group caused heat to bloom on her face.

She wanted to run and hide.

She wanted to freeze this moment of perfection.

She wanted to pull him into a kiss and forget anyone else existed.

Despite her avalanche of feelings, Wilder's song never faltered. He sang with the same level of passion and fearlessness and grace from the first note to the very last. He held the final note longer than necessary. A gentle reminder he was perfectly in control of both his song and the soft breeze that swirled around her, causing the lantern at her side to flicker wildly.

His lips closed gently on the last note. The wind floated away, and the flame settled into the same glow as the others. She sagged against the wall, trembling from the emotions he stirred and her inability to breathe while he sang.

His dark eyes glowed with the knowledge of her response to his song. He knew how he had affected her, and it pleased him. It wasn't the pleasure of defeating her, though Rose had to admit, he surely won that round in their battle of Discipline. Instead, it was the pleasure of giving someone a gift and enjoying giving as much as receiving.

It was several long moments before the crowd began clapping and cheering. Apparently, she wasn't the only one he had moved with the song. There were girls and guys still swooning as they cheered with dreamy expressions.

It surprised her to realize she didn't feel jealous. Wilder knew he'd charmed the crowd, and he turned to bow to each corner of the cavern. His wide smile caused more sighs from the crowd, and for once, Rose didn't feel the need to roll her eyes.

They could sigh for him all they wanted. It didn't change the fact that he'd written the song for her.

She straightened from her sagging position against the wall, her pride in the song giving her strength. Wilder moved away from the center of the cavern and took a spot on the wall directly across from her. She was glad he didn't walk to her side. She was still too breathless to hold a proper conversation.

But she had plenty of strength to admire him from afar.

She barely noticed as Kieran took the floor. The cheering for Wilder settled down, and Kieran waited until the cavern fell silent before he began his song.

Rose was staring at Wilder when she saw his expression change. He broke eye contact with her and looked at Kieran with a frown. Only then did she listen to Kieran's words.

She had heard a few explicit songs at the nightclub in Chaos, but Kieran's lyrics were a work of art in their filthiness. She was trying to understand the logistics of a few maneuvers being described when she realized Kieran was stalking closer to her with each note.

Her eyes widened when she considered his predatory moves along with the lurid song. She had worried that Wilder might be in danger, but she had never considered it for herself. She placed a comforting hand on her blade when Kieran took hold of her other hand.

She only had a moment to notice the tear on his cheek before she was suddenly not herself.

She was Kieran, leaving the performing arts school to come to the competition. She turned the corner and saw Lark talking to two Sentinels. Rose as Kieran pulled back around the building and peeked out again. Lark pointed up to the balcony of a student's room. Wilder's room. The Sentinels handed Lark something, and she slipped it into her pocket.

Rose blinked and opened her eyes back in the dark cavern. Kieran was still singing the raunchy song, his eyes locked on her face and asking her a question.

She nodded imperceptibly. She saw what he'd shared with her. The vision had been blurry and not as precise as a trained Knowledge Priest's, but not losing the thread of his song was impressive.

He let go of her hand and moved back to the center of the floor for the rest of the song.

Wilder was looking at her, questioning if she was okay. She smiled, but inside, her stomach churned with questions. Why were the Sentinels looking for Wilder? What were they planning to do to Wilder when he returned from the competition? And why did Kieran show this to her now?

Rose realized she didn't know exactly how this competition would end. Lark had said it would end with a vote or when one of them fell. Maybe Kieran considered the possibility that he couldn't warn Wilder later and had to do it now. After Wilder's song about Rose, it wouldn't be suspicious for Kieran to exert power over her. A quick glance at Lark told Rose that she had no idea what Kieran had done.

Her first reaction was to run straight to the performing arts school and take on both Sentinels alone. However, she also realized that was exactly what had gotten her into trouble before. So instead, she thought through her options.

She could wait until the end of the competition and then warn Wilder and the others as they walked back to the school. But what if the Sentinels were waiting for them to come out? Just because they found out Wilder's room didn't mean that's where they were planning their attack.

What she needed to know was where they were hiding and then surprise them before they could attack. She needed to gather more information. That was the thoughtful thing she had been learning lately. How to not run in, but to be quiet and listen. She needed to sneak up on the Sentinels before they expected her.

She was proud of this plan, and when Wilder started his

next song, she slipped quietly into the dark tunnel. It took her several moments to convince her feet to continue beyond the entrance, further into the darkness, and then suddenly a fuzzy white light tangled around her feet.

"Ladies!" she hissed. The wolves continued circling her feet. "Storm Fang! Pickles!" She pointed at them with a harsh whisper, and they dropped to their haunches. They had been sitting by Quinn earlier but had apparently noticed her leave. So much for a sneaky exit. She sighed. She wasn't the one who needed them most. "Go back in there and watch Wilder. You claimed him, so you better do it right!"

They bowed their heads, then trotted back into the cavern. Without their white fur shining at the entrance, the tunnel seemed just as terrifying as it had on her way inside. She took a deep breath and headed through the tunnel alone.

27

The tunnel seemed much darker without Wilder by her side. She clung to the wall for support, though the walls were so close she had little choice. There were no branching paths, but she couldn't stop the fear from racing through her mind that she would get lost and never find her way out of the darkness.

When she saw the faint glow of the Grotto ahead, she ran the last few steps to the cave exit. But before running outside like a fool, she took a few moments to catch her breath and let her eyesight adjust. She was going to be smart about this. Gather information, then get back to the group. That was the plan.

Once her breathing was calm and she'd checked all the blades hidden on her body, she stepped out of the cave. There were no Sentinels waiting to ambush her, at least none that she could see. She began walking to the performing arts school, looking in every location that the Sentinels might hide. Sentinels couldn't blend into a crowd in a fight club or hang out in a bar. They would find somewhere private they could hide while watching the school. She grinned with wicked glee when she found them.

The Sentinels lurked in the shadows of a doorway half a block away from the school. They would have a clear view of the crew as they passed, and unless the crew was checking every shadow as closely as she was, no one would notice them. Her fist tightened around her blade.

They were stalking Wilder. The same Wilder who had written her the most beautiful love song, then sang it in a completely public yet totally intimate way. Her heart pounded fiercely as the memory of the song wrapped around the anger that these Sentinels would try to hurt him.

She would kill them.

But no. Wilder would be furious with her if she tried to take them on alone. And Wilder's opinion mattered to her more now than ever. So, she took a deep breath and simply watched them. She analyzed their height and weight, their possible method of attack from this location, other places where she could monitor them without being seen. She gathered everything she could from the situation, then turned to head back to the cave.

The little boy who looked like Kai peeked at her from behind a stack of boxes. Her eyes widened as she recognized him. What was he doing here? The last she had seen him, he was heading with Vaylan to the Haven. Had he left to make it on his own? She had seen the boy try to fight. There was no way this little Kai would survive alone. She had to help him.

His eyes widened in fear as he saw her approach. He looked around for a direction to run, and in his haste to leave, he pushed over the stack of boxes in a crash.

A crash that startled the Sentinels into turning her way.

Her head moved back and forth, watching the Sentinels heading her direction and the boy sprinting off. She couldn't run after him without leading the Sentinels trailing behind her. There was no choice. She had to stand and fight.

Her entire life, Rose had watched in fear as the Sentinels stalked the City. They often killed with poison dust because few people in the City were trained to fight.

They would not find her such an easy target.

She pulled out a blade for each hand and dove at the first Sentinel to approach. His lightweight armor protected his chest and forearms, but she aimed her blade at a tendon in his shoulder, and he pulled back with a hiss. When they realized Rose wouldn't fall without a fight, they pulled back and began circling her in a slow, menacing crouch.

She moved fast, lashing out with quick blades, then ducking under their much slower attacks. She cursed how slow it felt to fight without the wind, but she was glad to see she was still faster than they were. They continued to circle her, and she realized it would take a long time for her to injure them enough to cause them to give up. She would tire long before then. She needed to end this fight quickly or escape.

She kept one eye on the Sentinels and searched the street for anything that could tip the balance in her favor. Besides the scattered boxes, there was nothing else in the empty street. She would have to run. As she slashed out again, she glanced down the street to plot the direction of her escape.

Wilder skidded around the corner and stared at her with terror in his eyes.

The first emotion she felt was guilt. She knew he was going to be angry that she had run off alone, and it was going to take time for her to explain her reasoning and how this fight was not her fault. She imagined fighting with him, explaining, and making up in the space of a heartbeat.

In the next heartbeat, a Sentinel stabbed her.

She heard Wilder's scream, then his running footsteps. She lashed out blindly with her blade, but the Sentinels backed away, their masked faces focused on Vaylan's mark revealed by her unzipped jacket. She pressed a hand against her bleeding stomach and stumbled toward them, but the Sentinels ran off in the opposite direction.

Rose's knees buckled, and she slid to the ground. Her mind felt oddly dull. She blinked, trying to clear away the shadows.

"Rose!" Wilder dropped to her side and pulled her into his arms. "Are you okay?"

Her thoughts scattered to the edges of her mind, and she couldn't fit them together in a clear response. She opened and closed her mouth several times before she remembered how to form words. "I'm fine." She gritted her teeth into a smile as he pressed a firm hand against the wound. "You can yell at me now, if you want." She tried to make the words lighthearted, but her voice was strained.

His eyes weren't on her face, but on his hand covered in her blood. He looked up as the two wolves raced down the street and slid to a stop at their side. They whined in fear, and Storm Fang began licking blood from a wound on Rose's hand.

Wilder's voice was an urgent growl. "Go find Tayeh," he commanded the wolves. "Now!"

They both yipped and sprinted away.

"Did you win?" asked Rose.

Wilder's fearful eyes shot to her face. "What?"

"Did you win the competition? I know you did." Rose's thoughts felt light, as if she were relaxing with Wilder on a warm spring day. "Your voice is always so lovely, but tonight you were magnificent."

He pressed his hand tighter against her wound, but she barely noticed. "Don't talk, Rose. Just relax. Tayeh's on her way."

"I loved your song," she said dreamily. "*My* song." She

smiled up at Wilder, but she wasn't sure if her eyes were still open or not.

"Yes. Your song." Wilder's voice was rough with emotion. "Don't close your eyes, Rose. Please, stay with me."

She blinked her eyes open and saw tears shining in his eyes. "Don't cry. You won tonight. You beat Kieran and me." She tried to laugh, but her body just tensed with pain. "You always win."

He blinked a tear out of his eyes, and his voice was a ragged whisper. "Not always." He pulled in a shaking breath. "Tonight, I know what I will lose."

Icy wind blasted through her, and she sat up straight with a gasp. Every nerve in her body woke back to life with sharp clarity. The shadows at the edges of her vision cleared, and she could see Wilder in perfect focus.

He was relieved she was okay. And he was crushed under a mountain of guilt.

"You healed me," she said simply. He couldn't meet her eyes but nodded. "You have more than one Gift." He swallowed and nodded again. "All of them?"

He finally met her eyes, but his voice was still a whisper. "Yes."

She was perfectly healed, but her mind still felt like it was moving too slow. Wilder had all the Gifts. That's why he was different from the other Seven.

And he'd kept it secret the whole time.

She wasn't sure what her expression looked like, but she could guess by Wilder's shameful glance away. She blinked, trying to decide what to say.

"Rose!" Tayeh's voice sounded from the end of the street. She began running, the wolves and the rest of the crew close on her heels.

Wilder flinched, then looked at Rose with fearful eyes. He stood up and offered her a hand to rise. She looked at his hand, but her emotions were a tangle of emotions, and she couldn't bring herself to touch him. She pulled herself up and stood tall. Wilder drew in a shaking breath through his nostrils.

Tayeh skidded to a halt in front of them. She grabbed Rose's hand, then cocked her head to the side. "By the wolves' reaction, I assumed you were dying. But you're perfectly fine." She studied the blood on Rose's shirt with suspicion in her eyes. "How are you perfectly fine?"

"She's okay," said Wilder. "We should get out of here before we discuss anything further."

Tayeh looked between the two of them, then straightened to her normally erect position with a sharp nod.

Wilder looked at the crew as they approached, out of breath. "We should get back to the school."

The crew looked at Rose with concern but nodded in agreement. They headed back to the performing arts school, but once they arrived, they found the students in shock.

Lark had been found dead.

The crew packed their things and headed out that night.

INSTINCT

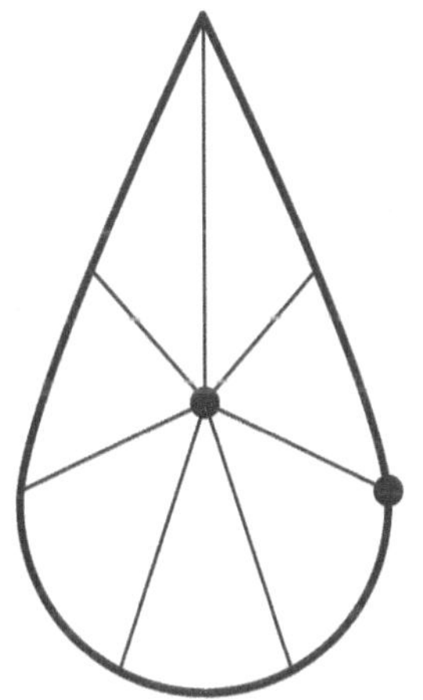

28

───────

Rose pulled the thin sheet over her face and tried to fall back asleep, but it was no use. She was going to have to face the day eventually, even though her mind locked up at the thought. On the other side of the sheet, she could hear the crew milling around in the large common room of the safe house. As a Priest, she'd had her own room, but now she was stuck with eight roommates. The thought of interacting with that many people so early in the morning was insufferable.

She threw her blanket off and sat up. Tayeh, Fitz, Rev, and Quinn sat at the rickety table, having a quiet conversation. Feather sat on one of the many mattresses scattered across the floor, pulling her dark hair up into a neat ponytail, while Kieran lounged on another mattress nearby. Wilder looked up as Rose looked his way, then his eyes dropped quickly back to the small notebook in his hands. The two wolves sat next to him on the mattress and stared at Rose with wary eyes.

Kai flopped down onto her mattress. "Are you okay?" he whispered.

She was perfectly healed without even the hint of a scar

182

but didn't think that's what he was asking. "That's a complicated answer."

Rev twisted her chair around to face the room. "Good. Now that you're awake, I think it's time we had a crew meeting."

Rose rolled her eyes. Not only did she have too many roommates, now they had to have early morning meetings together.

"We need to discuss what happened last night." Rev crossed her arms and eyed Rose and Wilder. "Who's going to explain?"

The walk from Rivalry to Instinct had been a quiet one. Traveling through the tunnels between Grottos could be dangerous, but with a group their size, they usually walked without fear. But last night, the crew was silent the entire trip, and when they arrived at the safe house, they all fell asleep without a word. The same awkward silence fell now, and Rose avoided looking in Wilder's direction.

"I think Rose should explain why she ran off alone to fight Sentinels," said Wilder.

Rose's head shot around to glare at him. "Me? You think *I* am the one with the most explaining to do?"

His eyes were flat, with none of the emotion she had seen in them last night. "Don't worry. I'll get my due. But I don't want to gloss over the fact that once again you reacted blindly out of anger, and as a result, I had to come save you."

Rose nearly vibrated in anger. "You had to save *me*? I was the one saving you from the Sentinels!"

"How did you know that?" Kai's voice was quiet but didn't calm her.

"He showed me!" Rose pointed at Kieran, who scowled at being brought into the conversation.

"I showed you Lark pointing the Sentinels to Wilder's

window. I didn't expect you'd be stupid enough to go after them on your own." He rolled his eyes in disgust.

"I didn't go after them to attack them." She ground out her words between clenched teeth. "I followed them to see where they were hiding."

Tayeh raised an accusatory eyebrow. "And you couldn't have taken at least one other person with you?"

Rose couldn't dispute that Tayeh's plan was a good one, so she had to find another tactic. "I'm not the one you should question right now. You should ask Wilder what he's been hiding from us this whole time."

Rev looked at her with a narrowed eye. She had told Rose that if Wilder confessed, she better not muck it up. Well, Wilder didn't confess. He got caught. And since he started this conversation with blades drawn, Rose wasn't afraid to fight back.

Wilder locked eyes with Rose, and his expression was unreadable. His words were for the group, but his eyes never left hers. "The night I saw the Goddess, she gave me all seven Gifts."

Rose didn't see how the crew responded since she continued glaring at Wilder, but they were silent for some time before Fitz spoke.

"It makes sense."

Rose broke her stare with Wilder to glare at Fitz. "It makes sense? I'd love to hear you explain how any of this makes sense."

He didn't flinch, only continued his explanation. "It makes sense why there are eight of us. We thought since Wilder and Kai both had Discipline that was a sign there were others like us. But we've heard no rumors of anyone else with a Gift. It makes sense that the seven of us each have one Gift each, and Wilder is something different with all of them."

Rose grumbled under her breath. "Something different sounds right."

"It's fascinating!" said Quinn. "The only two people who manifested all the Gifts were the Goddess and Ylena."

Feather leaned forward on her mattress with bright eyes and breathed, "Wilder, are you a goddess?"

Rose rubbed her forehead with both hands.

Wilder's voice to Feather was kind and grated on Rose's nerves. "No, I'm not a goddess. She just gave me all her Gifts for some reason."

"That's why Rose didn't need me to heal her last night." Tayeh looked at Wilder. "You already did."

Wilder nodded grimly.

"Thank the Goddess you were there, Wilder." Kai rested a hand on Rose's arm. "You saved Rosie's life."

At his use of her childhood nickname, something within her cracked. She shook him off and scrambled to her feet. "Yes, let's all thank the Goddess for saving my poor pathetic life with her big, strong, Gifted Wilder, who came to rescue me. She's so generous! Aren't we all so blessed to know the Goddess's favorite person?"

Wilder stood slowly and met her face to face. "I knew it." His voice was a low growl. "I knew you would react this way."

They stared at each other in silence as the wolves swirled around their feet, alternating between growling and whining.

"That's our cue," said Rev. "Time for the rest of us to go out for breakfast."

Rose barely noticed as the crew slipped quickly out the door. She couldn't think beyond the fire churning in her gut.

"I tried to keep it secret." His voice was an angry whisper. "If you hadn't been dying, I would have kept it secret even longer. Because I knew as soon as you found out, you would blame me for everything, even though I've done nothing wrong."

"The Goddess isn't here to blame." Rose spit out the words as if they burned her tongue. "And since you are so special to her, blaming you is like blaming her."

Wilder's shoulders tensed as if he was fighting off an attack. "Maybe I am special to her. So what? Why should your relationship to the Goddess take precedence over mine? Why do you need to be the most important?"

"Because I've served her my whole life!" Rose's yell sounded too much like a sob, but she couldn't hold it back any longer. "I've given her everything! My whole life has been for her, and now at the end, she's taken it all away."

Wilder's shoulders softened, and his whisper lost its growl. "I know it doesn't make sense, but you aren't alone. The crew is here for you. I'm here for you."

She pressed her lips together to keep another sob from escaping. When she spoke, her voice was still as a grave. "When I look at you, I see everything I'm not. Everything she's taken from me." She took a deep breath, but it did little to calm her. "I need to not look at you for a while so I can sort it out."

Wilder took a step backward as if she'd punched him. She turned quickly for the door so she didn't have to see his face.

The wolves fell in beside her, but she spun around and pointed at them to return to Wilder's side. They began pacing between her and Wilder, whining softly. From the tear in his eye and the concentrating expression on his face, she knew he was giving them a reasoned explanation on why they should follow her.

She growled loudly and thrust her finger at Wilder.

They lay down at his feet with a final muted whine.

She nodded and moved to open the door. His soft voice stilled her hand.

"If you were the one with all the Gifts and I had none, I would be strong enough to handle it." His voice was raw with emotion, and she couldn't turn to look at him. "I wouldn't feel intimidated or insecure that you were more powerful than me. I would support you. No matter how strong you were." Though his voice was soft, it was absolute. "I would still love you, Rose."

She didn't let him see the tears streaming down her face as she pulled the door shut behind her.

29

Rose wandered around the Grotto with her emotions screaming through her mind. She looked desperately for a place to drown them out but couldn't find anything loud enough. There were no nightclubs like in Chaos, and the loudest place she could find was a fight club where the people gambled on the results. She soon lost interest when she realized the fights were all prearranged and she couldn't do any of the punching.

Flickering lights and clanging bells filled Grotto Instinct, and it set her nerves even more on edge. Since there was nothing to soothe her, she decided to take out her angry feelings on someone who deserved it.

Two Adopted led her into a room that appeared to be Vaylan's study. She didn't know who'd formerly owned the Den, but Vaylan lounged in a chair before the fireplace as if he'd lived there for years and not since that morning. He waved her into the chair across from him with a concerned expression. "Are you okay? You look tired."

Rose stared at him for several moments without speaking. He wanted to pretend like he hadn't sent his Sentinels after Wilder last night? She wondered if he thought she was an idiot or if he enjoyed living in the delusion that he was a good person? She settled into the chair and said simply, "I had a rough night."

He frowned. "I'm sorry to hear that. You'll be glad to know that the children from the arena got moved into the Haven and are doing well."

She raised an eyebrow. "All of them? I saw one child wandering around the Grotto last night."

He shrugged. "They aren't my captives. Many of them roam around during the day but return home at night knowing they have food and a soft bed waiting for them."

"You consider the Havens their home?" she asked.

"Yes, of course." His voice turned fatherly. "This could be your home, too."

"Me?" She barked a laugh. "I have a home."

He leaned forward slightly. "Do you?"

She squirmed under his penetrating stare. "Yes. I have a family and a home."

He leaned back and adopted a philosophical tone. "They assigned you to a family based on the Goddess's so-called 'Gifts.' Now that those Gifts are irrelevant, what is your family?"

She ground her teeth together. "Family is more than just having Gifts in common."

"Really?" he asked. "It seems like having Gifts in common is what draws people together. It's why your crew exists at all right now."

Vaylan's casual words hit her with the force of a threat. The fireplace suddenly felt hot, like it was drawing out all the air in the room. "Why are you so interested in my crew?"

"Because they're the Chosen. I keep a very close eye on anyone involved in Brother Owyn's prophecies."

Her mind raced, trying to figure out what he knew about

the crew's Gifts and specifically about Wilder. She couldn't live in Vaylan's delusion any longer, so she attacked, hoping to throw him off guard. "You sent the Sentinels to kill Wilder last night."

Vaylan's face turned colder than she had ever seen it before. "I don't want to kill him, Rose. He's the Scion."

She blinked several times. "Is that some sort of prophecy?"

Vaylan sighed, and his face smoothed back to calmness. "Yes, it's prophecy. It says, 'Hear the prophecy and believe, O Scion. Life awaits those who follow the founder of a new day.' That's why I know he will eventually come to me."

"Because you are the 'founder of a new day?'" she asked skeptically.

"Yes."

He was so convinced that it sent a chill down her neck despite the warm fire. "Wilder will not come to you," she hissed. "And I will not deliver the crew into your hands. You can do what you like to me, but you will not have them."

His smile was affectionate, as if he was proud of her. "I appreciate your loyalty, because soon you will be that loyal to me, too. There's no need for you to worry how or when you will deliver them to me, because it's inevitable. The benefit of prophecy is that you can relax knowing that everything will turn out the way it should."

"Why should they come to you? They owe you nothing. Just forget about them and continue with your own life."

"They do owe me something. And they owe you something. They owe the whole City." His usually twinkling eyes turned flat and cold. "I told you I will set this City free. The poor women and children who live here have less than what is fair, so I give them what they need. And if someone has too much, I will take it from them. The Chosen were given something beyond what is fair, and I plan to take it."

"And how do you plan on that?" She didn't voice her sacrilegious thought: if there was a way to take someone's Gift, she might have already done it for herself.

"You will help me do it. When you darken the crystals." He shrugged as if it was obvious.

"I will do no such thing!" She stood up to leave. Her anger was stoked, but it wasn't the relief she thought it would be. "I'm tired of your cryptic messages, Vaylan. I thought our conversations would help me discover your schemes, but it's all pointless. It's great you are creating these Havens, but other than that, leave me and the crew out of this." She stalked to the door, but his voice stopped her.

"I know the question that haunts you." His unwavering certainty was entrancing. He stalked closer, but she couldn't walk away. "You ask yourself every day and every night why she didn't return your Gift. You wonder what you did, or what you didn't do, that caused her to forsake you. But I think the bigger question is, why did she give you a Gift in the first place? Was it because you're special? Did she love you more than the others? Or is it truly what you fear, that she didn't choose you at all? It was merely a random chance that made you the Priest and not someone else."

Rose refused to look at him and stared blankly at the door in front of her. He paced at her back, as if he was having a theoretical conversation, not one that had consumed her life for the last few months.

"Now you see what it is like on the other side. What it means to be unchosen. To be Gifted and loved by her must be glorious, but for the rest of us, we live in this reality every day. She could have given her Gifts to everyone, but she didn't. She chose to withhold her blessing. The power imbalance in this City is her fault. I plan to eliminate the injustice. I will see all her Gifts removed from this City so that everyone is on equal footing."

Rose gathered her strength into a rebuttal. "Everyone equal except yourself. You still have a Spark ..." She bit her lips, remembering that he didn't know what that meant. "You still control crystalline. You'll take everyone's Gift but keep something for yourself."

"No. When the crystals go dark, so will the crystalline. Even my power will be gone."

She widened her eyes. She hadn't expected that. "So, you aren't planning to rule the City?"

He smirked. "It's not my power to control crystalline that makes me the founder of a new day. It's because I'm the best one for the job."

She examined his dark eyes like Wilder's and his dimpled grin yet still couldn't decide if he was crazy, evil, or both. She shook her head and left to roam the Grotto, continuing her search for peace.

30

R ose found nothing in Grotto Instinct to comfort her, so eventually, she wandered back to the safe house. She couldn't bring herself to go in but sat sulking on the stoop outside. As she formulated her list of who made her the angriest, Fitz, Quinn, and Tayeh stepped outside.

Tayeh studied her with a look somewhere between pity and disgust. "Are you just going to sit out here all night?"

"Maybe." Rose didn't like how pouty her voice sounded.

Quinn gave her his usual cheerful smile. "The wolves told me you were out here. They really are an excellent resource!"

Rose looked at the three of them. "Are you going somewhere?"

"Yes," said Fitz. "It's best if you join us."

Rose's eyes widened. "Really? I assumed you would all be furious with me."

"Some members of the crew are very upset," Fitz admitted.

"Some?" Rose looked at Tayeh. "I thought you would be one of the angry ones."

Tayeh's eyes were hard as stone, and her hands rested casually on her blades. "That's one thing you got right. I'm only here to protect these two."

Fitz shrugged. "Okay, so *most* of the crew are upset. I thought you might want to join us on a little trip and let everyone settle down a bit."

She stood with a resigned frown. "Sure. I can't find anything else to do."

Tayeh grunted. "Glad we can entertain you." She walked ahead with Quinn and let Fitz trail behind with Rose.

"Are we going to a casino?" asked Rose. "Because I've gone inside a few of them, and I honestly don't get the appeal."

"Did you have any money to gamble with?" At her frown, Fitz rolled his eyes. "Then you kind of missed the point."

She walked quietly for a while, considering how she still hadn't earned any money for herself. Everything she had eaten, worn, or slept on the last few weeks was courtesy of the crew. She had never felt indebted to someone before, and she didn't like it.

"Why do you guys keep me around?" she asked.

Fitz stared at her with a truly confused expression. "Why do we keep you?"

"Yes. It makes no sense." She kept her eyes on Tayeh and Quinn in front of her but didn't stop her questions. "I'm not like you. You are all connected by history and now Gifts. You all have money and know how to make it on your own. Why do you need to keep someone like me around?"

He chuckled, but the sound held no humor. "Wow, Rose. Every time I start to believe you are the most arrogant person I know, you prove instead to be the most insecure. If you don't know why we want you, then you wouldn't believe me if I told you."

Quinn and Tayeh stepped into a narrow alley between two buildings, with Rose and Fitz close behind. When Fitz ushered her through the nondescript door and into a room filled with books, Rose's mouth fell open.

"A library …" she whispered.

It was nothing like the giant library that existed in Knowledge directly overhead, but she found it charming. Neat rows of dark wooden bookshelves lined the edge of the room, and in the center, cozy seating areas gave the guests plenty of space to read. A man sat on a leather couch, a woman resting her head in his lap, each with a book in their hands, while a mother sat in an over-sized chair reading a book to the small boy in her arms.

"I didn't think there were any libraries in the Underneath," she said.

Quinn's eyes lit up. "It's new. Isn't it beautiful?" He wandered dreamily down an aisle, and Tayeh took up a place near the door to watch.

Rose walked to the nearest shelf to read the titles. They were organized in a way she didn't understand, but it appeared they had quite a variety of topics.

"So, you thought if you brought me to a library, I'd settle down and stop being so mean?"

Fitz snorted. "Will that work?"

"Maybe." She plucked a book of poetry off the shelf. It reminded her of the day she had caught Wilder reading ancient love poetry. "Reading occasionally distracts me from my other bad habits."

"At least you know you act terribly. That will help when you finally decide to apologize again."

She narrowed her eyes at him. His self-righteous tone was making her suspicious. "Why did you bring me here?"

"I was with you the day you realized the Priests were charging people to use the grand library Upstairs. I remember the murderous look in your eyes when you claimed they were heretics. You wanted to run across the entire City to fight anyone selling Knowledge."

She remembered the day, too. She had been so naïve, not knowing that selling access to Knowledge was the only way she had food to eat. Since then, she was being supported by a crew that earned money in ways she didn't even ask about. When did heresy stop mattering to her?

"Wilder was there, too." Fitz's voice grew more accusatory, and she suspected that she was being set up for a fall. "Without him, you would have run off on your own again, and Goddess only knows what would have happened. I'm curious … how did he convince you to stay?"

She thought back to that day and remembered Wilder convincing her with nothing more than a look in his eye. The look promised her that one day, they would storm the library and defeat the heretics together. He was not afraid of her passion. He reveled in it.

Fitz took her expression as answer enough. "Whatever he said, he believed it. He provided the funds to start this library and found enough people willing to donate to keep it going."

How had Wilder found the time to not only start this library, but to get others to support it? She looked around the library, trying to understand why Wilder would do something so extravagant when there were so many other things to be done.

Fitz's normally sweet face was hard, and he tapped a finger in an irritated pattern against the edge of the wooden bookshelf.

A wooden bookshelf carved with roses.

She spun around the room. Carved roses curled up the sides of each bookshelf, the dark wooden rose garden sending a subtle yet clear message.

He'd built a library for *her*.

But not *only* for her. A library only for herself was sacrilege. He gave her something more precious. He gave Knowledge freely to all who would seek it, and he did it for her.

Rose wanted to curse or sob or both, but it was a library, so she bit her lips to stay quiet. She was still angry with Wilder, even though she could barely explain why, and in the midst of all that, she had to discover he built her a Goddess-cursed library! He was infuriating yet wonderful.

She couldn't shake the lingering anger, but a part of her knew she would eventually apologize to him once again. And this time, she might need to grovel. A simple apology wouldn't cut it. She wondered if this would be the time he chose not to forgive her. The thought made her feel sick.

She turned back to find Fitz leaning casually against the bookshelf with his arms crossed. "You brought me here to make me feel guilty," she accused.

His lip curled in a cunning expression. "Oh, yes."

She huffed. "So, when you said *most* everyone is upset with me, you were included in that group?"

"The only two people that aren't furious with you are Quinn, because he's literally the nicest person alive, and Kieran, because he couldn't care less. I think even your brother is upset with you."

She sighed. "It's not the first time."

He straightened from his lounging position. "Well, I did my part. Now it's up to you to figure out how you are going to fix it. I'm going to find a book to read. You can wait and walk back with the rest of us or run off on your own if that's what you prefer." He gave her a mocking bow and left her to explore her library on her own.

31

––––––––

Rose chose to walk back to the safe house with the others. Fitz had run out of ways to make her feel guilty, so he ignored her by walking alongside Tayeh. Quinn had his head buried in a book, and Rose occasionally pulled him out of the way of obstacles in his path. Each step toward the safe house felt heavier than the last, and when it finally came into view, she swallowed. Everyone inside had a reason to hate her.

It was quiet when they entered, and Rose breathed a small sigh of relief when she realized that Rev and Wilder weren't there. They were the two that she was the least ready to face. Rev would glare at her until she made amends. And Rose had too many feelings about Wilder to know where to start. She was still angry but also ashamed of how she treated him. She didn't trust herself to apologize without her lingering anger bubbling up and getting her in trouble again.

Kai's disapproving stare was a familiar one. "Are you finished sulking?" He crossed his arms on his chest as she came in the door.

"I'm not sulking." She tried her best to not whine but wasn't very successful.

Rose sat down on her mattress with a huff, and Kieran gave her a look that said she was pathetic. Feather shot her a brief look out of the corner of her eye before going back to arranging a vase of flowers.

Kai stood over Rose with a disapproving glare. "First, you explode in anger. Pretty typical, though I'm pleased to see no weapons were drawn this time."

She rolled her eyes and tried to ignore him.

"After that, you spend a day or two sulking. By this point, you realize you were wrong, but you're still too mad to do anything about it. Plus, knowing you were wrong makes you cranky in a whole new way."

She glared at him. "If you know me so well, you should know I don't want to be lectured right now. Just leave me alone."

He nodded wisely. "And then this stage ... when you lash out at others because you are angry at yourself."

She jerked to her feet. "That's enough, Kai." She looked to the table where Quinn sat reading, and she dropped her voice to a quiet snarl. "I'm going to go do something you can't manage—have a thoughtful conversation with Quinn without blushing."

His lips tightened with embarrassment, and she stomped off, knowing she had proven his point exactly right.

She flopped into the chair across from Quinn, and he looked up from his book with a smile. At least someone was happy to see her.

"Did you find anything interesting at the library?" she asked.

"Yes! I'm currently reading this book about wolves and their pack structure. I can talk to them using words, but they communicate back to me with pictures and phrases that don't always make sense. For example, their relationship with Wilder. They call him 'pup' but not like he's their child. More like how you might call a boyfriend 'baby.'" He chuckled. "It's much different from their word for 'mate,' which has sexual connotations, but it's clear they have a crush on him."

Rose considered how possessive they were of Wilder and nodded. "It makes sense, even though I would never have guessed wolves could have crushes."

"Me neither! That's why it's so fascinating! Their relationship with Wilder is complicated, but with you, it's clear."

"Their relationship with me?"

"I knew they called you 'Lady Fire Wolf' as if you were a red-haired wolf, but the 'Lady' honorific was odd. But I realized it's the way they were calling you 'alpha.'"

"Alpha?"

"Yes. They have a sharp memory of the first time you reprimanded them for not taking care of Wilder. That memory is tied to your name in their minds. They are highly attuned to what you want, which is why they will obey you even though you can't communicate with them like I can." He smiled as he remembered something. "Or like Wilder can."

She had yelled at them several times for not guarding Wilder like they should. Apparently, growling and pointing was all the communication she needed.

"It's also curious that they refer to you as Wilder's mate," said Quinn.

"His mate?" The word came out as a squeak.

Quinn explained as if it was a fascinating educational discovery. "Yes! They can clearly recognize the difference between their relationship with Wilder and your own. That's their best word to describe why Wilder looks at you the way he does."

Rose's heartbeat sped at the memory of how Wilder looked at her when he sang the song he'd written for her. While she had sagged against the wall, breathless with desire, his eyes had glowed with the knowledge of how much he'd pleased her. She didn't want to think about that now, so she reached for one of Quinn's stacked books as a distraction.

She flipped mindlessly through the pages before realizing she couldn't read any of the words.

"What is this?" she asked.

Quinn's eyes lit up. "I couldn't believe they had this book at the new library! It's one of the old books from before the City was founded. I recently started translating some of the old language, and every time I find another book, it gives me more clues to piece together the vocabulary."

She studied the strange marks, and a memory clicked into place. "I've seen this writing before." Quinn's eyes followed her hungrily as she went to her pack on her mattress and dug inside. She pulled out a crumpled piece of paper at the bottom and brought it back to him.

She had mistaken the strange scribbles as part of Walter's odd behavior, but now she could see that the marks were in patterns of language.

Quinn took the note with gentle fingers as if studying a precious artifact. She had to admit that it was a lovely work of art with the roses and butterflies sketched around the edges.

She remembered Walter handing her the note before leaving. "He said that this is what a butterfly whispered to him when it led him to his new home."

Quinn flattened the note gently against the table, and Rose found his slow words ominous. "*You aren't the only one with a Spark. Beware of anyone who wants to rule forever.*"

She looked at Quinn with confusion. "Walter has a Spark?"

His eyes lit up again. "Walter? You didn't say you met Walter!"

"Fitz and I met him at Jaida's house. How do you know Walter?" she asked.

"I've never met him, but his Spark is the first one we discovered. He can grant long life. That's why the High Priests lived so long."

She looked at the paper with a frown. "It seems Walter's butterfly gave him this message a little too late to be helpful." Walter had said the butterfly told him a joke that made him laugh for hours. He must be a fan of irony.

Quinn studied the paper with a thoughtful expression. "The Goddess must have given him this warning when she hid him. But this isn't about the High Priests—it's about someone with a Spark. Maybe it's about Vaylan?"

She leaned back in her chair with a thump. What would Vaylan do if he could live forever?

"We have to hide Walter," she said.

"He *is* hidden. I'm one of the few people in the City who knows what he can do, and I had no idea where he was. Even Ylena never discovered where the Goddess had hidden him."

But now that Rose knew, she thought Walter was a shining beacon for Vaylan to find. She began considering places in the City that she could hide him.

"Rose." Quinn's quiet voice snapped her out of her planning. "Vaylan is watching you. If you make any suspicious movements, such as traveling across the Grottos to get a random person out of a group home and taking them to a secret location, he will start asking questions. You might be the one who draws his attention to Walter when he otherwise might have remained hidden."

Her breath hitched in fear when she realized the wisdom of Quinn's words. She wouldn't be the one to deliver Walter or any of the crew into Vaylan's hands. She had to stay away and pretend she had never met him. It was the right thing to do, but a terrible fear wound its way around her heart.

"What if he already knows?" whispered Rose. "What if someone followed me there and swept into the house behind us? Vaylan could already have Walter, and we are so far away from Grotto Peculiarity that we would never know what happened."

Quinn reached across the table and took her hand. "We can't control what's in the past. All you can do is act wisely now."

He handed the note back to her, and she studied the delicate roses Walter had drawn. When he'd given her the note, he said she needed this message more than he did. If she couldn't hide Walter without risking his life, she would at least take his words to heart. Beware of anyone who wants to rule forever.

32

———

Rev and Wilder didn't return until late that night. Most of the others were already asleep, but Rose couldn't stop tossing and turning on her mattress. When she heard the door open, she stilled and pretended to sleep. She heard them talk quietly to Quinn, who was still awake and reading his books next to a small crystalline lamp. Her eyes stayed firmly closed as they settled onto mattresses on the floor near her own. She listened closely, waiting to hear Wilder's breathing settle into a pattern of sleep, but she fell asleep before he did.

The next morning, she faked sleep again as she heard them all wake and leave the safe house a couple at a time. She cracked open her eyes when Quinn hunched down next to her.

"The wolves know where we will be training," he said. "If you decide to join us, they can show you the way."

The wolves sat calmly staring at her, and Quinn ruffled Storm Fang's fur as he stood. They watched him close the door, then turned their attention back to Rose.

"What are you looking at?" she grumbled. They continued their silent stare. "Maybe I want to keep moping, okay? Nothing is fair, and I just want to lie here and complain about it."

The wolves' blue eyes were unrelenting. She sat up with a huff. "What do you want me to say? It wasn't that bad. I was just overly passionate about stating my opinion."

No response.

"I was perhaps a bit too harsh."

A very low growl.

"You're right." Rose sighed. "I was mean to our ... boyfriend."

A dual yip of agreement.

She rubbed her forehead. If she was going to be reprimanded by wolves, she might as well face the rest of the crew to finish the job. She dressed in sturdy brown training leathers and sheathed all her knives. The few times she made amends, sparring was involved, and she wanted to be prepared if she was about to be thrashed.

The wolves led her down the street to a large training room the crew had paid to use. She took a deep breath and opened the door.

The first person to notice her was Wilder. He stood next to Feather, and they moved their hands in sync as a vine curled its way around Tayeh, who was attempting to cut the vines as fast as they grew. The three of them looked her way, then coolly went back to their tasks.

Fitz's hand rested against the stone that made up the entire back wall of the training room. As he concentrated, the stone flowed into shapes that looked like they had been carved directly into the stone. She wasn't sure he noticed her until the wall formed into roses carved like the bookshelves in the library. The wall settled into perfect stone blooms before a muscular stone hand crushed the roses. She sighed and kept walking.

The wolves leaped away from her side and skidded to a

halt in front of Quinn. He flopped down on the floor beside them and began a silent conversation.

Even Kieran had joined the training. He was inside a boxing ring, training with Kai. Kieran appeared to be a scrappy fighter already, but Kai was an excellent teacher and showed him how to adjust his stance for more stability.

Outside the ring, Rev sat on a long bench. She gave Rose a tight smile and patted the seat beside her. Rose sighed in resignation and took a seat.

"I'm glad to see you joined us," said Rev. "I wasn't sure how long you would continue sulking."

"The wolves convinced me to come."

Rev nodded as if that were perfectly reasonable. "Good. At least you listen to someone."

"I have a question," said Rose. "What can I do to earn money?"

Rev's eyebrow raised. "That's not the question I expected."

"Well, I heard I need money to pay you to listen to my confession."

Rev's head tilted as if Rose intrigued her. "That is the usual way of things, but I'll make you a deal. I'll hear your confession if you'll hear mine."

Rose's eyes widened. "That's it?"

"The only condition is that when I give you my confession, you can't respond at all. Not a sound. If you utter a single word before I walk away, I will demand immediate payment in full. And I will collect it one way or another."

Rose blinked at the fierceness of her tone but nodded. No matter what Rev confessed, Rose was sure she could bite her tongue long enough for Rev to walk away.

"Wonderful!" Rev gave her an open smile. "What would you like to confess?"

Rose had planned her confession on the walk over, but now that she was here, she found the words difficult. "I left the competition without telling anyone and once again put myself and others in danger. I only considered how Wilder's Gifts affected me, with no regard for how he might feel keeping a secret so large. He kept the secret because he knew I would react poorly, and he was right. I lashed out at him when none of this is his fault."

Rev nodded slowly as Rose talked. "Is that all?"

"Um ... I can keep going, I guess. I've been sulking for two days because I still feel the anger bubbling in my chest, but I can't decide who deserves it. Wilder, the Goddess, myself ... which makes me even angrier."

Rev nodded. "Yes, and?"

"I don't know what else you want me to say. I'm sorry for all of that, and I'll try to do better next time."

"If that's all you've got, then you can hear mine. And remember ... not a word." Her eye was so serious that Rose literally bit down on her tongue to help her stay silent. Rose nodded, and Rev began.

"I was the youngest child of a single mother of three." Rose's eyes widened in surprise. Were confessions supposed to start that far back? "My two older brothers were eight and ten years older than me, so they always considered me the baby of the family. My mother worked hard to provide for the three of us, but it was never enough. She was always tired, always hungry, always *angry*."

Rose felt a chill at the emphasis Rev placed on the word. She bit her lips for good measure.

"One day, when I was four, I was sitting at the kitchen table while my brothers ran through the house, yelling. I'm not sure if they were playing or fighting or both, but even at four, I know my mother was one step away from screaming at them to stop. I hated it when she got loud. She was scary when she was mad. I wanted to hide, so I jumped down from the table.

"I had lost my eye in an accident the year before and still hadn't adjusted to the loss. In my hurry to escape, I tripped and knocked the bowl of soup off the table, sending it crashing to the ground. I remember staring at the doorway, waiting for her arrival in terror. When my mother entered, she stared at the soup as it slowly seeped under the cabinets and bellowed a furious roar.

"As an adult, I can guess what she felt: overwhelming despair. She had come home from work; cooked a meal that would barely be enough to feed the four of us, leaving her hungry as always; but now, there would be no dinner. Everyone would be hungry. And she alone would pick up the broken shards of pottery and clean the soup from underneath the stove. Her scream was one of despair, but all I heard was the rage.

"She looked at me standing in a puddle of soup, with my single eye blinking in terror. I trembled as she drew closer, and she bent down until she looked me right in the eye, and said, 'Rev, this world is a terrible place, and I honestly don't know if you will survive it. You will always be different and out of place. If you can't figure out how to be like everyone else, no one will ever love you.'"

Rose held her breath. She didn't need to bite her tongue anymore. She couldn't speak if she wanted to.

"Yesterday, when you spoke to Wilder as if he was some type of freak, it transported me back to that moment. I heard my mother's rage and despair in your voice, and I was suddenly four years old again. I wanted to fight you, as I couldn't fight her then. And I wanted to run away in fear, hiding under my bed like a scared child."

She cocked her head, as if waiting for a response, but Rose's lips were locked shut. Rev gave a brief nod and walked away.

33

———

Rose sat alone on the bench a long time after Rev walked away. At some point, Fitz went out and got lunch, and he handed Rose a sandwich, which she accepted with a surprised nod. The crew gathered to eat in a circle around the piles of vines Wilder and Feather created, but Rose stayed on her bench, unsure of the welcome she would receive.

As she ate her sandwich, she watched Kai smile shyly while Quinn told a story he had read in one of his library books. She realized that when she thought of "the crew," Kai was now included. When had he officially become part of the crew? Was it just because of his Gift? Or would they have welcomed him in even if he had none?

She was still mulling it over as they broke into new pairs to continue their training. Kai walked over to her bench in front of the boxing ring and gave her a comforting squeeze on the shoulder and a quiet smile. He had always been quick to forgive her, even when they were little. She didn't deserve a brother as kind as him.

He removed his shirt and hopped into the ring. Wilder strode over, removing his own shirt with a challenging look at Rose. He wanted to get a reaction out of her, either positive or negative, but she wasn't sure which one would be most beneficial. She kept her face as neutral as possible as he stepped inside the ring with Kai.

They bowed to each other in the formal tradition, then fell into fighting stances. She kept her lips clenched together to keep a sigh from slipping out. They were both amazing fighters without the wind, but with it, they became pure artistry. She had always enjoyed watching Discipline Priests fight, but she had never appreciated the beauty until the moves were lost to her.

Quinn sat down beside her, and she was grateful for the distraction from her melancholy thoughts. He patted Storm Fang's back absently as he watched the fight.

Rose saw the moment Kai noticed Quinn watching. He lunged too far to the left and stumbled before pulling himself back into a proper stance.

Rose sighed and turned to find Quinn still happily watching the fight. She couldn't ignore it any longer.

"Quinn, I don't know if you realize this, but my brother is usually a pretty tough guy."

He turned to her with an amused expression. "Yes." He waved toward the boxing ring. "It's very obvious."

"No, I mean, he's sporty and tough and level-headed. But lately ..."

Quinn just stared at her with his usual smile. He wasn't going to get it unless she came right out and said it.

"Kai likes you."

Quinn's usual smile curled into a smirk. "I figured that out already."

"You already know? I thought he was swooning over someone who was totally oblivious! Why haven't you said anything about it? You keep saying sweet things to embarrass him, and I can't count the times I've seen him stumble when you watch him fight. Why are you teasing him like this?"

Quinn stared at Kai in the boxing ring, and his lips twisted into a wry grin. "I think he's cute when he blushes." Kai stumbled, and Quinn chuckled softly.

Rose leaned back against the bench with a groan. "Ugh. You've spent too much time with Wilder."

Quinn turned back to her with his usual cheerful smile. "There's no need to worry. I don't plan on breaking Kai's heart. But I have to be smart about it and take it slow. I don't want Rev to lecture me about disrupting the crew dynamics."

Rose sighed. "Like I did."

He gave her a pitying smile. "Yes, you did. But we're a very forgiving group if you take the time to ask."

She looked around at the crew training as hard as usual. They were each brilliant in their own way, and it was time for her to make things right. "You're right, Quinn." She pushed herself to her feet. "Time to stop moping and move ahead. And as usual, I must start by apologizing for being an idiot."

He hopped off the bench. "Sounds fun!"

She whistled loudly, and the sounds of training stopped.

"Time for a crew meeting," she announced.

Everyone except Quinn stared at her in shock. She avoided eating lunch with them, and now she stood up, demanding they stop for a meeting.

"Please?" she asked kindly.

There were only a few mumbles as the crew gathered in a circle near the bench where she stood. She was glad to see that Wilder and Kai had put their shirts back on. Quinn didn't need any more encouragement to make Kai blush.

Once they settled, Rose took a deep breath. "I would like to apologize for running off on my own the night of the competition. I thought I was being smart about it, but it was the same bad habit that I always have. Instead of taking backup or relying on someone else, I rushed off on my own. I'm sorry. I'm going to do better."

Feather piped up. "I forgive you, Rose. And if you ever need backup, you can always ask me."

Feather was definitely not the first person Rose would call if she needed backup. And she also wasn't the one person she really wanted to forgive her. Wilder lounged casually against the wall and studied her with penetrating eyes. She needed to answer Feather well, or else Rose would be the one apologizing for how poorly she apologized.

"Thank you, Feather. I appreciate that. And I've got your back when you need it." She felt pretty good about her response, but Wilder watched her with a skeptical glare.

"Is there anything else you want to say?" asked Rev coolly.

"I have more apologizing to do, but I will save that for a more appropriate time," she said. Wilder's eyebrow made the slightest twitch up, and her gut twisted. The more appropriate time was when she finally figured out what she would say to him.

She cleared her throat and continued. "But I do have something else to say. Discussing your Gifts usually makes me a little irritable." Tayeh snorted at the understatement, but Rose ignored it. "Despite my feelings, I have noticed how skilled you have each become. Feather, the way you were collaborating with Fitz by using stone to strengthen your vines was remarkable. I've never seen it done before."

Feather's face lit up in delight, and Fitz's cool expression softened.

She turned to Kieran. "You kept singing while you showed me your memory. That's a highly advanced skill for a Knowledge Priest, and you did it on your first attempt."

Kieran's normally bored expression actually contained a bit of interest. "Quinn, there are Harmony Priests who would love your insights into wolves. And Rev, I've seen your water sculptures, and they are truly breathtaking."

She turned to Tayeh. "You healed me before you even knew what you were doing. The relief you gave me was far beyond what a beginning Priest could ever accomplish." She looked at Kai and shrugged. "What can I say about you? You've always been a great fighter and a brilliant Priest. That hasn't changed. And Wilder …" Her breath caught as she considered all his Gifts.

He called the wind the night they ran away from Vaylan.

He kissed her in the middle of a whirlwind.

He saved her life.

Her mouth moved, but she couldn't form those thoughts into words. She coughed and continued in a different direction. "All of you have shown such amazing progress with your Gifts, and I should have said it before now. I'm sorry I let my own problems distract me. But I'm really proud of your hard work."

Rev gave her an approving nod, and a little sigh of relief escaped Rose's lips. She looked at Wilder, but his face was still an unreadable mask.

The crew gave various smiles and nods of approval as they stood to return to their training. Something about it felt off to Rose, but she wasn't sure why. "That's it? You're going right back to training?"

"What else do you want?" asked Rev.

"I don't know," she said. "I guess a conversation about what comes next?"

Tayeh waved around the training facility. "This comes next. We train."

"Yes, but for what?" asked Rose. "What are you training for?" She looked at each of them, but no one had an answer.

Wilder still leaned casually against the wall and spoke in a slow drawl. "It sure would be nice if there was someone in this crew who liked to take action. Someone who could look at the raw talent in a crew and see potential." His voice sounded bored, but she felt every word as a challenge thrown at her feet. "Someone who didn't just run in blindly by herself, but who thoughtfully considered who would be the best person for each job. Some might call this person bossy because she always has an opinion about what's right and who should do what. Maybe if we had a person like that in the crew, we could accomplish something. Together."

His words stirred something deep inside her. She had been looking at the crew and seeing the ways she was different, the ways she didn't fit. But Wilder's words opened up the reality staring her in the face. She *was* different, and the crew needed someone like her. She belonged to this crew, and they belonged to her. There was a place for her. And it required her to be the best version of herself.

When she spoke, her voice was determined. "We need to find out how Vaylan's plans extend beyond the Havens. He is hiding something in the Heart of the Grottos. I won't go there alone. We all need to work together to figure out how to do this without getting killed."

Wilder's face was still unreadable, but the rest of the crew grinned at the challenge before them. The wolves gave a sharp yip, and Rose didn't need Quinn's Gift to translate.

Alpha.

DESIRE

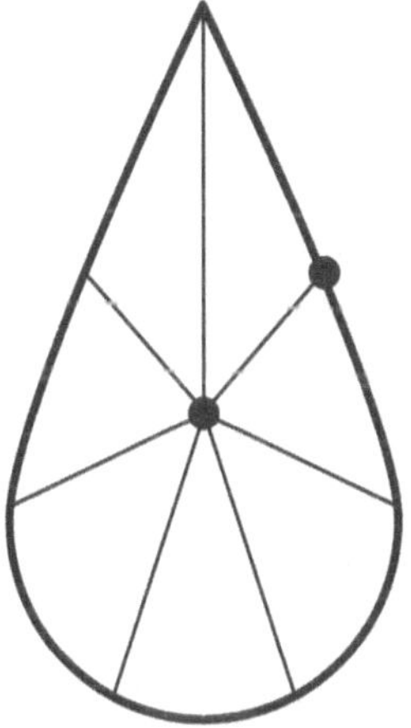

34

———

Rose's first recommendation for their plan of attack was to move on to the next Grotto. There was no real reason for it other than Grotto Instinct held too many bad memories.

Although there was a secret library. That memory, she still held close to her heart.

As they entered Grotto Desire the next morning, the discussion turned to where they would stay.

"We could stay at Vivi's." Rev studied Wilder with a strange expression, and Rose couldn't interpret it. "It's a cheap place to stay."

Tayeh snorted. "Cheap for everyone except Wilder."

Rose still hadn't apologized fully to Wilder, so she was trying to be on her best behavior, but something about the tone of the conversation made her feel twitchy. Who was this Vivi? Rose wanted to know but kept her mouth shut.

Rev gave Wilder another curious look. "We can stay with Vivi if you want to send a clear message to someone ..." Rev's eyelashes fluttered innocently, and Rose got the distinct impression they were talking about her.

He ducked his head, but his low voice was resolute. "Honestly, Rev. You know my choice."

She tapped him on the chest. "Good. It's always helpful to remind yourself what you want." She pointed down a busy street to the right. "I have some friends in the area. It will be a lot more expensive, but Wilder's made his choice so …" She shrugged but looked pleased.

As they walked down the busy street, Rose was stunned at the variety of services that were being offered. Even though Wilder was currently ignoring her, he paid attention to everyone throwing propositions his way. He answered most with his usual cocky grin, but a few lucky people got winks and kisses blown their way. She didn't have the time to feel jealous, because the sheer number of invitations was staggering.

Plus, she received plenty of offers herself. She was shocked by the audacity of the first man, but after a dozen propositions, along with a plenty of the goods displayed, she quickly became numb to it.

"They really are quite … enthusiastic," she said to Kai.

He laughed. "They are very devoted to their Vice. You'll eventually get used to it."

Her head spun to look at him. "Have you been here before?"

He smirked. "Not everyone pouted in their room following the Uprising. I did a bit of … exploring."

She snorted. "Is that what you call it?"

They pulled to a stop with the rest of the crew in front of a massive building glowing with thin lines of crystalline along the curved trim. "This is where we are staying?"

Rose thought Rev would answer, but she was hugging two beautiful women.

"What is this place?" she asked Kai under her breath.

"Ecstasy Theater. They have some truly fascinating ... performances."

Rose raised an eyebrow but didn't ask more. Rev kissed her friends goodbye and circled up the crew to discuss.

"Good news!" she said. "It won't be as expensive as I thought. I can get us two rooms here."

Tayeh narrowed her eyes suspiciously. "What's the catch?"

Rev adopted an innocent expression that was anything but. "Two of us will need to perform in the show."

Quinn clapped his hands. "Just what you always wanted, Rev!"

"Alas, I don't fit the costume. I'm not tall enough." Her eyes slid over to Rose.

"Me?" she choked.

Tayeh snorted. "Definitely not me."

Feather was the same height as Rev, but she looked up at Rose with a confused smile. "I have no idea what we're talking about."

Rev took Rose by the arm. "Come on. You're a talented dancer. You'll fit the costume. Believe me, I know exactly how great you'll look in it." Rose frowned at her. Rev had seen her change clothes a lot, but she didn't need to brag about it.

"So that's settled!" said Rev merrily. "Now we just need a male volunteer. I think that choice is obvious." She turned to Kieran. "Unless you'd like to compete for the role?"

Kieran let out a bark of laughter. "No. I think I'll pass this time."

"Wonderful!" said Rev. "Rose and Wilder will be in the show."

Wilder studied Rose with unreadable eyes, but since she didn't know what she had gotten herself into, she didn't think he could tell much from her expression.

Rev pulled Rose closer, as if making sure she didn't run off. "You are just backup dancers and still have some time before they need you. Let's get some coffee and discuss our plans, shall we?"

As Rev pulled her into the coffeehouse, Rose thought that even though Rev wasn't a bossy alpha, she still usually got her way.

It was challenging to make plans in a coffeehouse when the barista was also a stripper. Their crew of nine had a hard time finding enough chairs to pull around the two tables they pushed together, and once they were finally settled, their barista approached them with glee. Rose thought she must really enjoy serving coffee until the private show began. Then Rose realized she enjoyed a large crowd for the group interaction.

After she delivered each cup of coffee, the woman pulled a pin out of her hair, shaking her long black curls around her face. Rev turned her chair around so she had a front-row seat. She bit her lip as she smiled, occasionally tilting her head for a better view. Kieran smirked and leaned back in his chair to fully savor the performance. He even saluted her with his cup of coffee as a sign of encouragement.

Wilder was more reserved, but he definitely paid attention. He watched her with the same penetrating look he'd leveled on Rose before. He saw the woman, recognized her beauty, and acknowledged something deeper within. His eyes pierced to the core of who she was. Despite the woman's carefree attitude, she blushed under Wilder's gaze.

The rest of the crew watched the performance with varying levels of enthusiasm. Kai appeared to be his usual confident self when the woman sat on his lap. He laughed when she ruffled her fingers through his black hair. Rose thought Feather's eyes would bulge out of her head when the woman twisted her dark ponytail around her fingers and gave it a gentle tug.

Rose sighed when it was her turn. She appreciated the woman's skill but wasn't a fan of strangers pawing at her. The woman sensed her reluctance and took it as a challenge. She leaned over Rose, black curls framing her face, and trailed a slow finger along the collar of Rose's shirt. The woman's eyes caught on Rose's mark, and her hand pulled back with a start. She straightened and gave Rose a slight nod before moving on to Fitz.

Rose frowned. Not that she was upset about missing her own private performance, but why did a random coffeehouse stripper know about her mark? That the Adopted who roamed the Havens knew about her was bad enough, but now she was recognizable outside as well.

She couldn't focus on the rest of the woman's performance and only looked up when she heard the crew clapping. They handed her a pile of coins in appreciation, and she blew them kisses as she walked away.

To Rose, she gave one last bow of the head.

"That was terrific!" said Rev. "I wish all crew meetings were this thrilling."

"She recognized me," said Rose.

"She did?" asked Rev.

"I guess you weren't looking at her eyes," Rose said drily. "She saw my mark and knew what it meant."

Wilder turned in his chair to see the woman come out of the back room fully dressed again and ready to serve more coffee. "I didn't realize Vaylan's reach extended so far beyond the Havens."

"I thought all of Vaylan's followers wore white," said Quinn.

Tayeh shrugged. "Maybe it doesn't matter what color you wear when you wear so little."

"One thing is clear," said Rose. "We can't discuss any plans here."

"No, we can't," agreed Wilder. "We need to find another place to train and have conversations in private."

"I have another contact here who might know a place," said Rev. "The rest of the crew can come with me while you and Rose go to your dress rehearsal." She bit her lip with excitement. "I can't wait to see you both in the show."

35

───────

Rose and Wilder said bye to the crew outside of Ecstasy Theater. As they walked up the steps together, Rose realized this was the first time she had been alone with Wilder since the night she walked out on him. She had finally pieced together some words to say when one of Rev's friends found them.

"Oh, aren't you two a beautiful couple!" The woman wore her blond hair pulled into a tight bun and was dressed in a simple leotard and tights. She led them through the empty tables in the audience and into a door that led backstage. "We're rehearsing our opening act right now, so you can head to costume fitting while you wait. Your part is simple. You basically just need to stand around being gorgeous. I can already tell you will be great!" She pushed them into a room filled with glittering costumes, gave them both a smack on the rear, and left them with a wink.

An older woman popped up from behind a stack of costumes and studied them. She held pins between her lips and shoved a pencil into her honey-colored hair streaked with gray. Her dress was dark amethyst, of a simple but perfectly tailored cut. She pulled the pins out of her mouth and stuck them in a cushion.

"You're the new flesh?" She waved them forward. "Come here. Let me get a good look at you."

Wilder stepped forward, and the woman ran her hands casually across his chest. He blinked in surprise.

The woman noticed his expression and laughed. "Sorry. I forget new dancers expect to be introduced first. Nice to meet you. I'm Hazel."

"I'm Wilder. Nice to meet you, too." He gestured to his chest. "I guess you can continue?"

She gave him a wry smile. "Don't mind if I do." She circled him and rubbed her hands across his back, then stepped back to study him while tapping a finger absently against her lips.

She nodded to herself, then went to a rack of clothes and began flipping through them. "You will both be in two numbers. One is the finale, and you will wear what everyone in the chorus is wearing." She handed Wilder a flimsy silver piece of fabric with straps that hung oddly on the hanger. Rose had no idea how the fabric scrap would cover him.

Hazel moved to a second rack of clothes and studied them more thoughtfully. "For your second number, you are a couple in the background. Everyone has different costumes, but I need the two of you to match." She pulled a pair of white leather pants off the rack and handed it to him. "I'm pretty sure these will fit you ... who am I kidding? I *know* they'll fit you," she said smugly. "Take both costumes out there, and one of the guys can show you to a dressing room. I'll check on you before dress rehearsal to make sure everything is in the right place."

Wilder gave her a slight bow, then swaggered out of the room. Hazel watched him go with an appreciative eye.

Rose groaned. The woman had to be sixty, yet even she couldn't help but admire Wilder.

Hazel turned to Rose with a businesslike movement. She lifted her hands to Rose's waist, then stopped and looked her in the eye. "I'm Hazel."

"Rose." She sighed and raised her hands to the sides.

The woman slid her hands down Rose's waist, then patted her hips with calm efficiency. She gave Rose the same calculating stare she gave Wilder, then nodded.

"I have a few ideas." Hazel walked over to a rack and began looking. "The guys' costumes are always much easier. Yours will take a bit more trial and error. We've got a lot more moving pieces, if you know what I mean."

"It might take you longer to pick his costume if you also gave him a shirt to wear," Rose said drily.

Hazel gave her a flat stare. "That boy doesn't need to cover up with a shirt, and you know it."

Rose rolled her eyes. "Yeah, and he knows it, too."

Hazel sniffed. "Good for him. He's confident in who he is. You could learn a few things from him."

Rose's body tensed with the fear that she had stumbled into another one of Vaylan's followers. "What do you know about me?"

Hazel chuckled. "I can tell a lot about a person by what they're wearing." She gestured at all the costumes. "I've been doing this a while."

Rose used to love picking out new clothes when she was a Priest, but she hadn't thought much about what she wore since she fled to the Underneath. Her clothing used to be very intentional and a clear sign of her identity, but now, her clothes were just a way to cover up. Hazel wouldn't be able to read anything from what she wore.

Rose held her arms out to the side and twirled in a circle. "Tell me what you see."

Hazel didn't look her over again but spoke like she had already seen it all. "You're wearing a purple crop top under that big sweater, which tells me you are confident about your appearance. You're obviously a dancer, or you wouldn't be here, but I think by the way you carry yourself, you are also a fighter. So, you're confident in your own abilities and appearance, but you're covering up with a big gray sweater. It's possible you are feeling under the weather, but I think it's more likely that you are doubting yourself and don't want to be seen as too commanding. Or maybe you're in a fight with that boy and aren't sure if you want to appear too sexual. That part of your life is complicated right now, and you don't want to make it any worse."

She walked around Rose like a hawk circling her prey, and Rose trembled under her gaze. "Your choice of colors is odd. Normally, that means you are from Peculiarity or maybe a new arrival from Upstairs, but I sense something different about you. The gray sweater is dull, but you've got the purple top, red plaid skirt, polka dot socks inside turquoise boots. It seems like you are choosing colors with wild abandon, almost like a child does. You're too old to be exploring your personal style for the first time, so I think you've recently gone through some traumatic experience that has caused you to reconsider your whole identity. You aren't sure who you are right now but desperately want to grow into something new." Her voice softened. "So, what was it, child? Did you lose someone? Did someone hurt you?"

Rose stumbled backward until she thumped against the table full of clothes at her back. Her shoulders sagged from the exhaustion of having her whole life laid out before her. The woman saw everything, so Rose shared the only thing Hazel missed.

"I was a Priest," she whispered.

Hazel sighed, nodding as the pieces fell into place, and spoke in a tender voice, "Goddess blessing upon you."

"And also upon you." Rose's response was automatic but halting as she considered the woman.

"That definitely explains the colors," Hazel said. "Finding a new color palette is going to take some time. Keep exploring, and you'll figure it out. The larger question about your identity might take even longer, I'm afraid." She gave Rose an encouraging squeeze on the shoulder, then walked to a rack and pulled a costume off. "All I can offer is a new color for today." She held up a long, flowing white dress.

Rose sighed. "The color white is just as complicated."

Hazel narrowed her eyes. "Are you tangled up with those folks who wear white at the old Warden's Den?"

She pulled down the collar of her top, revealing her mark. "You could say that."

Hazel eyed the scar warily. "I don't know what that means, but it doesn't look good."

"No, it's not good. And it might be best if it's hidden under whatever costume you chose."

Hazel raised an eyebrow as if challenged. "Finding costumes that cover up unusual parts while revealing the fun bits is part of my job."

Hazel made Rose try on several white costumes until she found one that hid the scar and lived up to her exacting standards. As Rose squeezed into costume after costume, she grew more irritated that Wilder got to wear a simple pair of leather pants.

The finale costume was complicated on a whole other level. What Rose thought were jeweled undergarments was actually the costume. Once she squeezed into the shimmery tights and tiny glittering top and bottoms, she required Hazel's help to put on the rest.

First, a feathery pink puff that trailed down the back of Rose's legs and floated along the ground as she walked. Next, Hazel draped sparkling beads in loops across Rose's chest and back. The beads irritated her scar, but she applied some of the medicine from the apothecary to numb the pain. She shook off the memory of Wilder's gentle touch and rested the beaded necklace against her collarbone.

Hazel handed her sparkling high heels and long, pale pink gloves, then made Rose kneel so she could pin the tall feather headpiece in place. With the headdress on, Rose felt very tall. Her heels added four inches, but the headdress added two feet. She looked in the mirror and cocked her hips to one side, watching the feathers swish along the floor. She felt powerful, as if she could conquer the City.

Hazel walked behind her with approval written on her face. "It suits you. Whatever you decide to do with this next stage in your life, keep in mind that you can always have a career as a showgirl."

Rose tipped her head to the side, and the feathers tickled her neck as she considered the thought. She finally found a paying job.

36

Hazel shoved Rose out of the costume room with firm instructions that under no circumstances was she allowed to fidget. Even though Hazel had fitted the costume so precisely, it was hard not to fidget when the tiny costume felt like it was riding up her backside. Rose spotted the other dancers applying glue to their costumes, and she quickly became their new friend.

As they helped her get glued into position, a short man wearing a teal suit with a thick purple scarf approached her.

"You must be one of the warm bodies." His voice was nasal and instantly grated on her nerves.

She looked at him fully dressed, while she and the rest of the girls clearly weren't. "Well, I wouldn't say I'm warm."

He gave her a flat stare. "Funny. Don't worry. You'll be sweating soon enough. If you want to get paid and keep your room and board, you will do a good job during this dress rehearsal. Your part isn't hard, so I expect it to be flawless, or you're cut."

She straightened to her full height, which was more than a foot above him even without the headdress. "Oh, I am flawless." When she said it, she heard Wilder's confidence in the words. Maybe Hazel was right. She could learn that from him.

He raised his eyebrows and walked away as if he would wait and see if that was true.

Backstage was a sea of pink feathers and rhinestones. Rose and the other girls finished gluing and adjusting and wiggling, locking their costumes firmly into place, then lined up in order of height and quietly waited for their cue.

Their job was to walk gracefully down twin curving staircases. All Rose had to do was to walk in time with the girl in front of her, smile, and not trip. She had lost confidence in a lot of her abilities lately, but she was certain she could accomplish that.

As she studied the crowd of women in pink feathers around her, she considered Wilder's role. There weren't any men on the upper portion of the stage where the women waited, and she wondered if his assignment would be as simple as hers.

The curtain opened, and she plastered a smile on her face. She was close to the end of the line, so she heard the lead singer's voice before she saw her. The song was as racy as Rose expected, but the tune was catchy, and it was easy to walk down the stairs in time to the slow rhythm. Rose was halfway down the staircase before she found Wilder.

The lead singer lounged in a palanquin at center stage, carried by Wilder and three other men. They were all very attractive, but at the sight of Wilder, Rose's ankle buckled in her heels, and she had to take an awkward step to get back in time with the girl in front of her. So much for her flawless performance.

Wilder wore little silver shorts with straps crisscrossing his chest and arms. His biceps bulged from the strength required to lift the heavy palanquin, and Rose had to look away or she thought she might stumble again. She thought back to Hazel saying she would check on Wilder to make sure everything was in the right place. Goddess bless Hazel, everything surely was.

Rose made it to her predetermined stopping place without another stumble. She lifted her arm in a move of gentle presentation and prepared to hold her place for the rest of the song. Her eyes followed Wilder as he and the others lowered the palanquin to the ground with careful slowness. They walked to either side of the singer, and Wilder offered a hand to help her rise gracefully. The woman never lost the flow of her song as she trailed a playful finger down Wilder's chest.

Rose was grateful the music was loud enough to cover the low growl inside her throat.

The singer gave the same attention to the other three men, but Rose's eyes were still locked on Wilder. She thought her cheeks might crack at how stiffly she was holding her smile. The woman stepped forward, drawing all eyes to her, and Wilder and the other men faded back into the sea of pink feathers.

Wilder took up a position next to Rose. He was so close she could feel the heat radiating off him. She wanted to say something to break the silence that had lain between them since her last hurtful words, but she couldn't speak without breaking her smile.

Because of the angle at which he stood, Wilder could speak a bit more freely. He was close enough that his low voice could barely be heard over the music.

"My Gifts disturbed you so much that you said you couldn't even look at me." His voice was a strange mixture of sadness and cockiness. "Apparently, that's changed."

"Wilder, I—" The swarm of pink feathers changing position interrupted her apology. She glued her fake smile back on and shifted to her new place on the stage. Wilder moved to a new location, and she was so far away that they couldn't speak.

The rest of the song seemed to last forever, but eventually the woman sang her last naughty word, and the lights faded. Since this was only a dress rehearsal, only the backstage crew and a couple of people in the audience clapped. When the lights came back up, the swarm of feathers exited off into the wings, but Rose remained on stage looking for Wilder. The short man in the purple scarf caught her eyes first. He gave her a sharp glare that told her he had seen her stumble, but it wasn't bad enough to cut her yet. She bowed her head submissively as he walked past.

Once the other dancers had cleared the stage, she found Wilder. His shoulders looked slightly hunched, and he trudged to the stairs leading off the front edge of the stage. Closing in on him from her place in the audience was a blond woman stalking toward him with purposeful steps. The look in the woman's eye caused the hair on the back of Rose's neck to stand on end. Rose narrowed her eyes and walked just as purposefully to the front of the stage, her heels clicking fiercely across the boards.

The woman had already intercepted Wilder by the time Rose walked down the stairs to join them in front of the stage.

"Hi, Vivi," said Wilder. "I'm surprised to see you here."

Rose raised an eyebrow. So, this was the Vivi whose house they could have stayed at? Vivi's blond hair was piled in artful curls on top of her head, and her hot pink dress was so tight she appeared to be one deep breath from falling out of the top of it. Her pink lips curled in a slow smile as she studied Wilder from head to toe. A tremor worked its way down Rose's spine.

Vivi's voice was a low purr. "I come to the dress rehearsals to scout new talent. I had no idea I'd find you here. You should know by now; you never need to stoop to work so low as this. I pay much better."

Wilder's voice was clipped but still polite. "No, thank you, Vivi. I'm quite happy where I'm at."

Her smile froze on her face. "Really? Who's your coworker?"

Wilder looked at Rose with an apologetic look, as if he was offering her up to a wild animal. Rose perched eagerly on the balls of her toes with a feral grin. She was not easy prey.

"Vivi, this is Rose. We're ... friends."

Vivi heard the hesitation in his voice and pounced as if scenting blood. "Friends. How ... sweet."

Rose tried to not let Wilder's hesitation throw her off. He had good reason to doubt her right now, but she had no doubts about him. She needed to make sure Vivi knew that.

"Vivi ... that's such a lovely name. I can't believe I've heard *nothing* about you."

Vivi smirked. "Wilder's not one to kiss and tell. He's good about keeping special moments *private.*"

"Really?" Rose asked innocently. "In my experience, when he truly cares about someone, he's not afraid to talk about it."

Vivi leaned forward, and Rose wondered if she was as glued into her clothing as Rose was. "When it comes to attraction, words aren't necessary."

Rose pulled herself up to her full height and casually flipped her feathered headdress to reveal the long line of her neck and shoulder. "Everyone is attracted to Wilder. The question is, what does *he* want: something real or a meaningless fling?"

Vivi stared at Rose without blinking for several moments. A muscle in her jaw twitched, then her pink lips tightened into an angry pout. "Wilder, you are always welcome to come visit me if you tire of *this*." She gestured to the stage as if she meant the show, but her implication was clear. "If you're ever in the mood for a fling, you know where you can find it."

She spun around and began a slow sashaying walk up the aisle leading out of the theater. Rose's eyes followed her the entire way, not willing to relax her guard until this predator was safely out of range. When Vivi reached the last step, she turned around with a grin to confirm Wilder had watched her magnificent exit. At Vivi's fallen expression, Rose grinned with bared teeth, knowing he hadn't. Vivi huffed and stormed out.

Rose gave a smug grin but promptly lost it when she turned to see Wilder staring at her. His lips were slightly parted as he stared at her in surprise.

"Was I too much?" she asked tentatively. "I know I don't have a right to be jealous, but seriously, that woman was staring at you like a piece of meat. Well ... I admit I was also staring at you earlier, but still ... There was something about her that just set my teeth on edge. If you don't like that whole competitive vibe, I won't do it again. The last thing I want to do is make you mad—"

"I'm not mad," he said. "And I don't have any right to complain about competitiveness like that since I've done the same myself."

She sighed in relief. "Good." His comment made her think of Ylena, and Rose scowled as she stared at the last place Vivi stood. "How did Ylena not have a problem with that woman?"

She almost missed his soft laugh before he answered, "I think it's more accurate to say that Vivi didn't have a problem with Ylena. I think she sensed something ... different in you."

Rose flipped her feathered headdress over her shoulder with a smug grin. "You bet she did."

37

After her showdown with Vivi, Rose and Wilder split up to go to their respective dressing rooms to change back into their regular clothes. It felt strange taking off the pink feathers and putting back on her mismatched collection of clothes. The sparkly costume felt like one of the truest things she had worn recently. She hung the feathers and sequins as neatly as she could, then checked her old outfit in the mirror. It wasn't her, but she could at least stop hiding underneath the big sweater.

She walked to the performers' apartments and found the rest of the crew piled inside one of the small rooms. As she stepped inside, Feather handed her a slice of cheesy flatbread, and Fitz gave her a bottle of beer. She savored the delightfully stringy cheese, while watching Tayeh and Wilder across the room. He looked up and gave Rose a small nod of greeting.

Rev hadn't noticed Rose come in, but she sat on the bed, telling a Kieran a story with a wicked glint in her eye, and he threw back his head and laughed. Quinn and Kai sat together on the floor, having a quiet conversation surrounded by both white wolves. Her brother seemed genuinely happy and not as shy as before.

Rose looked at the group of people before her and realized something that surprised her.

She loved them.

They were her crew.

Her family.

The thought was so shocking to her that she took a sip of beer to hide her open-mouthed surprise. When had that happened? Vaylan forced her to run away with them the night they gained their Gifts. She didn't choose them, and they didn't choose her. But they remained together. They were each so different from her. And yet, she belonged.

She leaned against the door and ate her flatbread, savoring the strange feeling of belonging. She had grown up in a large family and belonged to a whole temple full of Priests, but this feeling was different. Before she could fully sort it out, Rev noticed her.

"Rose is here!" Rev's voice cut through all the others, and everyone quieted down. Rev folded her hands together in her lap and looked at Rose expectantly. "So ... what's the plan?"

The entire crew turned to look at her, and Rose wanted to yell at Rev for putting her on the spot. Except that the moment Rev asked, Rose realized she had the answer.

"We need to get into the Heart. Tell me what the tunnels are like."

Tayeh answered. "The tunnels range from six to eight feet wide, approximately ten feet tall. A thin line of crystalline runs along the top, providing the only light. If I were guarding it and I had enough people, I'd station them at the inner and the outer edge of each tunnel."

Wilder nodded. "We should assume Vaylan has a large troop of Sentinels. He's convinced a lot of people to become his Adopted. Who knows how many Sentinels he might have?"

"Are there any other ways in?" asked Rose.

"It's possible," said Quinn. "Ylena built the stairway leading from the Heart into the amphitheater. Maybe Fitz can burrow us a new tunnel through stone or dig down deep enough from Upstairs to see inside."

Fitz nodded. "We'll need to bring lanterns, or we will walk in the dark. I could shape the stone to draw a thin trickle of crystalline with us, but I'm not sure if Vaylan could sense something like that."

"That's a good point," said Rose. "We haven't seen the full extent of his Spark, so who knows what he is capable of."

It shocked Rose when Kieran took part in the conversation. "I don't know about you, but I don't like the idea of walking down a dark tunnel, unsure of what we will find at the other end. What's keeping someone from following behind us? We'd be trapped inside and forced to fight our way out, one direction or the other."

Fitz shrugged. "I guess I could close the stone up behind us as we go?"

Rose imagined being trapped inside a sealed tunnel with nothing but torchlight separating her from the darkness. "No!" Her voice was a little too high-pitched, so she coughed and said calmly, "Any other ideas?"

Feather raised a hesitant hand in the air.

"You don't have to raise your hand," said Rose. "You have just as much right to speak as anyone else."

Her voice was timid, but she spoke clearly. "Maybe we could wear a disguise?"

Rose cocked her head as she considered it. "Tell me more."

Feather seemed to gather her courage as she spoke.

"Well, the Sentinels walk in and out of the tunnels all the time. If we could get enough of their uniforms, we could all sneak in together." She bit her lip. "We would have to lure enough Sentinels at once to capture them and steal their uniforms before anyone got suspicious. Then we could sneak in, investigate, and get out as quickly as possible."

Feather nervously twisted her ponytail around her finger, waiting for Rose to respond.

Rose took a deep breath, then responded calmly. "Feather, why didn't you tell anyone you were a Goddess-damn military genius before now?"

Feather's eyes opened wide, unsure if that was a reprimand or a compliment. When Rose's lip curled into a smile, Feather giggled nervously behind her hand. Quinn patted her on the back, and the rest of the crew gave her encouraging smiles.

"Thanks to Feather, now we have a plan," said Rose. "Tomorrow, Wilder and I will go to our rehearsal, and the seven of you can work on a plan to trap at least nine Sentinels at once. Stone vines, water barriers—get creative, and see what you can do. Then we need to really focus on the tunnel exit. We'll need a distraction to lure several out at once. It must be something surprising enough to get them to follow, but not dangerous enough that they get suspicious."

Quinn tapped a finger on his lips. "I could send every cat in the Grotto stampeding toward their door?"

Rose imagined Sentinels trying to battle a herd of feral cats and grinned. "I love the visual of that, Quinn. First, see how easy it is to get a cat to stampede on command, then we will go from there."

He nodded as if she were his general giving him a direct order.

"Anything else we need to discuss?" When no one responded, she continued, "It looks like we'll be here a few days getting this plan into place, so settle in and get comfortable. But for tonight, let's just celebrate being part of the best Goddess-damn crew in the City!" She raised her bottle in salute, and the crew cheered in response.

She leaned back against the door and took a sip of beer before grimacing. Beer was not her favorite, but she drank it for the sake of the crew. As she took another sip, she looked across the room to see Wilder's eyes watching her every move. She held his eye contact, considering how to make up for the words she'd said.

She'd asked him before if this was how it would be between them—saying something stupid, then apologizing, over and over for all time. He said he hoped so. She had to trust he meant it.

He broke eye contact when Rev walked up to him. Rose couldn't hear what they said over the rest of the conversations happening in the small room, but she got the sense that they were talking about Vivi. Rev listened to Wilder's story with an open mouth until she suddenly burst out laughing. Rose smiled, then moved away from her place by the door.

Only the wolves noticed her as she walked toward the bathroom. She gave them a stern look, and they settled back down to their position near Quinn and Kai. She shook her head. Those girls were way too nosy about her business.

Rose pulled the bathroom door closed but since there was only one, she didn't lock it. Then she climbed onto the sink, unlatched the window, and slipped outside alone.

38

As Rose struggled to climb the outside of Ecstasy Theater, she realized she had been slacking off from her own training recently. The rest of the crew spent long hours sparring together, but she had spent most of her time watching them fight or lounging around debating Vaylan. Other than her poor performance against the two Sentinels, the last strenuous thing she had done was perform in the circus. She vowed that this climb to the top of the theater would be the beginning of her new training regimen.

She pulled herself up onto the highest point of the theater and took in the breathtaking view. The whole Grotto stretched before her, glowing in the crystal's constant white light. She looked over the edge of the roof, tracing the glowing crystalline trim with her eyes. Could Vaylan sense all the crystalline in the City? She shuddered to think how much crystalline wove its way through every building above and below.

"Rose."

She spun around at Wilder's voice. He wasn't even out of

breath, even though her pulse was still racing from the climb. "What are you doing up here?" he asked.

"I knew you would follow me. Well ... I *hoped* you would still follow me."

His jaw tightened. "You were testing me?"

"Yes," she said immediately. "And somehow, you always seem to pass."

He couldn't hide the smug grin that pulled at his lips. "I guess I'm exceptional."

"You are. You always have been. And now that you possess all the Gifts, you are exceptional beyond measure."

His smug smile turned hesitant. She cursed herself. Her truthful statement sounded too much like her mockery from the other night. She couldn't just rush into this apology the same way she barreled into fights. Her apology needed to begin slowly, with a confession.

"I was four years old the first time I remember calling the wind." His eyes widened at the strange leap in conversation, but he didn't interrupt her. "I'm sure I called it many times accidentally before that, but I remember that day clearly. I fell during a race and skinned my knee. It hurt, but most of my tears were in anger that I would lose the race." Her lips curled at the memory of her younger self, just as competitive as now.

"As Priests, we spend a lot of time learning how to use our Gifts, but no one really talks about what comes first. What produces a tear?"

She bit her lips, finding the words difficult to say. "It's a taboo conversation. All Priest children learn that it's extremely bad manners to ask what a Priest thinks about to stir their tears. It's private, between them and the Goddess. The only thing Mims told me was that I couldn't hurt myself to produce tears. She didn't tell me what I *should* think about, but she said self-harm wasn't the answer."

Other than a gentle wind that ruffled Wilder's hair, he stood unmoving, with his eyes focused only on her.

She took a deep breath. "Early on, I could cry when I thought of a childhood pet who died. But as the years passed and the pain faded, the tears no longer came, and eventually, my mind turned to darker thoughts. I imagined what it would be like if Mims died. The thought was so shocking that it brought immediate tears to my eyes. So, every day as I trained, I imagined Mims dead. Caed dead. Kai dead. I imagined gruesome and heart-wrenching deaths. Over and over, every day. I felt on edge, constantly terrified, and guilty over the images that my mind produced. Was there something wrong with me because I imagined their deaths every day? Did they know what I imagined? To stir their own tears, did they imagine me dead? I might have continued that strategy, except for one thing: the High Priest of Purpose killed Liam, Zain, and Ginger, my oldest brothers and sister."

She closed her eyes and pulled a shaking breath in through her nose. "I had imagined each of them dead so many times that even though I didn't see their actual murder, I knew exactly what it looked like. It was irrational, but I felt like I'd caused it. I imagined it, and it came true."

Rose's gaze unfocused as she mentally traveled back to those early days after their deaths. Even though they had been gone for five years, the crushing grief was still so near to the surface that it threatened to close her throat. "For a time, the tears came easily. Their dead bodies lingered behind my eyes day and night. Until one day, the tears dried up. I refused to imagine any more death, but the tears had stopped falling, and I didn't know how to start them again. I had no more sadness left to use. So, I used the only thing I had left. Rage."

Her voice dropped to a low growl. "I burned with an

anger so deep I couldn't contain it. I wanted to murder the High Priest of Purpose. I wanted to rip him apart with my bare hands. I wanted to fight every single High Priest until I ground them to dust underneath my feet. I took that rage buried deep within my heart, and I used it to train to fight. And the tears returned."

Her lips twisted in a rueful grimace. "But then the world turned upside down. The High Priests were defeated without my help, only to be replaced by the Wardens. My tears were no longer a sign of my purpose. Instead, I had lost my bond to the City, and every tear led me a step closer to death. And eventually, my tears meant nothing at all. I cried for days on end, weeping for everything I had lost, and nothing happened. My tears were completely useless." Her eyes flicked back to Wilder. He stood so still, the tears in his eyes the only sign that he had heard every word.

"Even though I don't need to produce tears anymore, I can't let go of my rage. Some days, it feels like the only weapon I have left. It's always there, simmering inside my chest, waiting to explode before I think through the consequences. I can call the rage to my hand and watch it cut before I've fully realized what I've done."

She looked deep into his dark eyes, willing a promise into each word. "I don't know how to lay down that weapon yet, but I will figure it out so I can be with you. You deserve someone whose first response is to trust you, not to lash out, and that's the woman I want to become."

Her confession had wrung her out, and she couldn't raise her voice above a whisper. "I'm so sorry, Wilder. You saved my life, and I responded by lashing out. I mocked you and your relationship to the Goddess, and I ran away from you instead of being strong enough to face what I had done. I'm still a mess in a lot of ways, but I'm no longer shocked by your Gifts. You don't need to hide them from me anymore. I want you to use them. Right now, in fact."

She moved closer to the edge of the roof, and Wilder jolted out of his calm stance, taking a step forward with a raised hand. "Rose! What are you doing?" He didn't approach her further, but remained hunched over as if he were afraid to startle her.

"I want to give you a sign. Proof that I accept you for who you are. I said a lot of words, but what are words compared to action?"

"Words are enough!" He edged a small step closer. "It's enough, Rose."

"But you gave me more than a few words, Wilder. You gave me an entire library."

He straightened slightly. "You saw it?"

"Fitz took me to make me feel guilty, and it worked. You backed up your words with actions, and so will I. I trust you, and I trust your Gifts. Don't hide your strength from me anymore. You can be your full self, and I will rise to meet you."

She balanced on a single foot. "You can pull me back from this edge in any number of ways. Or you can let me crash to the ground like I deserve. But even then, I know you will heal me again. I'm not afraid either way. I trust you."

He took another tentative step with his arm outstretched, but he was still too far away.

Her smile was tender, with just a hint of challenge. "I love you, Wilder." She stepped backward off the roof.

She didn't know how he would save her, but her guess was he would pull her back with a strong wind. That's what she appreciated about Discipline. It was simple and direct.

But Wilder was not just Discipline.

She hadn't noticed he had brought flowers with him until the vines sprang from his hands and wrapped around her waist, halting her fall. A ripple of the stone directly under her foot stopped her downward momentum. He held out a hand, beckoning her forward, and the wave of stone crested and deposited her back on the roof, directly in front of him, so gently she didn't even stumble.

Even though she was safe, the vines didn't stop growing. They slid away from her waist and poured in a massive profusion over the side of the building, and among the green leaves, giant red roses bloomed. The stone continued its rippling wave, and crystalline trembled in its wake. Without Vaylan's direct control, the crystalline flowed properly along stone at Wilder's command. He held out his arms, and a stone pillar formed at each corner of the roof. He raised his hands, clapping them overhead, and the pillars arched into the sky, melting into a delicate stone canopy. Crystalline flowed up along the stone, casting a warm glow where they stood.

The roses bloomed until they covered the entire roof. Rose and Wilder couldn't move without stepping on flowers. Luckily, neither of them wanted to leave.

Wilder lowered his arms to his sides, and a warm wind blew around them. Red petals swirled in the sweet-smelling air as the breeze tickled softly through Rose's hair.

He placed his hand gently on her cheek and lifted her face to meet his.

Her voice was a dreamy whisper. "You do nothing part way, do you?"

His mouth curled as he whispered across her lips, "I told you I was exceptional."

She grabbed him behind the neck and pulled his lips to her own. He was more than exceptional. He was all she wanted and more. She was not afraid of his power, not intimidated by him. Because she knew something that made her feel stronger than she ever imagined possible.

Wilder loved her, too.

She would battle Vivi for him. She would defeat Sentinels for him. She would storm the Heart of the Grottos for him. And because she loved him so much, she wouldn't go alone, but would lead a crew instead.

She pulled him closer, her heart beating like thunder in her chest. She would kiss him here atop a glowing tower, spilling roses onto the street below until the sun came up. And since there was no sun in the Underneath, she would kiss him even longer.

Except a yipping sound came from their feet. Rose tried to ignore it and even kicked out a foot to scatter the wolves, but Wilder chuckled and gently pulled away.

Rose growled. "I would look stunning in a wolf coat."

The wolves sank down onto their paws in the field of roses. Wilder cocked his head, then bit his lips to keep from smiling.

"What did they say?" she asked.

"Quinn sent them because the crew was worried you had run off to do something dangerous." Rose wanted to huff in anger, but she also knew that her entire plan was based on Wilder believing the same thing.

She narrowed her eyes. "What did they say about me?"

Wilder kept his face perfectly neutral. "They said they gave you time alone with me because you're the alpha, but it's not fair for you to monopolize all my time. You are a very selfish wolf."

"Hey!" She pointed at them with a stern finger. "I will spend time alone with Wilder whenever I choose, and you better get used to it!"

Pickles gave a short whine before ducking her head again.

Wilder covered his smile with his hand. "She says they knew me first."

Rose rolled her eyes. "Well, you ladies ruined the moment, so we might as well go back." Rose looked up at the glowing canopy arching overhead. "Also, maybe we shouldn't stand under a giant crystalline beacon?"

Wilder shrugged. "I assume Vaylan has people watching us at all times, so he probably already knew we were here."

A thought clicked into place in Rose's head. "That's why he cares for so many children. He's using them as spies."

A dark cloud passed across Wilder's face. "I was his spy when I was a child." He shrugged. "I have to give him credit for teaching me a valuable skill."

Rose frowned as she looked across the Grotto. She wasn't sure if Vaylan was in the Haven or maybe the Heart tonight. But she would stop him eventually.

She took Wilder's hand. "Let's get back before the wolves tattle on us. We should get some sleep. Tomorrow, we're performing in a show and planning an invasion."

He grinned, and they began the climb down the building together.

SHOWTIME

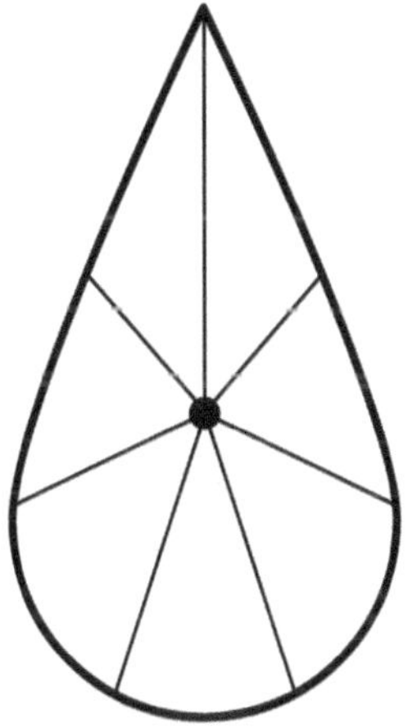

39

After they spent the night celebrating their plan, the crew slept late the next day. By the time everyone had dragged themselves out of bed, it was time for Rose and Wilder to get to the theater for their preparations before the show. Rose sent the wolves with Quinn so they could plan how to use them in their trap. As Rose and Wilder headed to the theater together, she gave a backward look to the wolves, who stared at her with cold eyes. She gave them a smug grin and put her hand in Wilder's.

When they walked inside, there was a lot of discussion among the performers about what had happened atop the theater the night before. Only Rose had seen Wilder's performance, but everyone could clearly see the effect. He had reshaped the roof of the theater into an open tower with arching stone, crystalline, and red roses spilling down the front of the building. Occasionally, rose petals would drift down from above, creating an even more stunning entrance. Every time a showgirl cooed about how romantic it looked, Wilder's face grew even cockier.

She loved that about him.

After the director gave them a few last-minute blocking changes, Rose and Wilder were free to relax until show time. They found a quiet corner backstage, and Wilder sat with his back propped against the wall as Rose lounged against him.

"I just can't wrap my mind around what Vaylan is trying to accomplish," she said. "I think I understand him, but then we have another conversation, and I feel even more confused than when we started."

Wilder sighed. "Yeah, sounds like Vaylan. He's so good at manipulation that he can spin his words until you stop believing what you know to be true."

Rose hesitated, unsure if she should ask the question. "What was he like?"

Wilder's face slid into a faraway expression, and she wasn't sure if he would answer. His dark eyes were filled with love and sadness as a single tear fell onto his cheek. She reverently took his offered hand.

Rose was suddenly a child. She found her shorter height disorienting but studied her small brown hands with interest. She was Wilder when he was around five years old, close to the time when Vaylan disappeared out of his life.

Vaylan stood above her and peeked around the corner of a dark alley in Chaos. His eyes narrowed as he focused on what he saw, and he ignored his child at his feet.

Rose sighed in relief, although she wasn't sure why. When Vaylan turned his dark eyes onto her, her flinch was out of her control.

"Okay, Wilder, time to do what I taught you."

She peeked around the corner and saw two scary-looking men having a conversation. Her heartbeat sped up, and her small hands felt clammy.

Vaylan lowered himself to look her in the eyes. He looked a lot younger, but to her small eyes, he was so large. "You aren't afraid, are you? All you have to do is sneak up, pay attention to what they say, then come back without being seen." His warm smile showed fewer wrinkles, but the dimple was just the same. "I'll be right here. You'll be fine."

The part of her that was Rose wanted to say a few words to him about using children for his goals, but instead, she turned and crept down the alley.

She moved along the edges, hiding behind boxes and discarded items until she was close enough to hear the men's voices. Most of it was a blur, but she picked out the words she was listening for.

"... The delivery is tomorrow at noon ..."

She locked the words in her mind and began her slow journey back to where Vaylan stood. As she ducked under a leaning stack of boards, she tripped, and the boards fell with a crash.

Her back stiffened in fear. The scary men's faces locked on her, and she fled. Their footsteps rang loud behind her, but she made it to the end of the alley where she would be safe.

Except Vaylan was gone.

Her small heart felt like it would explode from pounding so hard. She looked around the street in terror but couldn't find him anywhere. The men were a few steps away, but she ducked out of their grasp and ran.

She ran through the streets with no clear direction. Rose wondered how much of her confusion was from her own lack of experience in Chaos or from young Wilder's spiking terror. She wanted to stop and fight these jerks, but the thought of young Wilder's body in their hands made her run even faster.

As she skidded around a corner, she realized she hadn't heard their footsteps for several blocks. Her lungs heaved in gasping breaths, and she sagged against the wall. After her breathing returned to normal, she began the slow walk home.

Her feet knew the way even though Rose herself didn't. She studied the neighborhood from Wilder's small perspective and found it even more terrifying than she had as an adult. Her footsteps were quiet, and the people on the street ignored her. Rose realized that's why children made such excellent spies. No one wanted to look too closely and risk discovering that a child needed help they weren't prepared to give.

She approached a dingy little house that looked like all the dingy little houses around it. Her footsteps slowed as she approached, and she hesitated to go inside.

The door flew open. Inside stood the most beautiful woman Rose had ever seen. She realized her perspective was altered by young Wilder's eyes, but Rose recognized the beauty she saw every day on Wilder's face. The woman's skin was the same deep brown, and her cheekbones were just as defined. Her hair was raven-black like his and curled in thick waves past her shoulders. But her eyes were a bright amber gold. Wilder's eyes were dark as night, just like Vaylan's.

Rose stared up at the beautiful woman with a confusing mixture of love and terror. She scanned the woman's face, looking for a sign of her current mood, and when her eyes flared in anger, Rose flinched.

"Where have you been?" Wilder's mother grabbed Rose by the arm and pulled her inside without closing the door. "I told you to stay in your room!"

Rose wanted to run, but she couldn't look away from the woman. She desperately wanted to find the right words to make her smile. "I stayed in my room all morning, but Vaylan told me—"

The woman slapped Rose across the face so hard she stumbled backward and landed on the ground. Rose sat blinking, trying to figure out what happened. She felt disoriented again, surprised that she was so small and weak that a slap could knock her down. Then her mind caught up to the fact that this was Wilder's mother slapping him as a child. The part of her that was

Rose flared into a wildfire. She considered the best way to kill this woman with her childlike hands.

Before Rose could strike, she noticed Vaylan strolling toward the open door. He walked casually, as if he didn't have a care in the world. As if he hadn't just abandoned his son to escape thugs in an alley alone. Her murderous thoughts alternated between which of Wilder's parents to kill first.

Vaylan stepped through the open door and barely glanced at his son on the floor before turning his smiling attention onto Wilder's mother.

"Niara." His voice was a warm drawl as he reached his hands to her waist. "You look stunning today, dear."

She slapped his hands away. "Don't try to sweet talk me, Vaylan. I told your son to stay in his room, but you took him out on one of your schemes."

Vaylan smirked, and his dimple shone. "Those schemes are how we eat, dear." He twirled a lock of her hair around his finger as he stared into her eyes. "I will keep us fed, and you continue to be the most beautiful woman in the Underneath."

A hint of her anger dissipated, and Rose's body sighed in relief.

Niara's eyes were softer, but her voice was still an angry hiss. "Tell your son to stop calling you 'Vaylan.' It's unnatural."

Vaylan turned to look at Rose still sprawled on the floor. His eyes were unconcerned with how she got there.

"What did you learn?" Vaylan spoke as if his child were a soldier giving a report.

Rose straightened her spine and said in a clear voice, "Tomorrow at noon."

Vaylan nodded once, then turned back to Niara, all thoughts of Wilder gone.

"My current scheme is going to be very profitable." Vaylan's voice was a warm purr, and he took hold of Niara's waist with a possessive hand. "What should we do to celebrate?"

Niara's anger fled completely, and she melted into Vaylan's arms.

Rose's small body relaxed as Vaylan and Niara focused on each other, not her. She looked between her bedroom door and the open door leading outside, then slowly backed to the open door and fled out into Grotto Chaos, where it was safe.

Rose opened her eyes to see Wilder scanning her face for a reaction. She had so many emotions running through her mind that she wasn't sure what he would see first. Lingering fear from young Wilder's eyes. Sadness at the thought of Wilder's lost childhood. Burning anger at both of his parents.

"What happened to her?" she asked.

Wilder sighed. "I went back to Chaos a few years ago to look for her. A neighbor told me she died the year before. She had a wasting illness that struck suddenly." His eyes took on a faraway look. "I was both relieved and disappointed I didn't see her before she died."

"You loved her," she said simply.

"Yes." He gave a sad smile. "It's complicated."

She had felt the complex tangle of emotions even within his child's heart and nodded in understanding. "And Vaylan?" she asked.

"I wanted to please him. Even now, there's a part of me that is desperate for him to acknowledge me. But I know he can't. In many ways, he's as sick as my mother was."

Rose put Wilder's memory in context with the Vaylan she knew. Every time she talked to him, she felt confused, but she couldn't see the manipulation for herself. When she placed her memories alongside Wilder's, Vaylan came into focus.

Vaylan used Rose to accomplish his schemes like he used Wilder. She knew Vaylan was the one who ordered the Sentinels to attack Brother Owyn and make it look like the

High Priests did it. Yet he caused her to believe Brother Owyn was responsible for his own death.

Vaylan sweet-talked Rose, telling her what she wanted to hear like he did Wilder's mother. He showed Rose all the good things he appeared to be doing. He told her she was special even without her Gift. He made her believe she needed him.

"His true nature seems so clear to me right now, but I'm worried that as soon as he opens his mouth, I will fall for his tricks again." She looked into Wilder's haunted eyes and felt a cold resolve settle over her. "I need to keep you close to my side so I don't forget."

His lips curled into a smile, and he squeezed her hand. "It's a deal."

40

A stage manager called for the cast to begin their final preparations, and Wilder and Rose stood from their cozy place backstage with echoing sighs. Rose turned toward her dressing room, but Wilder grabbed hold of her hand and pulled her into an embrace.

She went willingly into his arms and rested her fingers lightly on his cheeks as he bent his head to kiss her. Her whole body relaxed, all the fear and confusion and anger caused by his memory floating away. He kissed her so long that she forgot where she stood, where she was going, what she should do next. As he gently pulled away from her, she blinked open dreamy eyes to see his same confident smile.

He was still close enough that she could feel his deep voice rumble against her chest. "I thought I should get one last kiss before we begin. You're about to put on a cute little outfit, then stand calmly next to me on stage, and I won't be allowed to kiss you like that again until it's all over."

Her heart skipped a beat at his words, but she was no longer angry that he had that effect on her. "There's always intermission," she said breathlessly.

He laughed, then gave her a peck on the cheek. "I'll see you on stage."

Rose had too much dignity to skip to her dressing room, but even she had to admit her footsteps were lighter than usual. She pulled on her first costume, a white dress with fluttering ribbons that fell to her knees but showed quite a bit of leg when she walked. Two wide strips of fabric crossed her chest and looped around her neck to form the bodice. Hazel had cleverly kept Rose's arms and back bare but covered up Vaylan's mark.

After the required amount of wiggling into place, strategic gluing, and a healthy dose of glitter, Rose made her way backstage to find Wilder waiting for her in the wings. Rose didn't know how Hazel had guessed the exact size of white leather pants Wilder needed, but he looked like he had been poured into them. The glitter supplier had also discovered him, and his bare chest shimmered with a faint glow, his tattoo of the Goddess's symbol the only adornment.

He gave her an appreciative look up and down, and she gave him the same. As she stepped closer, she realized her ridiculously high heels brought her almost to his eye level. She wondered if it would be different to kiss him from this height.

He appeared to have the same thought because he leaned forward and caught her in a kiss. His lips met hers from an equal height, but he stole her breath just the same. His fingers gently skimmed along her jawline, careful to not smudge her makeup.

As if she would have cared.

Before she could rub handprints through his glitter, he grinned and twisted out of her range. He took hold of her hand, and they walked on stage together right on cue.

Their part was almost as simple as it was for the finale. The little director had been correct. Rose and Wilder were just warm bodies.

As Rose looked at Wilder in his costume, her body felt even warmer than usual. Luckily, her look of desire was perfectly appropriate for the show. Wilder took her hand and spun her around in one of their few moves in the song. Her grin was permanently plastered on her face.

Until a pair of Sentinels stepped on stage.

No one had noticed their matte black armor in the shadows backstage, but when they stepped into the stage light, the theater erupted in screams. The crew and performers scrambled in all directions, and the audience began trampling one another in their attempt to flee out the back of the theater.

Rose stared at the Sentinels, kicked her shoes off, then fell into a fighting stance. She reached for her blades, only to recognize her costume was so small she couldn't hide any. And to her shame, she hadn't even considered the possibility.

The Sentinels' heads pivoted to Wilder at her side, and she realized that Wilder's extremely well-fitted pants meant he wasn't carrying a blade, either. She looked around for anything she could use as a weapon. The only thing remotely dangerous-looking was a prop lamp post, which she ripped from the stage and hefted like a staff.

The Sentinels hadn't moved, but they fixed their masked faces on Wilder. "Run!" she yelled at him, as she threw herself at the Sentinels, swinging the lamp post in a long arc.

The Sentinels fled as she approached, running off stage the way they came. She chased them backstage, still wielding the lamp post. They ran past screaming performers and crew and out the back door onto the street.

Rose took two steps to follow them outside before pulling herself to a halt. What were these Sentinels trying to do? They hadn't even tried to attack. Why would they give up so easily? And why would she follow them? The crew was planning to sneak inside the Heart, and she didn't want to ruin that. And what would happen to Wilder as she ran after these Sentinels? What if there were more hiding in the theater waiting for him?

She turned with a gasp to run back onstage to Wilder, only to find him standing behind her.

"I'm surprised you didn't run after them," he said.

Rose read the shock in his raised eyebrow, and the anger in his tightened lips. She tried to explain. "I thought there might be more waiting for me to leave you alone."

A slow blink of exasperation. "You attacked two Sentinels with a prop lamp post."

She shrugged. "It's all I had."

His head cocked—a setup before his final strike. "I have all the Gifts, Rose. All of them. And you ran after Sentinels ... with a lamp post ... to protect me."

She chewed on her lip, unsure how to answer his good point.

He sighed. "When are you going to stop trying to protect me?"

She knew the answer to that question. "Never," she growled.

His eyebrows rose at her fierce tone.

They were alone backstage now that all the performers had fled, and she slowly stalked toward him. "I will never stop trying to protect you." She stopped directly in front of him, and even though she was shorter than him again without her heels, she straightened her spine to give her every inch of height she had.

She spoke with the ring of command. "You are mine, Wilder. Now and forever. I will not let Sentinels take you. Vaylan will not touch you. If your mother was still alive and raised a finger toward you, I would *crush* her. I know you are stronger than all of them, stronger than me, but I don't care. I will fight anyone who tries to hurt you. I will change so I don't lash out at you in anger, but here's one thing that I refuse to change—if anyone tries to hurt you, I will destroy them."

All the conflicting feelings on Wilder's face shifted until one of them shone brighter than the others.

Desire.

They grabbed each other with ferocious hunger. Back to her usual height, she clung to his neck to keep her knees from buckling. His hands tangled in her hair, spilling her carefully styled curls into disarray. She pulled him closer, her fingers sliding across his strong back, smearing glitter in riotous streaks. They kissed until they were both a mess of glitter, smudged lipstick, and disheveled hair.

Wilder was the first to pull away. Despite his breathlessness, he was able to form a coherent thought. "We should find the crew. They need to know what happened."

Rose's thoughts lingered on Wilder's lips, but she forced herself to remember why they were standing alone backstage in the first place. She wondered sadly if she would ever get to perform with Wilder again. "You're right," she sighed. She noticed her pink lipstick on his lips and smothered a giggle. "Is my lipstick as messy as yours?"

His eyes dropped to her lips, and his sultry whisper caused her breathing to hitch. "It's fairly obvious what we've been up to." He rested his palm on her cheek as he rubbed his thumb gently along the curve of her lower lip.

She leaned into his palm, and her eyes dropped to his glitter-streaked chest. "We should clean up before we go," she whispered. She rested her hand on his tattoo, preparing to wipe off the glitter.

She felt his heartbeat leap beneath her palm before he caught hold of her wrist. He cleared his throat and said, "I don't think we have time for glitter removal, dear."

She sighed, then followed him to find the crew. She didn't know what Vaylan was up to, but she was finally ready to make a plan together with her family.

$$\sim$$

The crew's rooms were empty. The silence sent a shiver of foreboding down Rose's spine.

"They're probably training." Wilder injected his voice with confidence, but Rose could hear the doubt below the surface. She didn't call him on his false optimism but merely stared at him with a question in her eyes.

He took a deep breath, then nodded, agreeing to her unasked question by pulling a stash of weapons out from under the bed.

She pulled on her turquoise boots and started strapping daggers on top of her costume.

After fully arming themselves, they walked in nervous silence to the training space. Rose expected to see Sentinels around every corner, but the streets were empty.

Just like the training room.

All their training supplies were stacked neatly, with no sign of a struggle. With nothing out of place, it looked like the crew had simply stepped out for a break. Rose felt a tingle of wrongness but couldn't identify it.

Wilder's voice sounded shaky as he struggled to hold

onto his confident demeanor. "Let's look nearby. Maybe they are picking up dinner or gathering supplies."

Rose nodded numbly but knew he believed his words as little as she did.

They looked inside restaurants and shops for two blocks before they saw the child watching them. The girl looked like one of the many children wandering the Underneath, except when Wilder nodded at her, she fled into the shadows.

"He knows where we are," said Rose.

Wilder frowned. "Yes, it appears he does."

Rose looked toward the crystalline beacon highlighting the Haven. "Do you know what I'm thinking?"

Wilder raised an eyebrow. "That you'd like to run all the way to the Haven, see if Vaylan has the crew, and then murder him?"

Rose growled, "Yes, but not necessarily in that order."

"For once, we agree," he said.

Her face lit up. "Really?"

"Well, I think we should find the crew *before* we murder him, in case he's hidden them somewhere. But if he's taken them, I will gladly watch you tear him limb from limb."

Rose's lips curled in a feral grin. "That's the most romantic thing you've ever said to me."

They stalked toward the Haven together.

41

The two women in white outside the Haven stepped apart quickly to let Rose and Wilder pass. Rose didn't have to show her mark to gain their entrance, so the women were expecting them.

Which meant Vaylan was waiting for them.

Rose's senses buzzed with the exhilaration before a fight and the lingering desire from her passionate kiss with Wilder. The muscles in his back tensed in preparation for attack, and his eyes burned with a hard determination. She matched her footsteps to his as he stomped down the inner hallway of the Haven. She had dreamed of this moment since the first time she imagined defeating heretics with Wilder by her side. When he slammed his hands into the giant doors of Vaylan's study, her heart almost exploded in ecstasy.

They burst into the room to find Vaylan calmly sitting in his chair near the fire. Rose recognized his smile as the same on he had used on Wilder's mother to distract her from her anger.

"I'm so glad you arrived," he said warmly. "Come have a seat." He gestured to the two cushioned chairs before him.

Rose and Wilder didn't move. "Where are they?" she said, a blade held in each hand.

"I assume you are speaking about the Chosen?" he asked eyes twinkling. "They are safe for now."

"Tell us where they are," Rose growled. "Otherwise, I will kill you first, then look for them myself."

He clicked his tongue like a disapproving parent. "There's no need to get nasty, Rose. They are safe. But if I don't return tonight, I have instructed their guards to execute all seven of them."

Rose clenched her fists so hard her whole body shook. He was casually talking about murdering the crew. Her crew. Her brother included. If she wasn't already planning on murdering him, this would have secured his death in her mind.

"What do you want, Vaylan?" said Wilder coldly.

Vaylan's eyes lit up, pleased that Wilder finally spoke. "I want to see prophecy unfold as it should. Rose delivered the Chosen into my hands just as the prophecy foretold."

"I didn't deliver them to you," hissed Rose. "You kidnapped them!"

"There was no need for me to kidnap them. They came right to me." His smile revealed his dimple. "And you led them there."

"No, I did not! I haven't seen them since this morning!"

"Yes, but they saw you." He leaned back in his chair as if perfectly relaxed.

Rose couldn't piece together his logic, but Wilder did. "They were at the show."

"They were lucky enough to receive seven free tickets and went to watch your performance." He chuckled softly. "And you performed exactly as expected, Rose."

Her mind raced as she thought through his words. The crew had been in the audience. They saw the Sentinels.

They saw Rose kick off her shoes, pick up a prop, and chase the Sentinels off stage. The crew wouldn't know she stopped before following them outside. They would expect her to do as she usually did—follow the Sentinels back to their lair.

And the crew had followed to rescue her.

Rose staggered back a step. The crew attacked the Sentinels' lair, storming the Heart of the Grottos and disregarding their planned trap. They'd assumed she had rushed in like a fool and had put themselves at risk to save her.

Because they loved her.

She bellowed in rage. Vaylan had used her again, the same way he used her to kill Mayra and the other High Priests. He knew he could count on her to attack without thinking, and he'd used that knowledge to manipulate his prophecy into coming true.

She took a single step forward before Wilder grabbed her hand in a tight fist. "Rose!" His whisper was a low rumble. "Think!"

Vaylan aimed his dimpled grin at Rose and shook his head like a fond parent. "Brother Owyn's prophecy took into account how rarely you think before rushing into danger. I assumed you'd deliver the Chosen to me back in Rivalry, but instead, you managed to get yourself stabbed by a Sentinel." He chuckled, then folded his hands in a serene pose. "But the prophecy worked itself in its own time, as it always does."

She couldn't think. All she could do was feel. The heat pouring out of the fireplace was smothering her, and her lungs boiled like an inferno. She felt rage bubbling up inside of her, the same rage she had channeled into tears when she had her Gift. She wanted to surrender to it, wanted to let it consume her. She would kill Vaylan without a hint of regret.

Until it got her crew murdered.

The thought doused her back into reality. Her rage was pointless and would accomplish nothing. Her muscles slackened, and Wilder's hand fell away. Her voice felt scratchy from her scream, but she spoke calmly. "What do you want, Vaylan?"

He sank further into his chair, a patronizing smile on his lips. "I wanted peace, which is why I made a truce with the Priests. As long as no Priest attacked me, I would leave them be." He shook his head sadly. "Unfortunately, my Sentinels were attacked by seven Priests, so now that truce is over."

"They aren't Priests, and you know it," she hissed.

"Everyone saw the seven of them use their Gifts to attack my people." His dark eyes glittered. "The Priests have ruled too long. I won't stop until the Goddess's religion is dismantled. And the two of you will join me."

The hair on the back of her neck stood on end at his cold threat. She shook her head. "We will never join you, Vaylan. You're insane."

A flicker of anger passed across his eyes, the first authentic emotion she had seen from him other than amused condescension. "It's a good thing I believe enough for all of us, because your lack of faith is exhausting."

Wilder spoke first. "What will happen to our crew if we join you?"

Rose glared at him. How could he even consider surrendering?

"Not *if* you decide. *When* you decide to follow me, we will work together to accomplish my goals. Rose will darken the crystals, removing every scrap of the Goddess's power from this City. When the crystals' light fades, the Chosen's Gifts will fade with it. Your *crew* will return to normal people like everyone else. I will drain the last drop of her power from the City and then rule it correctly."

"I've been trying to get the Goddess to return her Gifts.

What would convince me to darken the crystals if I even knew how?"

Vaylan shrugged. "I don't know. I only know that you will."

Rose shook her head. It had to be insanity. She started to say so, but Wilder cut her off again.

"What about me?"

Vaylan raised an eyebrow. "You mean your Gift? Yes, I know you called the wind the night the two of you fled from me. You will lose your Gift along with the others. Once the crystals are dark, I will destroy all the crystalline, then rebuild this City as its new founder. And you, Wilder, will follow me."

"You will not take anything from me," said Wilder with cold determination.

Vaylan's eyes twinkled. "I guess it's possible you'll surrender your Gift willingly. On that point, the prophecy wasn't specific." He stood slowly from his chair. "While you are both here, let's sit down and have a meal together. The sooner the two of you submit to my leadership, the easier this process will be. Let me call someone to bring us a meal."

"No," said Wilder sharply. "We are leaving." He stepped closer to the door but didn't take his eyes off Vaylan. Rose adjusted her knives in her hands and watched for Sentinels.

"I'd rather you stayed," said Vaylan, a hint of frustration coloring his voice. "This is what's best. You both should realize this by now."

Rose and Wilder continued their slow steps out the door, then began their way down the long corridor.

Vaylan stepped into his doorway and raised his voice for the first time the whole night. "I said, don't leave!" He raised his hand in the air, then tightened it into a fist, and trickles of crystalline began dripping down from the ceiling. The few Adopted roaming the hallway scattered in all directions.

Rose bared her knives at the dripping crystalline but was unsure how to battle it. The knives were useless against crystalline, but she could take Vaylan out in a heartbeat. She focused her sights on him and raised her knife to throw.

Wilder stepped in front of her, arms outstretched with palms facing up. As a tear trickled down his cheek, he flexed his fingers, and stone flowed from the ceiling, covering the crystalline inside stalactites before they could touch Rose or any of the Adopted.

Vaylan's upraised arm fell limply to his side as he tried to understand what was happening. When he finally did, his voice broke in a ragged scream. "Wilder! You will surrender all your Gifts to me immediately!"

Wilder flinched at Vaylan's voice, but he didn't move. Rose saw the memory of childhood terror flash behind his eyes, with his instinct freezing him to the spot. Vaylan's wide eyes fixed on his son, and Rose saw senseless fury within.

She had to get Wilder out.

"Wilder!" She pulled at his arm, but he stood as unmoving as stone while Vaylan stalked toward him down the long hallway. "Let's go!"

Wilder's eyes were viewing some memory from his past and didn't see her. Her voice rose in panic, and she pounded her fist against his muscular chest. "Wilder! Look at me, Goddess-dammit! You are mine. I will not let him have you."

Wilder blinked and appeared surprised to see Rose in front of him. He looked at Vaylan stalking closer and turned and ran for the door out of the Haven. The second they crossed the threshold, he raised a hand palm out and swiped downward. A thin stream of stone slid down over the opening, trapping Vaylan inside.

Rose tried to pull Wilder away from the stone-covered

doorway, but he watched it with unseeing eyes and wouldn't budge. The two women Adopted who had let them pass stared at the stone and whispered frantically at one another. Wilder looked up at their panicked voices and spoke to them kindly. "The stone barrier isn't thick. Find someone who can chip through it to help them escape."

The women stared at him with wide eyes but nodded at his instructions.

Wilder turned and walked away, and Rose hurried to his side.

"Why did you tell them that?" said Rose.

"There are Adopted inside. I don't want them trapped." He sighed. "Plus, Vaylan needs to get back to the Heart, or else they will kill the crew."

Rose didn't respond. That hadn't crossed her mind the moment she'd hefted her knife to throw at Vaylan.

Wilder's footsteps slowed, and he turned to face her. "What should we do now?"

Her eyes widened. "You're asking me? My decisions tonight have been questionable, so I was hoping you had an idea."

He shrugged. "You're the crew leader, Rose. The only thing I can think of is to walk around aimlessly until we think of the next step." His shoulders sagged, and his usually confident face looked fragile and sad.

She took his hand and gave him a gentle smile. "That sounds like a good plan to me. Let's walk."

42

R ose and Wilder wandered for several blocks before the wolves found them. Wilder had stopped in the middle of the street and cocked his head in concentration, and a few moments later, Rose saw the wolves come into view. Both wolves ran around them in narrow circles before rubbing against Wilder's legs and licking his outstretched hand.

Rose had been angry when they'd interrupted her kiss with Wilder the night before, but sensing their relief at finding Wilder soothed a bit of her irritation. He murmured quiet words to them, and they stopped their frantic licking. He cocked his head to the side, listening as they strode in anxious patterns around his legs.

"What are they saying?" asked Rose.

Wilder's face grew grim the longer he listened. "Vaylan told the truth about the crew. A guy outside the theater handed them tickets to the show after Rev flirted with him."

Rose nodded. "Sounds typical. That wouldn't seem suspicious."

Wilder continued listening. "The crew saw the Sentinels on stage but were too far away to help, so they exited the

273

theater with the rest of the crowd. They saw a Sentinel run around a corner, followed by a woman with red hair. They were far away but knew where the Sentinel was headed, so they took a shortcut to arrive at the Heart."

The wolves began whining, and Wilder leaned down to stroke their fur and still their frantic circling. Rose was jealous of the attention; she felt just as anxious as the wolves looked.

"They attacked the two Sentinels standing guard, but then an entire troop swarmed them before they could even enter the tunnel leading to the Heart. They fought back and took down several Sentinels, but there were too many of them."

If anyone had been watching, they would have seen exactly what Vaylan planned: a group of Priests attacking the Heart. Rose held her breath, terrified to hear how the story ended.

"A Sentinel got hold of Kieran and held a knife to his throat. The rest of the crew surrendered. The Sentinels bound them and forced them to drink the tea that blocks their Gift. Before Quinn took a drink, he told the wolves to run and find us. The wolves fled but watched from a distance as the Sentinels led the crew inside the tunnel leading into the Heart. The wolves have been roaming the Grotto trying to follow our scent ever since."

Rose loosed her breath in a rush and sank down next to the wolves. She patted them affectionately on the scruff of their necks. "Thank you for finding us. At least we know for sure where they are without just blindly trusting Vaylan."

"Should we keep walking?" asked Wilder.

Rose stood up and took his hand again. "Yes, but I'm ready to leave the Underneath." He gave a nod of understanding, and they walked toward the looping bridge leading Upstairs.

Rose expected to find Sentinels searching for them at every turn, but few people paid attention to them at all. The wolves got a few strange looks, and Wilder always received attention, especially in Desire. But tonight, his face was drawn and his swagger non-existent, so he wasn't propositioned as much as usual.

They made it to the top of the bridge, and Rose was relieved to find it was still dark. It was easy to lose track of time in the Underneath, and it often felt like perpetual night. Even though Rose was not fond of the dark, she wasn't ready for the bright light of day yet, either.

The City had changed even more while they had been in the Underneath. People roamed freely through the streets, despite the late hour, and the anti-Priest factions had grown. A mob of people stood outside of Temple Purity, heckling a row of Priests standing guard around the perimeter. A few of the hecklers threw things and yelled obscenities, but the Priests didn't move from their position, not even when one pushed an older male Priest. Rose moved to attack before Wilder pulled her back.

"Rose, this isn't your fight. Not today." His voice was calm but did little to soothe the anger inside. But she recognized the truth of his words and followed him deeper into the City.

It had only been a few weeks since she had been in Purity Diocese and believed that a Pageant was all it would take for the Goddess to restore her Gifts and to return Rose's life to normal. But now, Rose couldn't imagine going back to her old life. Would she ever be content to live in a room by herself in Temple Discipline, training in her Gift day and night? To live that life would mean giving up her current life with Wilder and the crew. She wouldn't give up the new life she had discovered for anything.

Not even for the return of her Gift.

The thought shocked her in its honesty. There was a time when she'd thought the Goddess had returned a Gift to Mayra or one of her cronies. Rose had been prepared to use violence to force the Priest to confess how they'd kept their Gift. She would have stolen the Gift from them if she could. It had been Vaylan manipulating crystalline, not a Purpose Priest, but that hadn't erased Rose's thought.

Back then, she would have given anything to have her Gift returned. Now her Gift was meaningless compared to her desire to rescue the crew.

She knew where Wilder had been leading her for some time. His aimless wandering had eventually turned in a straight line toward the center of the City, and Rose didn't object. Worry lined his face, and his fragile expression broke her heart. Rose wanted to murder Vaylan for causing that look on Wilder's face. She added it to the list of all his offenses.

Rose was relieved to find the amphitheater empty. Since Vaylan had taken over the Heart, she assumed it was just a matter of time before he claimed the amphitheater as well. But for now, he had drained it of all its crystalline, leaving it the darkest place in the City because of its distance from each of the seven crystal spires. The only light at all came from the crystal basin directly at center stage.

Wilder walked toward it with purpose and a hopeful expression on his face. Rose ground her teeth, irritated that he believed the Goddess had anything to offer. And then she was ashamed of how little faith she still possessed.

She walked reluctantly to his side. He still wore only his white pants, and his tattoo blazed against his dark skin in the basin's light. She remembered asking, why did the Goddess choose Wilder and not her? But now, the question seemed ridiculous.

Of course the Goddess would choose Wilder. Not only

was he stunning and gregarious and one of the kindest people she knew, but he also possessed a level of faithfulness that Rose just didn't have. His devotion to the Goddess was written across his face as clearly as the tattoo on his chest. In that moment, she realized he was truly worthy of all the Gifts, and the Goddess had chosen wisely when she picked him.

She gasped as a thought clicked into place. "Wilder. It's you."

He turned away from the basin and looked at her with confusion. "What are you talking about?"

"Vaylan keeps talks about the prophecies and interchanges the word 'Seven' with 'Chosen.' But they aren't the same. He captured the Seven. But the prophecy about the Chosen is about you."

Wilder's face took on a faraway look as he considered the prophecies they had read. "But he calls me the Scion, not the Chosen."

"Believe me, Wilder, if the Goddess chose anyone, she chose you. The prophecy is about you." She considered what that meant, and the breath hitched in her throat. "I'm going to deliver you into his hands?" Her voice raised in fear. "Oh, Goddess, Wilder, I'm going to deliver you into his hands!"

Wilder took her by both arms. "Listen to me, Rose. That is ridiculous. You swore to me earlier that you would destroy anyone who tried to hurt me. Do you honestly believe that you will suddenly betray me like that?"

"But I betrayed the crew! Look what happened to them! What if the same thing happens to you?"

"You didn't betray the crew. Vaylan tricked us all. He's twisting the prophecy to mean what he wants. He's doing exactly what he always does—manipulating people to get his way."

Her voice dropped to a whisper as she revealed what she feared the most. "But what if he tricks me again? What if he manipulates me into handing you over to him? What if he captures you and never lets you go? What if he—?"

Wilder rested a warm palm against her cheek and stilled her words. "He will try to manipulate you, and he might trick you. That's who he is. But lucky for me, I know exactly who you are. You're the one who won't rest until you rescue those you care about. So even if he captures me someday, there is no one I trust more to rescue me than you."

He leaned down and brushed a soft kiss against her lips. The kiss was a promise. A promise that they would rescue the crew and a promise that they would do it together.

She opened her eyes and caught her teardrop before it fell to the ground. She took a deep breath and held her hand over the basin. "I'm ready whenever you are."

His smile was gentle as he blinked a tear from his own eye. They clasped hands, then touched their tears to the basin.

The City exploded in white.

43

R ose hadn't truly believed they would summon the Goddess again. If she had considered it, she might have changed out of her showgirl costume. But even if she had been appropriately dressed, she would not have imagined meeting the Goddess inside a dark cave.

The last time Rose and Wilder touched the basin, it had transported them to a completely white void with the Goddess and Companion in their full glory. But this time, they found themselves inside a cave with only the light of a single lantern on a dingy table. The fire flickered wildly behind the glass, and Rose felt as trapped as the flame, with the dark shadows at the edge of the cave pressing in.

"I wasn't expecting company." The Goddess's voice came from the shadows behind them, and Rose and Wilder spun to face her.

The Goddess's hair was a disheveled mess, and she wore a ragged sweater over a faded pair of pants. She seemed embarrassed to see them, as if a Goddess could be ashamed to be seen.

Rose struggled to understand the Goddess's changed

appearance, but as usual, Wilder was quick to respond with compassion.

"Are you okay?" he asked.

The Goddess looked at him, and the worry lines across her forehead softened. "You are kind as always, dear Wilder. It's not fair of me to distress you when I'm sure you have plenty on your mind." She took a deep breath, and the entire room flared white.

Where shadows had lurked, now the cave shone like a jewel. The light was almost too much to bear after the darkness, and Rose blinked her eyes to adjust. The Goddess stood in a long white dress with wide sleeves that drooped to the floor, and her chestnut hair was twirled in an intricate updo.

"Why don't you have a seat?" She waved an elegant hand to the dingy table, which had been transformed into an intricately carved table of deep mahogany. The lantern was now a single burning taper in a silver candlestick. Three matching chairs appeared as they approached.

The Goddess took a seat slowly, as if in pain, and twitched her fingers, and a delicate teacup appeared in front of each of them. She took a careful sip and closed her eyes.

Rose looked around the strange room with wide eyes. She didn't like being confused by new things, not when she already had so many confusing things on her mind.

The Goddess opened her eyes and looked at Rose and Wilder closely for the first time. "Costumes? I expected you to put on a Pageant by now, not just perform in burlesque shows."

Rose nearly choked on a laugh. "The Pageant? Seriously? That is low on our priorities right now."

The Goddess set her teacup down and stared at Rose. "Don't you remember I told you that's what I need? I need a symbolic event with a majority of the City watching so I can gain enough power to return all the Gifts. You still want that, don't you?"

Even though Rose had just realized her lost Gift was lower on her list than returning the crew, it didn't mean there wasn't a part of her that still longed for it. And the Goddess, the one who had taken it from her in the first place, was speaking to her as if she was an idiot.

"I thought I did." Rose sensed Wilder squirming in the chair next to her, trying to get her attention, but she kept her eyes firmly on the Goddess. "However, now I'm not so sure I want anything from someone so fickle."

The Goddess remained perfectly still except for raising one arched brow. "Fickle?"

"Yes. You rejected those who served you for their entire lifetime, only to bestow your Gifts on those who don't even follow you."

The Goddess's green eyes narrowed. "You disagree with who I've chosen?"

Rose wanted to expand on that point, only to realize that she didn't disagree. She thought the Goddess chose the Seven well, but the familiar sting of rejection still haunted her. The thought was too embarrassing, so she chose a different method of attack.

"Do you realize where they are right now?" At the Goddess's confused expression, Rose pressed forward in her assault. "Vaylan has them. He tricked us all and captured them. He's threatening to take their Gifts away, and he wants to add Wilder to his collection."

The Goddess's face grew sadder and angrier at each word, so Rose dove ahead. "You didn't know that? I thought you watched over the City now. Or are you hiding away again and allowing someone worse than the High Priests to take over?"

The Goddess's eyes flared, and she growled at Rose. "I have concerns right now that you know nothing about."

Wilder reached for Rose's hand under the table, but she shook him off as her hands clenched into fists. "I don't give a damn about your concerns. What I care about is my crew. I hoped I could trust you to care for the City, but it looks like I will have to take care of everyone on my own, with no help from you."

The Goddess's voice dropped to a deadly whisper. "I have given this City my blood, my tears, and my very soul. I care for this City in a way that you can't even imagine. And yet you have the audacity to appear unexpected and declare that I have not given enough?"

All the anger from the last few weeks burst back to life in Rose's chest. In her grief, she had lashed out at Wilder and the crew, but here before her was the true source of her pain. Over and over, Rose had asked, "Why?" but there was no reply. But now, Rose would make the Goddess give an answer.

She clutched the edge of the table, her fingers curling into claws. "I have served you my entire life, and when you had the chance to return my Gift, you refused. I have cried useless tears day after day, night after night, begging you to return what you took, but you haven't listened." Her voice raised to a shout, echoing throughout the glittering cave. "Instead, you have been sitting in this cave, waiting for *me* to act, while you do nothing. You ripped my soul to shreds, and you don't even care." Rose's body shook with the anger barely contained as she waited for the Goddess to explain herself.

The Goddess rolled her eyes. "Rose, if this is because I didn't return your Gift, I honestly can't believe you are so childish that you—"

She didn't finish because Rose dove across the table and closed her hands around the Goddess's throat.

The Goddess remained perfectly still, but her eyes widened in surprise. Wilder stood suddenly, and his chair clattered to the floor as he tried to pull Rose away.

Rose knew it was wrong, knew it was insane to strangle a Goddess, but she had never felt so free. She thought she understood what freedom felt like when she performed in the circus, but stunts without a net were nowhere as euphoric as strangling the Goddess who had caused her so much pain.

Vaylan would be so jealous of her.

The thought stilled her hands. Her fingers twitched, then released. She allowed Wilder to pull her back across the table and down into her chair. She tugged her dress back into place and smoothed out a piece of her hair, even though it was a complete wreck from her earlier kiss with Wilder.

The Goddess had not moved a muscle from when Rose attacked. Wilder walked to the Goddess's side of the table and lowered himself to look her in the face.

"Goddess? Are you okay?" When she didn't respond, he picked up her teacup and put it in her hand. Her fingers closed around the familiar object, and she lifted it to her mouth without looking at it.

She set the cup down, and her eyes focused on Wilder. "Thank you, Wilder." She rubbed her forehead as if she had forgotten what she was doing. "I'm afraid I'm not well."

A hint of shame wound its way around Rose's heart at the thought of attacking a sick person. But this was the Goddess! Even an unwell Goddess should be more than a match for Rose.

But the Goddess hadn't fought back.

Rose leaned back in her chair with a sigh. "We hoped you'd be able to help, but I guess that's not happening."

Wilder hadn't moved from his place near the Goddess's side, and he looked at Rose with a disappointed frown.

"What do you want me to do, Wilder?" Rose said with exasperation. "Vaylan has the crew and wants to destroy the City, and the Goddess doesn't know how to fix it either."

"What did you say?" The Goddess's voice had returned to its deadly whisper.

Rose was grateful to see any life in her at all. "He said there's a prophecy that says I will darken the crystals. That's how he plans to take the Gifts from the crew."

The Goddess's hand shot across the table to grab Rose's hand. "You can do that? You can shut down the crystals?"

Rose squirmed uncomfortably under her fierce grip. "It's just some ridiculous prophecy Vaylan believes."

The Goddess's eyes took on a faraway look, but this time, Rose could see thoughts running through her mind. She appeared to be making calculations, then blinked and focused on Rose's face.

"Do it." Her voice was a command.

"Do what?" said Rose. "Touch the crystals? I've done that before countless times. I was with Ylena when she touched the crystal and the City went dark, but I don't know how she did it."

"Yes!" The Goddess squeezed her hand harder. "That's exactly right! Ylena did it. You can figure it out, too."

Rose didn't like admitting there was something Ylena could do that she couldn't, but that had been clear from the first day Rose had met her. Over time, she had seen Ylena do so many miraculous things that shutting the crystals down wasn't truly that spectacular. But even so, it was beyond Rose's skill.

"I'm sorry, Goddess. I don't know how. Ylena has a Spark and can do a lot of things I can't."

The Goddess rolled her eyes as if Rose were being an idiot again. "Don't make excuses, Rose. Just use your own Spark and figure it out."

44

———

Every muscle in Rose's body froze in place. She had no energy to spend on moving or breathing or even blinking, because all her strength was focused internally, working through each word the Goddess just spoke.

She pulled in a ragged breath through her nose and asked quietly, "What did you say?"

The Goddess looked at Rose, then at Wilder, who was also perfectly unmoving. His eyes were locked on Rose, who could feel the hope boiling off him in waves. She didn't dare reach for hope yet. She didn't dare move at all.

"Your ... Spark." The Goddess's eyes flicked back and forth between the two of them. "Of course you knew about it. Right? Tell me you knew."

"I have no idea what you're talking about."

The Goddess put her head in her hands and gave a deep, shuddering sigh. As she breathed out, the glittering room faded back into the shadowed cave from when they first arrived. Wilder stood from his place at the Goddess's side and took the rickety chair next to Rose. He put his hand in hers and waited for the Goddess to look up.

The Goddess raised her head, and though she was back to her disheveled appearance, she still held herself with a regal posture. She spoke as a teacher to a student, though not as condescending as Vaylan usually sounded.

"Sparks are a remnant from our home before the City. They are very rare and are triggered by a traumatic event in life. No one knows exactly why the same traumatic events lead to a Spark in some people but not others, so don't ask me to explain theology that I don't understand. What I do know intimately well is what my Spark is. I gain the Spark of anyone I meet, even if I don't see them use it. Ylena's is similar, although I believe she has to see it first to use it. But the point is, I knew you had a Spark the first night I met you, because after that, I could do this."

The Goddess placed her hand near the lantern and twitched one finger. The flame jumped out of the lantern and shaped into the form of a running tiger hovering above her palm. Rose stared at the moving flame in disbelief. The Goddess closed her hand in a fist, and the cave was suddenly pitch black. Before Rose had time to panic, the light returned. The Goddess held her open palm flat and coaxed the flame to dance along her fingertips.

The Goddess looked at Rose. "You never noticed that fire acted strangely around you?"

"We rarely had an open flame in the City. And in the Underneath ..." She looked at Wilder and remembered the night he called down a whirlwind while they kissed. The flames had burned brighter as a result, but they thought it was only from the wind stoking the flame. But maybe it was more than that.

Rose stared in fascination at the fire dancing across the Goddess's palm. She let go of Wilder's hand and reached a tentative finger out to touch the flame. The Goddess's hand twitched, and the flame was suddenly back in the lantern.

"It's not real," said the Goddess.

Rose felt disappointment settle over her shoulders again. She hadn't noticed the hope building in her chest until it was gone.

"I mean, it *will be* real, dear." She patted Rose's hand. "It's not real *here*. Your actual bodies are currently crumpled in a heap on the floor of the amphitheater. I'm just showing you what it will look like when you are back in your body. Does that make sense?"

Rose nodded even though she had no idea what the Goddess meant.

"I honestly don't know everything you can do with your Spark. I only met you at the very end of my time in the City, so I didn't test it out much in that body, and now that I'm in this form, my Spark is irrelevant. But I believe your Spark could be the key to saving the City."

"What am I going to do with magical fire besides burn the entire City down?"

The Goddess snorted. "Please refrain from that instinct, dear. I need you to do what Vaylan suggests. Darken the crystals. Extinguish all the light, then bring it back."

"Why? Vaylan's already arrogant enough. He doesn't need the encouragement proving his prophecies are correct."

"The City is dying," she whispered. The Goddess covered her mouth with her hand, but Rose saw her lip tremble. She blinked her eyes repeatedly, holding the tears inside, then drew in a shaking breath and continued. "The Companion is more than linked to the City. They are one. The crystals are remnants of his bones." Her green eyes flashed with a hint of violence. "And someone has been manipulating his blood."

Rose leaned back in her chair. She had always felt like

Vaylan manipulating the crystalline was unnatural, but she had never considered the theological ramifications.

"The Companion is growing weaker each day. Some days, it's as if nothing has changed, and other days, I can't speak to him at all. I'd love to convince Vaylan to voluntarily give up manipulating crystalline, but I don't guess that's a possibility."

Wilder spoke in a gentle voice. "He says he will stop after all the crystals have gone dark. Then he will pull away all the crystalline, leaving the City without a trace of you."

The violence lingered in the Goddess's eyes. "And without a trace of the Companion. I made a promise long ago to not hurt the people of my City, but if I could appear in the flesh again, I swear I would rip Vaylan apart for what he has done to the Companion."

Rose's eyes widened at the threat. She had been angry at the Goddess earlier, but now Rose finally understood her.

Rose nodded. "Okay. I'll try."

The Goddess's face lit up. "Thank you, dear. I swear I will help you if I can. And I'm sorry for calling you childish earlier. I thought you knew you could control flame and were so greedy you wanted the wind back, too. I chose Kai so you trusted at least one person with a Gift."

Rose gripped Wilder's hand and smiled. "Everyone you gave a Gift, I trust with my life. You chose wisely."

The Goddess's smile was the last thing she saw before the cave faded into blackness.

Rose awoke tangled up in Wilder's arms. Even though her legs were twisted uncomfortably, she considered faking sleep to stay curled up beside him.

As usual, the wolves wrecked her plans.

She heard them before she saw them. Their tongues made disgusting sounds as they licked Wilder's outstretched hand compulsively. Rose swatted them away as Wilder opened his eyes.

"See? He's fine. Stop drooling all over him."

Wilder chuckled and wiped his wet hand on his pants. He hopped up with more energy than Rose felt, then reached down to pull her up.

His face practically glowed, and Rose found his smile contagious. "What are you so happy about?"

"I was right," he said smugly. "I knew there was a reason the Goddess didn't return your Gift. Well, first, I thought she returned your Gift but you didn't notice. I admit that was a stupid thing to say. But I had faith there was some reason she didn't return it, and I was right."

She considered their past conversations and fights. "Did you ever tell me you believed there was a reason she never returned my Gift?"

He laughed. "Absolutely not! You would have murdered me!"

"Yes. And you would have deserved it."

Wilder's face turned serious. "So, now what?"

She bit her lip. "I know, but I don't want to say it."

"I think it's the right decision."

Her voice dropped to a whisper. "I don't want to leave you."

"Do you want me to come with you?"

She swatted him on the arm. "Of course not! It's not safe for you."

He raised an eyebrow. "And it is for you?"

"We both know if Vaylan wanted to hurt me, he would have done it long ago. But despite his claims otherwise, both times he's seen you, he's tried to use his Spark to harm you."

Wilder sighed. "I know you're right, but I still don't like it. You can't let him know about your Spark. He will feel threatened. Please be careful."

It hurt to look at his sorrowful eyes, so she glanced at the wolves seated at his feet. They each had a corner of their mouth pulled up in what appeared to be a smug grin.

"You better watch over him," she growled. "Because if you let him get hurt, I swear I will skin you both." Neither of them blinked. They accepted her charge.

Wilder looked down at the wolves, then back at Rose with a startled expression. "They knew."

"Knew what?" she asked.

"About your Spark. Their name for you has always been Lady Fire Wolf. It wasn't about your hair. Somehow, they knew."

Rose looked at the wolves in surprise. Even though she couldn't understand their language, she was pretty sure they considered her a very stupid wolf at the moment.

Rose forced herself to look into Wilder's eyes. Her throat closed up, but she choked down the tears. "You better practice your Gifts while I'm gone, because I expect you to wow me with some miracles the next time I see you."

Wilder pulled her into a kiss that was desperate and fierce, but despite the tears on his cheeks, he didn't use any of his Gifts. It was only Wilder and Rose, without Gifts or Sparks, yet their kiss was still magic.

She pulled away from him reluctantly and poured all her hope and desire and promise into her last look. "I love you, Wilder. I will save the Companion, rescue the crew, then come find you. I swear it."

"I believe you, Rose." His lips curled up in a smile. "I'll be waiting."

She took a deep breath and slid back the door on top of

the staircase. Then she walked into the Heart of the Grottos
alone.

~

*To Be Continued in *Fight with the Heart -
City of Virtue and Vice Book 6**

ABOUT THE AUTHOR

Susannah Welch lives in sunny South Florida with her brilliant husband and a magically hypoallergenic cat. She enjoys singing and dancing and showing off. She likes her stories with a little bit of drama, and a whole lot of sparkle.

facebook.com/susannah.welch.author

instagram.com/susannahwelchauthor